The Scummers

The Crum Trilogy

CRUM • SCREAMING WITH THE CANNIBALS • THE SCUMMERS

To

Chuck Kinder, my identical twin cousin
who fixed it when it couldn't be fixed, and to
The Woman at Fallingwater
in the center of the room.

Vandalia Press

MORGANTOWN 2012

5

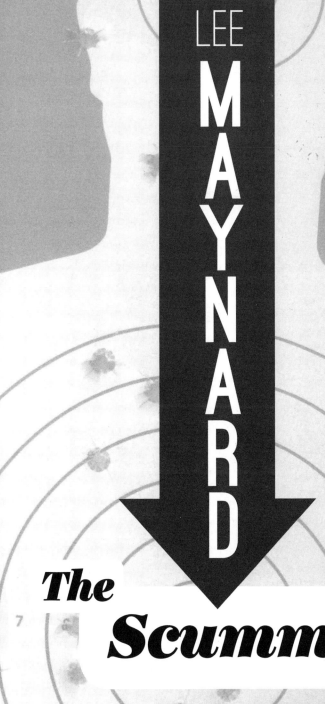

LEE
MAYNARD

The Scummers

Vandalia Press, Morgantown 26506
Copyright 2012 West Virginia University Press
All rights reserved
First edition published 2012 by Vandalia Press
Printed in the United States of America

20 19 18 17 16 15 14 13 12   9 8 7 6 5 4 3 2 1

Cloth: 978-1-935978-53-4
Paper: 978-1-935978-47-3
EPUB: 978-1-935978-48-0
PDF: 978-1-935978-57-2

Library of Congress Cataloging-in-Publication Data
Maynard, Lee, 1936–
The Scummers / by Lee Maynard. — 1st ed.
    p.   cm.
ISBN-13: 978-1-935978-53-4 (cloth : alk. paper)
ISBN-13: 978-1-935978-47-3 (pbk. : alk. paper)
1. West VirginiaÂFiction. I. Title.
PS3563.A96384S37 2012
813'.54--dc23
Library of Congress Control Number: 2011049268

When I was a child,
I spake as a child, I understood as a child,
I thought as a child:
but when I became a man,
I put away childish things.

1 Corinthians 13:11
King James Bible

CONTENTS

Prologue

How does a man come to this?

In 1961 I was ready to kill a man. I meant to do it. I was going to try, or so I thought. But somebody else beat me to it.

Question is, would I actually have done it?

That same year, I *may* have killed a man. I don't know for sure. I never found out.

Question is, did I mean to do it?

Death, time and again, in a single year.

How does a kid from Crum, West Virginia, come to this?

How does any man come to this?

In 1956 I was run out of Myrtle Beach, Horry County, South Carolina, because I worked with, and lived with, black people. I am not black. I am a blond, blue-eyed white man from Crum, in Wayne County, West Virginia, where no black people live. When I got to South Carolina, I had no idea I was not supposed to like black people. Or work with them. Or eat their food. Or live with them. Or make love to one of their women. All of which I did.

And so I paid the price.

It was painful.

When I lived in Crum, I wanted out. I wanted out so intensely that I would have done anything, *anything*, to make it happen. Even though I knew a girl there who would live in my mind for the rest of my life.

Yvonne.

But Yvonne didn't stay there. And neither did I.

I found my way to Myrtle Beach. I had never seen the ocean, and it was magic.

But that's when I made the crucial mistake—I fell in with those black folks.

I was an ignorant hillbilly with no particular skills. After Labor Day, when all the tourists went home, there was nothing for me to do. Couldn't get a job—there were no jobs. Except one. I could work on a small fishing boat, owned by a black guy, and worked by other black guys. It was hard, manual labor—pulling oars, paying out net so heavy it tore the skin off your hands, even through heavy, soaked gloves. But working with black men meant that no white people would rent a room to me.

And so I lived with the black people, in their rural slum.

And so I was "asked" to leave. By the white people.

But I did not want to leave Myrtle Beach. I was in love with a girl there, a white girl, a girl from my high school years in Crum, West Virginia, a girl like no other.

Yes—Yvonne—who had found her way to Myrtle Beach before I even got there. She was not looking for me, at least not in the beginning, but found me there, nevertheless.

But I had no choice. I had to leave. I had defied the written and unwritten laws of segregation. To stay in South Carolina would have been possibly fatal. I had to hit the road.

And so I did. Alone.

Without Yvonne.

I love being on the road, alone, no one knowing where I am, no way of finding me. But, even on the road, a life must be lived. And

I lived mine. I even kept journals that tried to say what was happening, and maybe why it was happening.

The journals did not work out too well.

For a while, on the road, life was made up of whatever the hell came down the pike. All in all, it wasn't bad, but it wasn't particularly good. It just . . . was.

But life has a way of fucking with your plans, even when you don't have any.

Because at the end of the road, I found the army.

No, that isn't quite true. The army found me.

And in a very short time, I wanted to become a killer. And I may have succeeded.

I put away childish things. It took a while.

I tried. At least I think I did.

How does a man come to this?

Fuck it. I'm tired of thinking about it.

It's over. I know that, now.

I don't keep a journal anymore.

In fact, I think I'll take the boat out and just read a book.

—Jesse Stone
Canada
or maybe Mexico
Honduras?
Who the hell cares?

Part I

THE ROAD WEST

One

I was naked, sitting upright in the center of the hood of the big sedan.

In my journal, I once wrote that I had been "run out of the county" there in South Carolina. That was not exactly true. I was given a ride to the county line—on the hood of the car—but then I was launched through the air. Technically, I was "flown" out of the county.

It started out by my being given a ride down a hidden country road in a car large enough to be a boat, being driven by a three-hundred-pound redneck named Wimpo. In the passenger seat was a sheriff's deputy named Polk.

Wimpo had held a shotgun on me, made me strip, and climb up on the car.

Now, Polk had the shotgun and Wimpo had his head part-way out the open window and was yelling at me . . .

"You come down here from the North, you mess around with the niggers, work with 'em . . . hell, that don't matter much, we all work with niggers now and again, when we have to.

"But you, hell, boy, you living with 'em . And that ain't right, boy. That's against the law of God, against everything we know is right and true."

The car started to roll forward . . .

The car picked up speed, tearing down the road, trees whipping by, a limb now and then catching me in the face or across the chest. I ran my hands around the hood, trying to find something to hang onto. There was nothing.

"And don't let anybody ever tell you," he screamed, "that I DIDN'T GIVE YOUR ASS A RIDE TO THE COUNTY LINE!"

And he slammed on the brakes, locking the wheels.

There are few times in your life when you are free, truly free, and I was free now, alive and vital and sensitive to the smallest things, the smell of thick rushing air, dust motes brushing my face, the sound a pine needle makes when it hits the forest floor, and I knew all of these things were there, all of them, in my world, in the black of night and the pushing wind against my face and the flailing of my arms and legs in freedom so complete, so pure, as I spun almost lazily through the air.

Freedom is a some-time thing. It seldom lasts forever. It begins, and it ends.

My face kissed the soft padding of the forest junk that covered the road, then kissed it harder, then dug into the junk and found the harder parts underneath and my body caught up with my face and passed it, tumbling and sliding, a huge, soft plow smashing open a furrow in the darkness and the dirt, skidding, twisting, bleeding, scraping.

I launched off the hood of the car, cleared the road, and hit a signpost. I had seen the sign before. It said Horry County Line.

Officially, I was out of Horry County.

"You think he's dead?"

The whining voice came through some dense wall of pain around my mind.

"Nah. Don't think so. Looks like he don't even have any broken bones. Got a pretty good head bleeder there, though."

My head moved and I thought he was adjusting it, checking out a scalp wound.

"He had a good trip, sure 'nuff."

"Yeah," I heard Polk say through the wall, "might've we set a record with this one. You think?"

"Maybe so. Went about twenty feet in the air. Bettah than most. Bettah than that nigger last month. He hardly get any distance a'tall."

"Too thick. Dense, they are. That's why they can't swim nowhere. Sink, like rocks."

"This 'un hit the sign, too. Head on. That never happen before."

Silence. The sound of breathing. My head was beginning to clear behind the pain, but, for once, I was smart enough to lie there and play dead. Damn near was . . .

And then I heard them laughing, both of them, and the laughing wasn't too far from me and it didn't move and I knew they were sitting there, just down the road, enjoying. They didn't care that I was there. They had disposed of me like a piece of shit in a brown paper bag thrown from a car window. I was no longer in their lives.

. . . I had knocked the sign post over and I lay partially on top of it. I slid off the thing and sat up, wanting to scream but clamping my mouth shut. I ran my hands over my body and they came away sticky. I was bleeding from a thousand tiny cuts and scrapes . . . But everything worked. I pulled my legs under me and stood up, careful to hang back in the edge of the trees. The car was there, a few yards down the road, pointed back toward the way we came. They must have turned it around while I was passed out because I never heard the engine.

. . . . I could hear them laughing, hooting, howling, a brotherhood of the Confederacy come to a safe place after the battle.

I knew I was finished there at the beach . . . in Horry County, in South Carolina. I finally got the message. I was standing naked and shivering in the fringe of black woods on a back-county road that led off into country I had never seen or thought about, hearing the howling of *men who lived by laws of their own making, laws which did not admit me to the safe places of the earth.*

It was ended.

They had won and all the rest of us had lost and that's the way it was going to be down here in the South and I wondered if there were other places in the world as good as this, with the soft air and the warm water and sand that toasted your feet and women who stood next to your chair and let you look down into the tops of their bathing suits. Places as good as this, but without . . . Polk and Wimpo.

Maybe I should go looking for a place like that.

Two

Goddammit, i wasn't a northerner. And from what I had seen, I wasn't a Southerner, either; didn't want to be; didn't want any part of it. Not after all the shit I had brought down on my own head in that wonderful place called "The South." I didn't know if there were any people called Easterners, but it didn't matter. I wasn't going east. I was just another West Virginian stuck in a hate warp that I didn't make but which, sure as hell, would suck me in if I stuck around and let it.

Had already sucked me in.

I was only kidding myself. I could not stick around. I had been run out of Horry County, South Carolina. I still had some of the scabs on my body to prove it.

If I went north I could end up back in West Virginia. If I went east I would hit the Atlantic Ocean. South? The South could kiss my ass.

I was going west.

I had grown up on Black Hawk Ridge, in the mountains of West Virginia; learned about tracking animals; moonshine; guns; blood feuds; the wisdom of relatives, especially my Great Uncle Long Neck. And fucking. I learned a lot about fucking.

But they sent me away from Black Hawk Ridge, sent me down to Crum, a tiny little town on the Tug River that had a high school. I don't think I wanted to leave the Ridge, leave Great Uncle Long

Neck, leave the security of the mountains and the forest. My mountains. My forest. But what I wanted did not matter—they sent me anyway. They knew what I would become if I stayed. I would become like them.

And so I left Black Hawk.

I left.

It was only the first in a long line of leaving things, whether I wanted to go or not.

Crum sucked.

Well, maybe it didn't, but I never gave it a chance.

I lived with some distant relatives on a hillside across the railroad tracks and above the school and from the day I got there the only thing that held me together was the thought that someday I would leave.

And so I went to Crum High School. That was what Great Uncle Long Neck wanted me to do.

I did learn a couple of things, however.

I learned what love was. And I learned that I could be stupid enough to make someone hate me. Unfortunately, I loved, and was hated by, the same woman.

Yvonne Staley.

I wrote in one of my journals that Yvonne was the only truly beautiful girl in Crum. She had a dignity, a presence, a way of way of seeming destined for better things than Crum. She was the quietest of the girls, and certainly the smartest.

I think I loved her. I'm pretty sure of it. Looking back on it now, I know I did.

Loved her.

And I still do. Oh, God, I still do.

She came to hate me.

One dark, rainy night back there in Crum, I actually got to make love to her. And then, true to form, I messed it up, the kind of messing up that stays in your mind as long as you are alive, the kind of messing up that you might, one day, forgive. But you would never forget. And Yvonne never did.

You see, I thought she was a whore, and I tried to pay her for making love to me.

Mistake.

We had made love in the thick, heavy dark of a summer night, on the front porch of her house, the house stuck on a hillside above Crum, locked together, naked, not caring where we were or what we were doing.

But we knew what we were doing.

At the end of it all, back in her living room, dressed, still weak and panting from what we had done, I pulled out a crumpled five-dollar-bill—the only money I had—and handed it to her. I thought that was what she wanted.

Mistake.

After Yvonne and I had made love . . . I didn't go to school for two days, and when I did Yvonne wasn't there. After school I walked in the cold and dim light down past Yvonne's house . . . There were no lights on.

The narrow highway was empty and I shuffled on the pavement past the tiny rough-plank garage where Yvonne's brother parked his old Chevrolet. The doors were open and I could see the grill of the car grinning out at me. I felt uneasy, walking past Yvonne's house like that. I didn't belong there; she had made that clear. I stopped in the middle of the highway, intending to go back. Before I could move I heard the en-

gine of the Chevrolet grind into life. The car rolled forward and turned in my direction on the road. It stopped, the engine idling. I figured Yvonne's brother was going to Kermit. I wondered if he would mind giving me a lift. But I didn't wonder long. The car's gears pounded and it lurched forward, the engine racing. Straight at me.

The whole thing didn't register. The car didn't have the lights on and the distance fooled me. I stood there almost too long before I leaped sideways, diving onto the gravel. As I rolled over the car raced by and I caught a glimpse of the driver. It was Yvonne. I got up and stared down the highway until I couldn't see the car anymore. And I knew then that she was gone for good.

Yeah, I'm pretty sure Yvonne hated me.

Three

Two Lane Blacktop
Western South Carolina
October 1956

What the hell was I doing there?

That seemed to be the central question of my life, the question that kept coming up, again and again, no matter where I went, what I did.

What the hell was I doing here, on that two-lane highway far and west and into the mountains?

Whatever I was doing there, I wouldn't be doing it for long.

I was leaving again, hitchhiking, catching rides with strangers who always looked at me sideways.

Leaving again, just like I had left Black Hawk Ridge and Crum, West Virginia.

I left the Ridge because I was sent away.

I left Crum willingly, even though I had found Yvonne there; left desperately, blindly; could not wait to get the hell out. Yvonne, the most incredible woman I had ever known—but then, how many incredible women could I have met in a place like Crum?—had come to hate me. I hated Crum when I got there; I hated Crum when I left.

But back there, right now, right this minute, far behind me, through the mist, was not Crum. Back there was Myrtle Beach. I had come to hate the South, but *I did not want to leave Myrtle Beach*. And maybe because of that—not wanting to leave—I had been driven out.

Maybe that was how I would spend my life: wherever I was, just leave, or be driven out.

I stood there at the side of the narrow road, staring back at the land that fell away to the east, back toward the thin pines and the sand and the ocean.

I did not want to leave.

Yvonne was in Myrtle Beach. And I don't think she hated me anymore.

I did not want to leave Yvonne. Yvonne of the midnight hair and the long, firm legs. Yvonne, who could raise in me feelings that I did not understand. There, in those final days back at the beach, for the first time in my life, I had no urge to leave. I never wanted to leave Yvonne. Ever.

And yet, here I was, on another no-name highway.

I had left Crum on a hard run and worked my way down through Kentucky, finally plopping my ass down in Myrtle Beach. I got a job as a lifeguard. The guy who hired me never even asked me if I could swim.

And that's how I found her again. Back there in Myrtle Beach. In a saloon.

I was just looking for a beer. I sat on a stool nursing a long-neck and looking past the bar and out the windows that bled the light from the beach into the room. The bar looked like one of those that was supposed to be dark and dim. Maybe it was, at night. But now the light flooded across the worn wood and battered counter top and glistened from unlit neon beer signs that cluttered the walls.

The woman behind the bar stopped in front of me.

Yvonne. She was there. In Myrtle Beach.

She stopped directly in front of me . . . The blood was rising in her face and she struggled to stay calm. She reached for my empty beer bottle, absently wiping the bar with the damp rag.

My mouth wouldn't work right. "Uh . . . howdy . . . Vonny."

She pulled her arm back and swung the beer bottle. I saw it coming in a brownish blur that cut an arc across the bright light coming in from the windows. I saw it coming in the light from her eyes and the heat of her body. I saw it coming in what she owed me, in the great justice of my being there on that bar stool within reach of her. I saw it coming, but I couldn't move. The bottle caught me cleanly on the temple and I crumpled off the bar stool, tumbling downward. My mind clicked to another time, some place far removed and safe, a place where there were tall hardwood trees with vines in them and I was swinging on one of the vines, clinging to the end of it, my body cutting great, sweeping arcs out and through the sunshine and far over and above the forest floor. And then the vine broke.

I fell into a pool of left-over mop water still standing in a depression in the wooden floor of the bar. I hit the mop water face first . . .

But we had gotten past that, Vonny and I.

Myrtle Beach, for a while, was as good, and as warm, and as safe, as I would ever find again.

There, with Vonny.

Even though, twice now, she had tried to kill me.

Four

Two Lane Blacktop
Western South Carolina
October 1956

Winter was coming on in the Carolinas. The land rose to the west and lifted higher into the mountains and I could feel the cold flowing down and out of the hills and wrapping itself around me in my beach shirt and old jeans and I wished I were back there, sitting on the sand, sweat running down into my eyes and a can of cold beer dangling from my hand. I carried a thin, tattered gym bag but there was nothing much in it but an old shirt.

I started walking down and around the mountains and farther into the South, my thumb out every time I heard a car, trying to keep my eyes straight ahead.

I thought about going home, but I really was not sure where home was. And it didn't seem to matter. I just ended up in places I didn't want to be, after taking off from some other places I didn't want to be.

Actually, I had no intention of going home, ever again. Wherever it was.

The rain was pissing down out of a sky I could not see and the tree did little to protect me. I sat under it anyway, pretending it was better than nothing. But it wasn't. I pulled the tattered shirt out of the gym bag and wrapped it around my head, but it was soaked instantly and all it did was feel cold and clammy as it slid down around my neck.

I clutched the gym bag to my stomach, trying to keep it dry. There was nothing in it now but a piece of soap in a plastic box. There wasn't even a book in there. No book. I squeezed the bag harder, and that's when I felt it. A book. I opened the bag. There *was* a book in there—well, not a real book, not the sort of book you buy in a store. It was one of those hard-backed notebooks with the pages stitched in. Composition books, the kids called them, dark cardboard covers, thick sheets of paper. It was my book, my notebook. I wrote in it. It was my journal, but I didn't remember putting it in the bag. I did not know what it meant to keep a journal. I just wrote. And it became a habit.

It is still a habit, but one I have been trying to break for years.

The tree was up a slight rise and back a ways from the road and I knew anybody driving past would not see me. I would wait until the rain stopped and then walk down to the pitted blacktop and keep on walking west. No one was going to stop and pick up a guy my size, soaking wet, carrying nothing but an old gym bag. It didn't matter. I really had no place to go.

The rain stopped and I stuffed the wet shirt back into the gym bag. Blue holes began to show in the overcast sky. The air did not move, an absolutely still wrapping of cold around my wet clothing, chilling me as I walked. The trees dripped with wet, their leaves still green but hanging limply, knowing they were dead but refusing to change color and drop.

The road came out of the trees and onto the side of a high ridge and I could see other ridges in the distance, identical to the one I was on, the heavy clouds capping the higher points, the valleys below so narrow and deep that they were black at the bottoms. I knew I was somewhere in the Western Carolinas, but I did not know where. I followed the road and the rolling ridges and I did not give a damn where they went as long as it was west. The entire world was wet and green and cold and steep and the narrow road just kept going and I knew I was not where I wanted to be. Yet. Maybe never.

But the road led west.

I walked for the rest of the day.

With nothing to eat.

When I knew I was not going to get a ride I started looking for a place to hole up for the night. A pile of concrete culvert sections was stacked off to the side of the road, left there by a road crew. The sections were big, at least three feet across the inside, and were stacked up like a pyramid, the top culvert maybe ten feet off the ground. The road crew had thrown a chain over the pile to keep it from coming apart. I hauled myself up the chain to the top section of culvert and slid inside. I used the gym bag as a soggy pillow. I lay there in my clammy, wet clothes, shivering. Finally, my body just gave up and I fell asleep.

I did not wake up until first light.

I wormed my way to the end of the pipe and looked out into the world. The world was wet, low clinging fog drifting through the trees, the pavement on the road shiny in the moisture. If I kept going west the land would keep on getting higher and the wet would keep on getting colder, but there was no other direction for me. I knew that. Maybe I had always known that. Maybe when I sat in the tiny library in Crum High School back in West Virginia reading the travel books for the third and fourth time, looking at the pictures of the mountains and the canyons, maybe that was when "West" began to have some meaning for me.

Maybe I would never know for sure.

I eased my arms and shoulders out of the pipe and dropped the gym bag to the soggy earth below. I started to twist around and pull myself further out when a head appeared from the end of another pipe below me, not far off the ground. The head was black and shaggy. All I could see was long stringy damp hair. The head was looking down at my gym bag.

I started to pull myself farther out of the pipe, but I was too late. The guy down below squirted out of his pipe like he was greased. His clothes were too big for him—heavy jeans and a floppy shirt—but that didn't seem to matter. In a single flowing movement his body drooped over the end of the pipe, his arms out in front of him as he dropped arms-first onto the ground, tucked his head and rolled. Somewhere in the roll he grabbed my gym bag. And then he was on his feet.

"Hey! You son of a bitch!"

I didn't even yell at him to drop the bag. I knew he wouldn't. But he did turn and look up at me, just as I lunged out of the end of my pipe and dropped on him like a 220-pound bag of shit. I hit him full on, drove him into the muddy ground, rolled off him and came to my feet.

And so did he.

I thought I would have at least addled the guy, maybe made him stagger around some. Instead, he was on his feet like a cat, starting away from me at an instant run, my gym bag still in his hand.

I had only one chance at it—I lunged at his feet, my arms stretched out in front of me. My hands hit his heels and he went down hard and I was on him, landing full on his back. I wrapped my arms around him and pulled him over, trying to get him in some position where I could drive a fist into his face. I squeezed him hard and we wrestled there in the mud. The guy was like an eel, long, slender and slimy, and I knew if I relaxed even a little he would squirm away from me. I got my left hand on his chest and tried to roll him over.

It took a moment for it to sink in.

I had my hand on a breast.

I flipped him—her—over and pinned her to the ground, driving my knee between her legs, separating them, and then shoving my knee up into her crotch. For a few seconds we lay quietly on the sodden ground, me holding on with all my strength, the girl tense but not moving, her head turned away from me, her arms flung out in some sort of almost-surrender. Still holding the gym bag. Her hair was black and wet, lying in a tangle against her thin, pale face. Her nose was straight, pointing to lips that looked black but I knew were not. I didn't know if she were beautiful, but I thought so at the time. Oh, God, I thought so.

And then I felt her hips move, slightly at first, and then stronger, her crotch grinding against my leg, slowly, slowly, all the time in the world.

She turned her head and finally looked at me.

Jesus, she really was good looking. Dark eyes, narrow face, full lips . . . and the best part was, she was grinding her crotch against my leg.

I relaxed my hold briefly and that was all the girl needed. She pulled an arm free, slapped me hard and stinging across the face, squirted out of my arms and was on her feet in an instant. I came up on my knees, still confused by what was going on. And she swung the gym bag with both hands. The hard-backed journal inside the thin nylon cracked me square between the eyes.

The girl was so slight that the whack with the book did not even knock me over, but it did freeze me. She turned and instantly was in full flight, heading for the road. She made a sharp cut to her right and darted into the heavy trees and brush.

I knew I would never catch her; I knew I would never see her again.

And she still had my gym bag.

And she had my notebook.

And my dick was still hard.

I slid back inside one of the lower culverts, squirmed around on my back and lay death-still against the casket-like feel of the stone pipe, my hand feeling my leg where she had ground her crotch into it. And I started to laugh. It just came out of me in great booming sounds, magnified and broadcast by the concrete pipe, the laughter crashing through the trees and out across the ridge.

I hope the bitch heard it.

Five

The Forest

Western South Carolina

October 1956

What was she doing there? What was she doing, sleeping in a culvert by the side of the road? What was she . . . .
　　She lived there! No, not there, not in the culvert. She lived . . . *there* . . . through the woods, where she ran.

I slid out of the culvert and looked toward the thick wall of trees where she had run like a small deer, kicking sodden leaves into the air, her feet punching marks into the forest floor.

On Black Hawk Ridge I had followed my uncle, Long Neck Jesse, through these same woods, Appalachian hardwoods, Long Neck carrying an ancient, single-shot rifle. The rifle was not originally a single-shot, but somewhere back in the years the rifle had lost a couple of small parts and would no longer feed another cartridge after the first one was fired. Long Neck never had it repaired. *Man shouldn't need more'n one shot,* he said.
　　We hunted deer. We hunted deer the way Long Neck hunted, going out into the damp woods and moving, always moving, crouching low to look slant-wise at the floor of the woods, finding that one leaf that was turned just so, and another, just a bit farther on. And the tiny branch on the undergrowth that had no water on it, the water brushed off by the passing of the deer. And on and on until we found the deer, the deer never knowing we were there. And then that one silent moment when Long Neck and the deer were wrapped in a universe of their own making. And Long Neck fired his one shot.

Gradually, I became the tracker, Long Neck squatting, studying the forest floor, me squatting beside him, Long Neck taking longer and longer to point out the direction of the deer. I did not know he was waiting on me, but finally I raised my arm and pointed, my fingers shaking a little. Long Neck nodded. I had picked the right direction. I was now the tracker.

And then one day Long Neck handed me the rifle and a single cartridge. And I became the hunter on Black Hawk Ridge.

I grunted my way out of the culvert and stood rubbing the knot on my forehead where the girl had hit me. I was still wet, still cold, had lost my journal and my only spare shirt, and had absolutely nothing in the front of my life.

I should have just walked on, down the road, to anywhere but where I was. But I did not.

And then I remembered that it was times like these when I always got into trouble.

I walked slowly to the edge of the woods where the girl had disappeared. I squatted, staring into the shadows along the soft floor. The girl had been in a hurry, knowing that her speed would be her advantage. Although she ran like one, she was not a deer—her feet had left large marks as she pounded the soft floor of the woods, large marks, easy to see, easy to track.

I could find her.

I could find the bitch.

But why? Was it the challenge? Was it being hit without hitting back? Was it my book, a book she would read, a book I did not want anyone to read?

I stood at the edge of the woods, staring into the shadows and the wet gloom.

And then I walked away.

My bag was gone, my journal was gone. The girl was gone.

And I was gone, down another road.

Was I changing? Was I putting away childish things?

Oh, hell, I hoped not.

I was on some other road that ran down off the ridge and into a valley where I knew there must be some little town where I could do something, some work of some kind, enough so I could save the few bucks I already had in my pocket. Buy some food. And maybe one of those cheap plastic raincoats.

I shuffled along the road, not really in a hurry. The rain had stopped and the night lightened a little. I found an ancient shed at the edge of the trees and I hunkered down in some old hay. I was almost warm.

I had to have a plan. A plan. Something that would tell me that I knew what I was doing there, so I would not have to ask that fucking question ever again. If I had a plan, I would *know* what I was doing here, there, anywhere. But most of all, I had to have a plan to give me something I could shoot for, something to keep me going, something to keep me from bottoming out.

I wondered if this was what it felt like to bottom out. I wondered if anybody really knew, at the time, that they had bottomed out. Maybe you didn't know. Maybe only later, when you looked back on it, did you know, did you understand that you were chin deep in shit back then. That you had bottomed out. Was there more than one way to bottom out? Could you bottom out, and then do it all over again? I thought about that for a while, trying to think deep philosophical thoughts. And then I began to wonder if I were smart enough to think deep philosophical thoughts.

A plan.

A plan?

The hell with it. I had never had a plan in my life. I had no idea what a plan really meant.

And right in the middle of all that deep philosophical shit I fell asleep.

Even in my sleep, I could feel the cold of the concrete culvert all the way into my stomach.

And I could feel the girl.

Six

Cattle Ranch
Wyoming
November 1956

Seems like getting to the Mississippi River was no trouble at all.
Just one short ride after another, the drivers talking about the same
things, the same trees going by the car windows, the same nights,
the same days, the same cafes where the drivers ate and I didn't,
pretending that I was not hungry. I had a few bucks in my pocket.
I could have bought food. I don't know why I thought I had to save
the money.

The driver pulled over to the curb. He did not even look at me,
just waited for me to open the door and slide out. As I swung the
door shut I started to say "thanks," but he did not wait for that, moving the car forward even before the door was fully closed.

Fuck you, I thought.

I did not know what town I was in, or what state, for that matter.
And, in fact, it did not matter. Wherever I was, I was not staying.

There was a tiny bus station across the street, one of those places
so small there was no place to park the buses. They just sat at the
curb. Where a battered bus sat waiting now, engine idling, heavy
diesel smoke rolling.

I remembered sitting on the steps of the high school in Crum,
watching the buses drive by on the narrow highway across the
railroad tracks. Sometimes I would sit on a fence right beside the
tracks so I could see the faces in the windows. I wondered where

they were going, those faces, those people, wondered if they knew they were passing through Crum, or if they cared. Maybe they didn't care about passing through anywhere, or anything. But at least they were going. They were *going*. Now and then I would see one of the faces looking at me, sitting there by the tracks, and for a second or two we would stare at each other. I wondered why they were going somewhere. Anywhere.

They wondered why I was staying.

I fingered the money in my pocket. I had never ridden a bus. Maybe now was the time. I walked across the street and stood by the grime-covered machine. Some others were standing there, waiting, heads hanging, hands stuffed into their pockets. The door to the tiny station opened and the driver came out. He must have weighed 300 pounds. His hat was shoved back on his bald head and he was still chewing the last bite of whatever he had eaten inside the station.

Whatever this was, it wasn't me. I could not do this. I knew which way was west, and I walked away in that direction.

Just east of St. Louis a guy driving a bread truck picked me up. As we crossed the river I couldn't take my eyes off the water, sitting up there in that bread truck, looking down over the rail. The driver was talking but I wasn't listening. The rail flashed by in patches just below my vision and then we were off the bridge and on the ground again. And I had that feeling that I have come to live for, the feeling that I was somewhere new.

I was in the West.

When the driver let me out, he gave me a loaf of bread.

It took another week to get to the real mountains.

The cattle truck was going north along the Front Range of the Rockies and I thought I might as well ride along. We finally came to a stop on a ranch near a tiny town in Southwest Wyoming. The ranch needed muscle. I had some of that. They hired me. *Jesus Christ! I was a cowboy.*

There was nothing much on the ranch to interrupt the hard flow of daylight and work and night, and then daylight again; of fixing fences in places where there shouldn't even be fences; of standing hip-deep in water so cold it seemed to crackle against your waders while you cleaned irrigation ditches; of keeping one eye on your job and the other on some loose-brained, flat-eared, rolling-eyed horse that was going to try to bite off your kneecap every time you stepped into the saddle; of just trying to stay alive through a long bitter winter of feeding cattle in ass-deep snow and wondering how many toes you might lose before spring.

What the hell was I doing there?

It didn't matter. It was one of the best jobs I ever had. I was happy. I didn't really mind hard work and I was working outside and there was no one there who knew I had ever been in West Virginia or Kentucky or South Carolina. There were no preachers. There were no sheriff's deputies. It was a good enough start, I thought.

It was on the ranch that I first saw a frozen fence. I was picking up strays on a high pasture and had spent the night in a line shack, a tiny cabin tucked into the side of a soaring ridge, partly shielded by thick pine growth up behind it. A sagging remnant of barbed wire fence ran beside the cabin and disappeared into some brush off to the east. The cabin was small and drafty, but it had a narrow bunk, a kerosene lamp and a rusty wood stove and was a hell of a lot better than sleeping outside. I put my horse in a shed that half-leaned against the back of the cabin. I got a book out of my saddle bag, closed the cabin door, fired up the stove and the lamp, wrapped my heavy wool coat around tightly around me, pulled my hat down to my ears, cleaned the grime from one of the tiny windows and watched as thick clouds began to roll along the ridge.

I liked it there. I liked the altitude and the sharpness of the thin air and the feel that whatever was up there belonged there and no-where else. And I was up there.

The ridge ran away to the north and in front of the cabin it fell steeply all the way to the valley. In the distance I could see the wagon road that eventually led back to the ranch house, miles away. The night had turned brittle cold, too cold to read. I had only a thin trail blanket with me and twice during the night I had to get up and feed the tiny stove. Finally, I took the blanket out to the shed and tied it on the horse, then went back into the cabin and pulled the bunk as close to the stove as I could without setting the damned thing on fire. I lay on the bunk, dozing as the stove burned, waking when it grew too cold.

The cold deepened, and then the clear light of early morning hit the shack's window, a promise of warmth, a light brilliant as only it can be in the pure fine reaches of the mountains where it hits the high country first, untouched by the rest of the Earth. I didn't really have to wake up; I had never really been asleep.

The sun came up and clattered through the sagging strands of the wire fence. As I came out into the dancing light the wire glittered, each wire wearing a coat of bursting crystals, thin layers of ice that cracked and caught the sun and sent flaring colors shooting past my face and through the cabin and into the far mountains. Like the fence, I was frozen, standing motionless before a kaleidoscopic display that changed with the very movement of my breathing and the delirious turns of the Earth.

I had seen nothing like it. A crystal fence. I stood, a prisoner held by light and color, transfixed. I was locked to it, as surely as if it were a totem.

And then another tiny click of time sent the sun a fraction higher, and the light and the color faded, passing from my eyes in an instant. I walked slowly to the fence and felt the wires. The ice cracked easily under my touch, falling away in thin, fragile shards. I grabbed the wire more strongly and shook the old, rickety fence, shook it until the ice crystals burst and sprayed into the sun.

For some reason, I wanted the ice to be gone.

I would see a frozen fence only once more in my lifetime.

In the army. At North Depot Activity. In Western New York State.

And I would want the ice to be gone then, too.

Seven

Cattle Ranch
Wyoming
Autumn 1958

On the ranch, to keep myself from going stir crazy, I ordered books through the mail, mostly history and biographies, some travel. I read novels when I could find the right ones. I made sure that all the books were paperbacks, so I could carry them in my saddlebags and behind the seat of the pickup truck. The books would become worn and fragile from handling and I would have to tape them, just to keep the pages from falling out. I wore out three different copies of *For Whom the Bell Tolls*. There was a small light nailed to the wall next to my top bunk and at night, reading, I would keep it burning until the other hands, or Tubbs, made me turn it out.

On every ranch I was ever on, or ever visited, there was at least one hand like Tubbs, a surly bull who took it upon himself to keep everyone else in line. Tubbs was older, maybe thirty, his hair so blond and sun-bleached it was almost white. His burly, thick arms, covered with white hair, drooped from his barrel chest like snow-laden limbs from a short tree. And he was mean.

He didn't like me—there was a possibility that he didn't like any-body—and particularly didn't like the fact that I read books, lying in my bunk with the light on. When Tubbs thought I had kept the light on long enough, he would simply pull the plug. More than once I had rolled out of my bunk and grabbed him, both of us straining and grunting and rolling on the floor. Tubbs would always end up on top and just as he was getting ready to drive his fist into my face the others would pull us apart. A night or so later, we would do it all over again. Nothing ever got settled.

Actually, I hated wrestling with Tubbs. Tubbs thought washing his body would make him weak, so he only took a bath when the foreman made him do it, or when the rest of the hands threatened to do it for him.

Finally, I moved out of the bunkhouse and into the barn. I built a small room out of scrap lumber in the corner of the loft where I could read in peace and wonder about the other corners of the Earth, while listening to the rats scurry across the tin ceiling of the tiny cubicle.

I found a cheap set of weights at the hardware store in town and I decided to develop my body, only to find out that a full day on the ranch left little time or energy for weightlifting. But I kept trying.

One of the ranch hands had been on a Judo team in the Air Force. I ordered a book titled *Learn Judo in Ten Easy Lessons*, and I and some of the other hands would practice in the late evenings and on Sunday afternoons, throwing each other into the loose hay in the barn loft and into the soft earth of the breaking corral, laughing and wrestling and working off the tension that can come from long periods of intense labor in front of the same set of faces. The book and the Air Force veteran taught us something; not much, but something. I even tried to get Tubbs interested, tried to entice him into the lessons, but the bastard would only grunt and walk away.

The hardware store had school supplies. I found some more of my favorite composition notebooks. And I signed up for some correspondence courses in English and history. In my room in the barn I would read the books aloud, listening to myself, trying to correct my pronunciation, trying to get the West Virginia out of my speech. I almost made it. My speech became a rolling gait of soft sounds and rumbles, country, but with no discernible origin.

All in all, the ranch was okay. I got bigger. And I got stronger, much stronger—the weights helped some, but mostly it was just the ranch—and I developed some sort of agility that I had never had before. Most of it came from my time on the horses, but some of it was the weights and the Judo.

And then the question hit me again.

What the hell am I doing here?

In the late summer I packed a small, gray duffle bag that I could carry in one hand, and in the first light of a cool morning I walked down the narrow dirt road to the gate of the ranch.

And then I changed my mind. I put down the bag and walked back to the ranch, into the bunkhouse.

Tubbs was sitting on the edge of his bunk, his thick body leaning forward, his elbows on his knees. He was surprised to see me up and dressed and already on the move. I walked over to him and squatted down so I could look him the eye, even in the dim light.

Neither of us moved.

And then I said, as softly as I could, so as not to waken any of the other hands, "You are a world-class stupid motherfucker."

I watched his muscles bunch under his tee shirt, heard his breathing sharpen, waited for him to hit me. But he did not move.

"I'm leaving, but I just wanted to make sure I said that to you."

And he still did not move.

I waited a few seconds, then slowly stood up and backed away, keeping an eye out for any movement he might make.

He did not move.

I went back to the highway, and was gone.

Eight

College
Colorado
Autumn 1958

Two hours after I left Tubbs sitting on his bunk I flagged down a bus. My first bus ride. I didn't give a damn which way it was going. I rode until I came to the first large town, got off, and discovered there was a university there.

The town was loaded with young people who looked as though they were lost, and I soon found out why: fall enrollment at the university had just begun.

I had read enough books on the ranch to know that I needed to read a lot more books. The novels got me into history, and history into biography, and biography into philosophy, and philosophy into everything else until I was deep into shit I didn't even understand.

I thought I needed college.

So, out of curiosity, and for no more reason than that, I enrolled. As an English major.

When the lady at the registration desk asked me for my address I didn't know what to tell her. In the hip pocket of my jeans I had a folded, worn letter from an elderly school teacher in Laramie, who had long since retired to a little town in Colorado. He was a gentle, intelligent man who had once spent several hours in a public park on a golden Sunday afternoon talking with me about books, about how all the things in books can never escape, once you've read them, once you've captured them with your mind. They are yours forever. It was one of the best talks I had ever had in my life, and not a single time did either of us mention cows. I pulled out the letter and gave the woman the old man's address.

She accepted it without question.

I stared at the letter, remembering the sunshine and conversation that went with it. The letter was important to me. And the address? Well, if addresses were really important, the address on the letter was as good as any I had ever had.

To tell the truth, I do not know why I enrolled. Within the first few weeks I realized I was in the wrong place. College was too pretty, too organized, too juvenile. Too fucking straight. Maybe I was smart, maybe I was not, but college, no college, would ever get it out of me. It did not seem real there.

Every day I saw hundreds of students moving around the campus, some of them with intent looks on their faces, some of them looking as lost as I was.

And, yeah, I watched the girls. I looked at their cute skirts and blouses and their cute haircuts and their cute butts and I wasn't particularly impressed. But then, some of them looked at me and I could tell from their expressions that they weren't particularly impressed with me, either. My jeans had frayed cuffs at the back where they hung down too long when I wasn't riding a horse. My boots were old—very comfortable, but very old—and the heels needed a transplant. I had on my only clean shirt, but it had a small hole in the left elbow. I only had one hat, and I was wearing it, my hair uncut and sticking out underneath like straw under a bucket. I knew there were sweat stains around the hat band and I knew the girls wouldn't know what it had cost me to put them there.

I was a lousy student. I had no interest in anything. I stumbled around the campus not really caring whether I got to wherever I was going on time, or whether I got there at all. I always carried some books. If I did manage to get to class, I wanted to give the impression that I meant to get there. The books were only props. Most of them were novels.

Usually, I veered off from the path to class—any class —and wandered into the student union. I played ping-pong for hours, gradually becoming good enough to enter tournaments. Once, in a tournament open to the entire student body, I placed ninth. Smashing a tiny white ball with a piece of rubber-covered wood was the crowning achievement of my college career.

I played ping-pong in cowboy boots.

Sometimes I went downtown and drank beer. I ran into some other guys, and a few girls, doing the same thing. We sat in darkened beer joints and sipped at our glasses, trying not to appear to be alcoholics, only to discover that no one cared whether we were or not. The discovery was sobering.

Now and then I wrote in my composition books, but, usually, I was too stoned to write anything that made sense.

Sitting in a saloon one day, I became bored with sitting in a saloon. Even philosophy class seemed more interesting than what I was doing. I bought a quart of beer, put it in my book bag and straggled off to class.

I had been to only a handful of the philosophy classes, preferring to just read the books and fake the quizzes. Then I got bored with the books and did not read at all. I was failing the course. I didn't give a shit.

I got the class time wrong; I was actually early. A girl asked me if I was a late enrollee in the class; she had never seen me before.

I do not remember if I sat through the entire class.

I remember the last exam I took. Actually, I do not remember the exam itself, but I do remember what happened. There was a bench in front of the library . . .

I knew I was lying on a bench at the side of the grassy quadrangle in front of the library. I could feel the bench beneath me. I ran my hands along the front of the bench, feeling the smooth, worn wood.

I had lain down on the bench an hour or so ago. I needed a nap. I had come out of the exam and the bench was there. Many times I had seen people napping on these benches. No one ever seemed to bother the nappers.

My eyelids seemed glued shut. I rubbed at them with my hands, then sat up, blinking. My book bag was on the bench beside me; I had been using it as a pillow.

I thought I should be jittery, but I was not. My head rang with soft pain but my hands did not shake. The reds must have worn off.

The reds, bless their little rounded, shiny bodies. They may have saved me again. Take a fistful of those, one of the girls said, and you can steam through the night, catch up on all that philosophy crap. Pass the final, and you pass the course.

What the hell, I thought, it was worth a try.

The reds cost me all my beer money.

I started popping them at mid-day. I kept at it though the night, popping pills and reading. I took the last red at three in the morning. Philosophy never seemed so exciting.

I forgot my watch and ran for the campus, barely making it on time. I do not remember the exam at all. I do remember odd looks from some of the other students, but, what the hell, it's a philosophy class. It's full of goddamn odd students.

The reds started wearing off. I managed to get through the exam and staggered out of the building around noon. The last exam. I was through with that shit. Maybe I was through with that shit forever.

I started across campus, my feet not attached to my legs. The reds were fleeing the country. I saw the bench near the library. I was hungry, *really* hungry. But I could hardly walk. I needed a nap. I lay down on the bench.

It was getting late, the sun far down behind the buildings and sinking fast. I had slept longer than I meant to, but it did not matter. No one was looking for me; no one knew where I was; I had nothing to do.

I stood up and stretched, looking carefully around the quadrangle, trying to appear casual. There was no one around.

Not anywhere.

I wondered about that. There should have been someone, some exam-battered student heading for the student union building, some dry slug or two heading downtown for a beer. Somebody. Going somewhere. But there was no one.

It did not register with me until I realized the fading light was not fading. The light was growing stronger. The sun was not setting, it was rising. There was no one on campus because it was just barely first light.

I had slept on the bench all day, and then all night.

I sat back down and stared at the growing light.

What the hell am I doing here?

College.

I gave it my best effort.

Well, maybe not my best effort, but at least some effort.

Bullshit. I didn't give it any effort at all.

I only lasted a single year.

I found out years later that I passed the exam.

Nine

Crested Butte, Colorado
Winter 1959

On a day in winter when I could smell the ice in the air, even through the frosted windows of the room, I raised my hand during a class that I do not even remember and asked to be excused. "Restroom," I think I said. I never went back. I just kept walking. I went to my room at a boarding house, packed another ratty duffle bag and caught a bus for El Paso, then changed my mind and got off in Pueblo, Colorado. I hitchhiked west to Gunnison. A tiny highway ran to the north and a guy in Gunnison said there was a town up there, Crested Butte, a village of some 200 people caught in a time warp. They lived in quiet and gentle peace at the end of one of God's most beautiful valleys. Unless you had a Jeep or a horse, the road ended in Crested Butte; once there, there was no place else to go.

Sounded good to me. I went.

For fifty dollars I rented an abandoned shack on Maroon Avenue, a single-lane dirt street beside the creek. The fifty dollars paid for the rest of the winter.

I nailed up the holes in the walls and heated the place with a small wood stove, burning scraps of lumber I dug from beneath the deep drifts out back. The snow from the high mountain Colorado winter drifted to the eaves of the house, forming a blanket of insulation that my small stove gradually melted back until I could squeeze along the outside of the walls of the house in search of wood scraps. I spent the rest of the winter reading.

That summer I got a job with a Gunnison outfitter who took tourists on pack trips into the high country. We worked out of an old ranch up a canyon just south of Crested Butte. I knew my way around the mountains, was good with horses and, since I was getting paid for it, was even good with the tourists. The outfitter had only two other employees, an Indian and a Mexican. The Indian pretended not to speak Spanish, the Mexican pretended not to speak English, and I pretended not to understand either of them. Some days, we didn't speak for hours, and it got so we didn't need to.

The outfitter stayed in Gunnison and let the three of us run the pack trips. We made a good team. We made an odd team. I was six feet tall and stocky, with blond hair that hung down almost to my heavy shoulders. I walked upright, almost too upright—I had a stick up my ass, the Mexican said—and when I moved I went directly about my business. The Mexican said you could watch me move and know what was going to happen next.

But not the Indian, Wendell Klah. With him, you never knew what was going to happen next. He had skin the color of a late sunset in New Mexico, a deep, rusty tint that seemed to glow even in the feeble light of early morning. His hair was straight, glistening black, and hung down longer than mine. He was slender, tall, with lanky arms and legs that he seemed to be able to fold at odd angles. When he got up to move, there was always a hesitation, a moment when he seemed on the verge of changing his mind, a split second when you couldn't be sure, not of the Indian, not of anything about him.

The Mexican was somewhere in the middle, not as heavy as me, not as tall as the Indian. Quicker than both of us. His name was Caton Baros, but no one called him that. They called him Cat, sometimes The Cat. It fit, in every respect.

Caton meant wise man, the Mexican had once explained.

"*Si*, my mother, she wanted a wise man. But she got a *payaso*, a clown."

But a tough clown, I thought. A very tough clown. The Mexican was good with his fists, had fought professionally in Mexico City. There had been some trouble in the ring one night, the other guy knowing he was losing and whispering something in the Mexican's ear, something about his mother, maybe trying to break the Mexican's concentration. Caton punched the guy into oblivion, and then kept punching him and punching him and punching him until he was dead. The crowd loved it.

But Caton had to get the hell out of Mexico.

He wore his dark hair short, held back from his forehead by a red bandana, until the day the Indian traded him a soft leather band for it. He kept the band on, even under his hat. And then one day I noticed he had added something to it—beadwork.

"Jesus, Cat . . . beadwork? I thought only Indians did beadwork."

Wendell was sitting at the base of a tree, his hat pulled down over his eyes. He didn't move.

"Yeah, well, I seen white guys do knitting. Why can't a Mexican do beadwork?"

I laughed. He was right.

Cat's forearms were sculpted with muscle and he could chin himself with one arm. As long as I knew the Mexican, I never really knew whether the man had a temper. I had seen him mad, but it always seemed as though the Mexican programmed it, made it happen, didn't wait for the rise of a temper that wasn't there. But that was good, I thought. God knows what the Mexican would do if he ever lost control.

Like back in the ring in Mexico.

So we took the tourists on horseback rides, ate huge lunches carried on a packhorse, and swapped stories of where we grew up, and how we grew up, and how we would not wish that sort of growing up on anybody.

In the early fall when the tourists stopped coming the outfitter took in hunters and turned them over to us, and we led the dudes by the hand into the mountains to hunt elk.

On the last trip of the season, on a bare ridge that rose far into the West Elk Range, in the storm-dark of early afternoon, with snow beginning to slice almost horizontally through the air, a greenhorn from Chicago shot my horse. He thought it was an elk.

I was riding the horse at the time.

The dude panicked, got on his own horse, and rode away, leaving me on foot in the wilderness. The dude didn't know which way to ride but that was no problem—the horse took him straight back to camp.

I walked six miles through heavy timber, around steep slopes, and through the hard snowfall of an early winter storm before darkness caught me, still and cold in the lee of a low stand of trees, the temperature dropping like a stone through clear water. My parka and boots were not heavy enough for what the weather was doing, and I knew that I would not survive if I did not find shelter. I spent the night under a deadfall, lying as far back under the fallen tree as I could. Before I crawled in, I piled all the dry forest junk I could find against the back of the tree, trying to block the movement of air underneath the trunk. I spread more on the ground, to lie on. I scraped a wide line in the snow in front of me, down through pine needles and twigs in front of the deadfall, scraped it all the way down to bare earth. The line was the length of my body and I built several small bucket-sized fires along it and kept them burning throughout the night. As each little fire died down I would build it up again, working the fire line constantly, grabbing a few minutes sleep between firings. I knew the temperature had dropped below zero, but the fires, radiating directly on me and reflecting from the deadfall, sustained me. I stayed alive. Barely.

An hour after first light the next day I ran into the Mexican and the Indian. They were searching in the general direction the dude rode in from, their horses moving easily through the snow that was now almost a foot deep. They gave me some hot coffee, wrapped me in a sleeping bag, and put me up on the horse behind the Mexican. I dozed all the way back to camp.

The Indian had the dude tied to a tree. He had tied the man there without a second thought, left him, and had gone off with the Mexican to try and find me. The dude was shaking inside the ropes, an almost terminal kind of shaking, a combination of the cold and abject fear.

They eased me off the horse, my body beginning to stiffen from the night in the cold and the long ride back on the horse. The Indian built a fire and the Mexican wrapped me in another sleeping bag and stuffed me with hot food and more coffee. They left the dude tied to the tree.

They tried to decide what to do about the dude. Finally, the Mexican took the dude's rifle and inspected it carefully, admiring the engraved, grotesquely expensive, hardly used weapon, checking to make sure there was a round in the chamber. He walked slowly and carefully around the fire, holding the rifle in front of him. And then he whirled and fired a shot into the tree just above the dude's head, the explosion of the shot cracking across the mountainsides and through the canyons. The Mexican worked the rifle's bolt in a blur of motion and fired another shot, and another, emptying the gun into the tree, the dude screaming all the while. When the firing was over, the dude had fainted.

The Mexican tossed the rifle to the Indian, who rammed it muzzle-first into the fire. He sat, singing some soft and unknown songs, his own rifle across his lap, and kept the fire burning for three hours.

Later, the dude swore to the outfitter that I had caused the whole mess by joking around and tying some small dead branches to my horse's head and leading the animal through the woods. Anyone, said the dude, would have thought it was an elk. The outfitter didn't believe him, and he didn't really give a damn about the horse—only the money it would cost him to replace it—but he used the opportunity to fire the three of us. Winter would be coming on hard and he didn't want to pay us for the long, cold time. He kept our last week's pay—to pay for the horse, he said.

That evening, while the outfitter and the dude were getting drunk in the Cattlemen's Bar in Gunnison, the Indian and I took the outfitter's two stock trucks to his hunting camp where the Mexican loaded them with horses. We drove the trucks to Montrose and sold the horses the next day to a Mexican with a crippled leg, bad breath, and a fat wallet; he left immediately in the general direction of Mexico.

The three of us split the money evenly.

We drove the trucks to a diner and parked them out front. I asked the counterman if anyone in Montrose wanted to rent some stock trucks to move cattle down from the high county, knowing full well that most of the cattle had already long since come down. The counterman sent us to a ranch south of town where the crew was getting ready to ship some cattle south for the winter. We made a deal to take both trucks south, loaded the cattle, and took the rent money in cash.

We split the money evenly.

We drove out of town and kept going until we saw some cowboys riding across a low meadow. We turned down a dirt road, stopped the trucks, and then walked away toward the road before anybody got around to wondering why two trucks full of cattle were doing parked just off the highway. The rancher in Montrose would probably get his cattle back, but we wondered how long it would take the asshole outfitter in Gunnison to find his trucks. We knew he would never find his horses.

To throw anyone off the trail, we decided to split up.

Wendell and I had never been to San Francisco. Caton had. He said it was a great place to get lost in. So that is where we decided to go.

"We'll meet up on the waterfront," Cat said. "There's a museum there, name of Ripee's Believe It Snot."

I looked at Wendell. Wendell was looking at Cat.

"What?" Wendell asked. "Name of . . . what?"

"Ripee's Believe It Snot," Cat said. "Damndest thing you ever see. All kinds of shit in there. We can just keep going down there, wait out front, 'til we all show up."

Jesus.

But Wendell and I didn't have any better ideas.

"Let's take our time on the road," Cat said.

"Why?" Wendell wanted to know.

"Make it last," Cat said.

"Make what last?" I asked.

"Life," Cat said.

The Indian caught a bus, the Mexican caught the next bus, and I hitchhiked, all of us heading toward San Francisco. We had a twenty dollar bet on who would get there last.

Not get there first. Get there last.

It was an easy bet for me to take.

Sometimes I do not get where I'm going in a straight line.

Sometimes I do not get there at all.

It took me four days to get to the city and two days to find them. And then, there they were, sitting on the sidewalk, leaning back against the side of some sort of tourist trap, passing a joint back and forth, people walking off the sidewalk to get around them, not wanting to come close to them. Not wanting to be in the same city.

They looked like hell. But to me, they were beautiful.

I looked at the big sign on the tourist trap. "Ripley's Believe It Or Not" the sign screamed.

Dumbass Mexican.

At about ten o'clock on our fourth day together in San Francisco a cab driver, for a twenty dollar tip, took us to the best whorehouse he knew of. We didn't come out until very late the following afternoon.

We shouldn't have come out at all.

It was raining.

Ten

Paradise Street Gentlemen's Club
San Francisco
April 1960

I never learned to get out of a whorehouse the easy way. Maybe I should have gone to whorehouse school to get my manners polished up. I just never got around to it. But, all things considered, I went to some schools that were pretty much like whorehouses, and I never got around to learning anything much at those, either.

So I was angry when I stumbled out through the door of the whorehouse, the side of my face aching from some fist that had come out of the darkness right after I tried to find the Mexican. I could hear the Mexican screaming and I thought they were trying to kill him. Turns out they were. They were trying to fuck him to death.

It was raining when I staggered outside, one of those cold, miserable far late afternoons in San Francisco that brought the sky down to touch the street. I stopped at the top of the short flight of concrete steps and let the rain stream down my face and felt it blow past me and down into the bowels of the city along distant steep streets that ran far out of my sight in the grayness, an almost silent misty downpour that took away the light and closed in the distance. The rain soaked my shirt and ran down the loose shirttails. My worn, faded jeans picked up the rain instantly and I knew it would be hours, maybe days, before the damn things would dry.

My boots were getting wet. Oddly, I didn't remember putting them on before I came out the door, and I wondered if I had ever taken them off. I must have taken my boots off, I thought, else, how the hell could I get my jeans off?

But I really didn't feel the rain too much; I was drunk. It was old drunk, tired drunk, started a couple of days ago, and I was in that stage where I was just trying to clear my head and force myself to see clearly. I held onto the door frame to steady myself, not wanting to trust my legs and my boots to the slick steps and the dark wet bricks of the tilted street.

The Indian came out and lurched past me, staggering down the steps and straight into the middle of the street. He stopped, stood there blinking, naked to the waist, his glistening black hair shedding the rain down his back. He rubbed his chest, seemed surprised at the feel of his own wet skin. The tilt of the street confused him and in his stupor he thought he was falling backward. He tried to stand up straight from the surface, causing himself to pitch face-first down the slick bricks. He hit the street, slid for a foot or two, and lay absolutely still. I thought maybe he was dead. And then he rolled slowly over on his back, his head downhill, the rain running up his nose. He was laughing.

"Hey, Jesse," the Indian yelled, still lying in the street, "you seen my shirt? I had a shirt. Damn sure did have a shirt, must have had a shirt . . ." His voice trailed off in the rain.

Even at that short distance it was hard for me to see the Indian clearly, partly because of the rain, partly because of the rapidly failing light, partly because of the old-drunk whiskey still running through my veins.

I wondered where the Mexican was. The Mexican had been down the hallway a couple of doors from my room. I had heard nothing from him all night. And then sometime later in the black of early morning I had heard the Mexican yelling. He was yelling in Spanish slang and I hadn't been able to understand all of it, but the yells had been real and loud and long and high pitched and they scared the hell out of me. I had gone looking for the Mexican. That was a mistake.

I eased myself carefully down the steps and onto the sidewalk and lumbered into the street, starting to say something to the Indian. Before I could get the words out the whorehouse door blew open and the Mexican blasted through, twisting forward as he came, a brown human curveball. He missed the short flight of steps completely, hit the sidewalk at a dead run, then tripped over the Indian and was airborne. He swapped ends in mid-air, turning and rolling into the street. He came to a stop sitting up, jubilantly holding up a half-empty bottle of whiskey. The bottle had never touched the ground.

I squinted through the rain at the doorway. A fat man the size of a cattle truck was just closing the door. I heard the hard clack of a bolt being snapped shut. I wondered if the fat man's fist was the same size as the ache in my jaw.

"Jesus, Cat, what the hell . . ." I started toward the Mexican, who was just sitting in the rain, staring at the whiskey bottle.

"Forget it, man, *no problema*," the Mexican said, his words sputtering as the water ran down over his face. "I'm okay, man. Was worth it. It was worth it, man! Shit, man, she was six feet tall and stronger than I am, man, and, and . . . shit, man, she held me upside down against the wall! Shit, Jesse, I never been fucked so hard in my whole *stupido* life!"

The Mexican was almost shouting now, his back straight and his arms flung out to the sides. "Jesse, we got to go back in there, man! We got to go back through that door and kick some ass . . . go back in there just so's you can see what she can do when she holds you upside down against the wall!"

The Mexican pulled his legs underneath him and seemed to float up from the street, standing, holding the whiskey bottle against his face, dancing back toward the steps of the whorehouse.

I thought about the fat man in the doorway. I wasn't sure whether the whole thing would be worth the trouble. And I knew that the Mexican was more than just drunk; he was totaled, polluted, drunk all the way to his scalp, drunk all the way back into other generations of his family. He was beyond ordinary drunk—he was in some special drunk class all by himself.

I thought he might try to go back inside, but he wasn't going anywhere. I watched as he collapsed gently onto the steps of the whorehouse. I had seen him this way a couple of times before, so drunk that he was edging back toward sober. It was almost as though the Mexican's body reached a point where it simply refused to accept any more alcohol and just started sobering itself up, knowing that the Mexican would need a sober body at some time in the immediate future. He was amazing, the Mexican, especially when he was drunk. His wiry body and quick mind seemed to respond in ways that magnified his actual need, as though only some larger response would do.

I staggered back across the sidewalk and sat on the steps next to the Mexican. It took a while in the pale light of the rain for me to notice the odd color of his shirt. He had a red bandana around his neck and at first I thought the rain was washing the color out of it. Then I saw the Mexican's face. Jagged scratches ran in all directions across his forehead and down his cheeks, tiny flaps of skin still oozing blood, the rain washing it down onto his white shirt. There must have been other scratches on his back because blood was soaking through his shirt back there, the rain diluting it to a pale pink, flowing down the dripping shirt. Cat took a long drink from the bottle and then poured some of the whiskey into the palm of his hand and rubbed it across his face, screaming at the contact of the alcohol against the newly raw flesh. I wondered which he thought was better, the fucking or the scratching.

"Shit, man," Cat muttered, "this damn whiskey ain't really whiskey. They must have made this stuff yesterday." He stood and rubbed another handful across his face, then looked past me and started to laugh all over again. In the middle of the street Wendell had gotten to his feet, dropped his jeans to his ankles and was urinating in a high arc, applying all the pressure he could. The urine made a graceful curve up and into the rain, seeming to disappear before it hit the street. He wore no undershorts. Except for the sodden pants piled down around the tops of his boots, the Indian was naked. The rain slid over his tall, slender body and ran along the grooves that pulled deep between his muscles. I knew he was probably pissing on himself by now, but there was so much rain it didn't make any difference. It all blended.

I got up, put my arm around the Mexican, and we guided each other over to the Indian, who continued to dribble piss into the street. The three of us stood in the stone-gray rain, the blood pounding in our ears, our stomachs churning from too much cheap whiskey and too little food. This was only our fourth day in San Francisco and if we had bothered to feel around in our pockets we would have known we were broke. The money from the horses was gone; our wallets stripped clean. But we didn't know that at the time and so we began to laugh, to laugh at ourselves, at the sight of each other, at the whole idea of the thing, of being in a big city with nowhere to go, nothing to run from, nothing to run to. We were totally useless and homeless and soberless and fucked out and broke. And so we just laughed, and weaved back and forth a little in the fading light, filling the street with our sounds and our presence. It didn't really matter what we knew or didn't know, we would have laughed anyway.

The Indian was still laughing, strands of his shoulder-length hair strung wetly across his face, his pants still around his ankles, his dick still in his hand, when the patrol car rolled quietly up the steep street, poked its nose almost into us, and came to a stop in front of me and the Indian.

The Mexican was gone.

The lights on top of the patrol car came on and we stared at them, fascinated by the effect of the rain on the red and blue flashers. Colors.

I remembered sitting with Wendell on the edge of a high mesa in the reservation country where he was born, chewing on a bitter button that Wendell had gotten from some Utes. Damn Utes, he had said. Wish they'd keep this shit to themselves. But he had a pocketful of them. We chewed, staring into the late evening sun.

And then I puked, falling over on the red rock.

As I lay sideways I saw that the sun was red, and then blue, and then some colors I had never seen before, have not seen since. My eyes blurred and the colors ran together, washing over each other and over me, blending and yet crisp, clear and individual. I could see each color separately and distinctly, and yet I could see the whole, flowing out over the mesa and covering the red land with a warmth that I had never seen before, never felt before. I remembered that the warmth had lasted two days. When it was all over, my head felt strangely empty, clean, and I was as hungry as I had ever been in my life.

I knew that I had been very screwed up. Shit, I thought, maybe the Utes aren't so bad, after all.

"Let go of your cock and pull up your goddamn pants!" a voice commanded from a loudspeaker mounted between the lights. Wendell didn't move.

"I said, pull up your goddamn pants, and get your ass over here!" The voice was harder now, metallic, tougher.

Wendell reached for his dripping, heavy jeans and began slowly tugging them upward, the sodden cloth clinging to his skin. He wore a braided horsehair belt with a large, oval rodeo buckle. He had won the buckle for bull riding at some small country rodeo outside of Flagstaff, Arizona. On the front of the buckle a bull rider and a bull were frozen in mid-jump, their tiny forms buffed and polished almost smooth by years of wear. Wendell gripped the buckle and tried to fasten his belt, all the while weaving on unsteady legs. He had trouble making the buckle connect. He leaned forward slightly and his hair hung in front of his face like a black waterfall, almost completely masking his features.

"Jesus Christ, Harry, I got me a goddamn Indian over here! Who you got over there?" The voice didn't come from the loudspeaker and I knew one of the windows of car had been rolled down. Wendell forced his hands to steady and got his belt buckled at last.

The other window rolled down. "Damned if I know. Looks like a cowboy fresh out of that cathouse, over there. A cathouse cowboy! Get over here, boy, and let's have a closer look!"

I felt the whiskey begin to slosh around in my stomach. I knew that no good things could happen if I went to the car. The headlights and the flashers created a wall of shimmering lights in front of me and I couldn't see inside. But there must be two of them, I thought. I wished I could see the Indian more clearly but it was raining harder. If I could just see the Indian clearly I might be able to work something out. We had been able to do it before, me and the Indian, without speaking a word.

I took one step toward the car, then turned and lurched several steps back up the street, stopped, and turned again. I was standing directly in the patrol car's path. I felt movement to my left and knew that the Indian was there beside me. I could hear faint cursing sounds from inside the car.

On the right side of the patrol car the window came down farther and a head eased into the downpour.

"Goddamn it, you shitbags, I said over *here!*" The cop hit the last word hard, then waited, sure of himself, sure of his position in the San Francisco Police Department, sure of San Francisco.

The Indian raised his arms to the sky, face full into the rain, and screamed. It was a long scream, a high-pitched wail slicing into the dim light and carrying away down the hill, a pure, timeless scream out of the Southwest, meant to be screamed from the edge of black-red mesa in that tiny moment just before dawn when the full dangers of another day are about to become visible. It was one of the most beautiful screams I had ever heard.

At the end of the scream the Indian turned his head slightly and said softly, "Let's see if that fucks 'em up a little."

For a moment, after the scream, no one moved. Then slowly, reluctantly, both doors of the patrol car opened and the two cops got out into the rain. They were wearing slickers and the long, shiny coats gave them a wavering appearance, black-suited apparitions drifting through the dancing dimness of the rain and the headlights and the approaching night. They eased the doors shut, engine still running, and moved to the front of the car. They stood just behind the lights and I couldn't see their faces.

"Okay, boys, the bullshit stops right here," the driver said. "Now you do exactly what I tell you and the rest will be easy. You got that? You, Indian, you step over that way!" he shouted, throwing his arm out toward his partner. "You hear me, Indian? I said *move!*"

Quietly, out of the corner of his mouth, the Indian said, "I ain't movin', Jesse. These white boys ain't gonna cut me no slack."

"Me neither," I muttered. "Screw them. Let 'em come. We're drunk. We can always say we were drunk. I'll take the one on the right."

"Just one thing, Jesse. My knife's gone. Must be they took it in the whorehouse."

I didn't even have to check my belt. I knew my knife would be gone, too.

Just as well, I thought. Knives would just get us shot.

The cops started forward, slowly, carefully, moving up into the glare of the patrol car's headlights, toward us. I moved backward with the Indian, matching the cops step for step.

On the sidewalk next to the car a tiny light flickered, almost obscured by the flashing reds and blues. It was a yellow light, and it curled and danced.

Flame.

The Mexican held the flame out in front of him, shielding it from the rain with his hand. He had soaked his bandana with the whiskey, jammed it down into the bottle, lit it. He held the Molotov cocktail carefully in front of him and slowly, quietly, opened the driver's door of the patrol car.

The cops took another step forward.

"I think you got a problem," I said, looking past the shoulder of the cop on the right.

"Jesus, you boys been seein' too many John Wayne movies," the cop said, not taking his eyes from me. "You hear what he said, partner? He said we got a problem."

"Oldest trick in the book . . ." the other cop muttered, but couldn't prevent himself from glancing quickly over his shoulder.

"Holy shit, Harry, there's somebody in the unit!" the cop yelled, clawing for his gun underneath the slicker.

The Mexican had eased into the driver's seat, still holding the burning bottle. He flicked the headlights off and held the bottle up in front of him, the flame flickering brightly through the windshield. The headlights came on again.

"What the hell's he got, Harry . . . Jesus, he's going to burn the car!" The cop cleared the pistol from the slicker and began to draw down on the windshield.

"Don't shoot!" Harry screamed. "He's got a bottle! If he breaks it, the unit's gone!"

"Well, who the hell is that? Where the fuck did he come from?"

"Jesus Christ, how the hell do I know? Maybe another goddamn Indian! Just try to get close!" Harry looked back at me and the Indian. He drew his pistol.

"You fuckin' people take one step, just one step, and I'm gonna blow your asses off! You got that?"

He didn't wait for an answer. Turning back toward the car both cops edged carefully down the street, moving tenderly, the way men approach a skittish horse. They took no more than two steps when the car's engine suddenly roared and the car slammed into reverse, tires spinning on the wet street, whipping twenty feet backwards down the hill.

"Hey, hold it right there, goddamn it! Let's talk this thing over!" Harry yelled, holding his pistol out to his side, showing it. "We don't want trouble! We can work something out! Let's just talk this thing over, okay?"

The cops moved toward the car again, carefully, slowly. The car took another violent jump backwards. The headlights went off again, the bright, flickering flame continuing to show through the windshield.

We watched silently as the cops made another move, watched as the car moved again, watched the flame dance inside the windshield, then watched as the process repeated itself, the scene growing dimmer in the distance each time the cops and the car moved. The cops talked constantly to the driver, never really seeing him behind the dancing flame. The Mexican never responded.

The Indian's pants were down around his ankles again, and he was once again pissing in the direction of the patrol car. I wasn't surprised. I grinned at him.

"Didn't get finished when they first drove up," the Indian muttered. "Damn white boys—seems like all they ever want to do is keep Indians from pissing on the ground."

I laughed, remembering that one of Wendell's favorite things to do was to take a leak, anywhere he wanted to, anytime.

"Jesse, you know what Cat wants us to do?"

"Yeah, Wendell, I guess I do."

"You think he'll be okay, Jesse?"

"Christ, I don't know . . . I guess so. Hell, there's nothing we can do about it anyway."

"Then let's get the hell out'a here," the Indian said flatly. He pulled up his dripping pants, reached inside and carefully arranged his penis, and pulled up the zipper.

We walked away up the street, in no particular hurry. At the top of the hill we turned and took a last look. It was difficult to see anything clearly now. We no longer could see the tiny flicker dancing in the windshield, could hardly see the car. The car and the cops and the Mexican faded into the far down distance of the wet and darkening street and the mists of San Francisco, shadowy players merging with the city.

And then a brilliant, billowing ball of flame blossomed in the midst of those far shadows, flashing out from the car toward both sides of the street and curving, curling, up into the rain. In the bright light of the flames I could see the silhouettes of the cops, standing rooted to the steep street.

The Indian fumbled at the waistband of his dripping jeans and untied a small leather sack. He fished inside the pouch with his finger and rolled two tiny bean-like objects into the palm of his hand. He put one into his mouth and handed the other to me.

"Here," he said. "My last ones. The rain's got 'em already softened up."

We turned the corner and walked away. When we were a hundred yards farther down the street we heard a heavy roar, the concussion pounding through the neighborhood like a giant wave among the pilings of a pier.

"Gas tank," I muttered.

"Yeah," the Indian said.

"You think Cat was still in the car?"

"Get serious, white boy."

Jesus, I thought, getting out of a whorehouse is never easy.

Eleven

Flophouse
San Francisco
May 1960

The dreams came and floated, then merged into a confused mess that I could not understand and would not remember. Except for the dreams about the ranch.

I was back there, on the ranch, and it was payday. But there was no place to spend the money.

Every payday I drew my pay and stuffed it in the war bag I kept tied to the end of my bunk and then, once a month or so, I and some of the other hands would take the old pickup truck and drive the rutted dirt road out to the highway, then the two-lane blacktop into town. We would go to a movie, hang out in the feed store or the town's one saloon. Or maybe visit the whorehouse. But the town was so small that the whorehouse only had two whores, both of them fat, and something about fat whores in tiny whorehouses made me a little crazy. We would drink a little, laugh a little, fuck a little, and then something would come over me—maybe it was the whiskey, but I always thought it was the sight of unrestrained flopping hugely fat breasts. I would see a pair of them heading toward me, drooping and bobbing through a doorway, like two small blimps in mating season, and I would just fall over, shaking, laughing, out of control. Fat arms would rise out of the flesh at the side of the tits and grab me, shoving me out into the tiny waiting room where I would rumble toward the door, trying to keep from choking on my own laughter. Always, always, I would stumble over someone's feet and there would be some words and maybe a half-assed punch or two thrown and somebody would end up being thrown out into the street. Usually me. Usually face-first. Shit. Getting out of a whorehouse was never easy.

I was face down on a mattress that smelled of dried sweat mixed with the faint, acrid scent of ancient puke. I tried not to breathe too deeply. I rolled slowly over and when I tried to open my eyes, my eyelids crawled upward, dragging like raw flesh over ground glass. The effort caused a rumbling dull pain through the center of my head. I knew my body was in serious trouble. It was probably the whiskey, or maybe the junk the Indian gave me. It didn't matter which.

I heard a noise to my left, the creaking of bed springs. I rolled my head slightly in that direction and even that small movement made a film spread across my mind. I lay still, without moving or changing the rhythm of my breathing, trying to make my eyes work in the near-darkness. My mind slowly cleared. Except for the creaking of the bed springs, the place was silent.

I was on a bunk, the cheap metal kind, a flophouse bunk. On the bunk next to me the Indian sat with his arms folded across his chest, legs drawn up in front of him, barefoot. As Wendell breathed his chest rose and fell and the springs creaked slightly.

Christ, I thought, sometimes he looked so damned . . . Indian.

"Where the hell are we?" I mumbled.

Immediately, I wished I hadn't spoken. My voice rattled in my head like stones in an empty oil drum.

"Don't know. Haven't thought about it." The Indian stared across the room at the filthy window with the pale light behind it. I knew he didn't want to be here, in this room, with no real light and no real air. So he wasn't thinking about it.

There were other bunks in the room, some of them with motionless bodies on them. At the far end of the room a naked bulb burned at the top of what must have been a flight of stairs. The thin light faded into the crumbling brick of the wall at the end of the Indian's bunk.

"How the hell did we get here?" I wondered aloud.

"Don't know. But I'll think about it now," the Indian muttered. "We were drunk, Jesse. We were very drunk."

"Yeah, and we were having a very good time. In fact, I think I had about as much good time as I can stand for a while."

"You done your part, white boy."

"Say, listen, Wendell, do you remember it raining?"

"Yeah, Jesse, it was raining."

"And do you remember some cops—and a patrol car?"

"Yeah, and I remember the Cat. The Cat, he did . . . something . . ."

"Yeah, but I'm not sure . . ."

I was worried about the Cat. I wondered what a good Mexican boy like Cat would do in a big city, being chased by the cops. I guessed he would be okay. Somehow, I thought it wasn't the first time Cat had been chased by people with guns.

"You got any more of those little buttons?"

"Nah. All gone. Good Ute shit, man. Do you good one of these days. It'll come back to you when you need it."

Wendell Klah turned and looked at me. Jesus, I liked that Indian. *Really* liked that Indian.

I thought about the Mexican, and about the police car, and about getting out of whorehouses. My mind drifted.

All in all, I felt like hell. It could have been worse, but I didn't know how.

Outside, somewhere in the weak light of morning, a siren drew nearer, then faded back into the San Francisco streets.

Twelve

Flophouse
San Francisco
May 1960

There was silence. I didn't know how long there had been silence. It bothered me. Where were the snoring sounds of the others? I lay there in the bunk, trying not to breathe the stink, but too full of hurt to get up.

I was motionless, almost asleep, trying to let my body purge itself. Confused images floated in my mind, twisted fragments of rainstorms and slick city streets, of cars and fire and doorways. I heard the Indian twitch on his bunk and I rolled slightly to the side, trying to see him. My shirt was gone and as I rolled I could feel my naked skin sticking to the dirty mattress.

Wendell Klah was lying on his bunk, flat on his back, his eyes closed. Just from the look of him I knew his mind was not here, in this room. It was probably back in New Mexico, lost in his being, floating on the winds and soft lights of the mesa. He was not here, not in this room with its stench and its dirty bodies.

Wendell did not hear the soft, fat, shuffling bare feet as they came to the side of his bunk, did not really feel the eyes on him, did not smell the stink that grew more acrid as it flowed down from the huge body and across Wendell's face.

But I heard the feet and I smelled the stink and I gaped at the size of the hulk that loomed over Wendell's bunk. It's just that my muddled mind would not accept what I saw.

Wendell did not see him, the hulk, but I knew he felt the hand. He felt it when it clamped his throat, felt it as it expertly cut off his breathing, felt the fingers tighten around his neck. And then an arm, an arm the size of a leg, rammed under Wendell's back and he was lifted as easily as a doll. And I thought Wendell Klah was going to die.

I raised myself on my elbow, trying not to attract anyone's attention. I could see Wendell more clearly now, but I could not see him breathing. The Indian's back rose slightly from the mattress, lifted, bowing upward, leaving his feet and the back of his head on the bunk. It was as if his middle body had decided to rise, to leave, without taking the other parts with it.

In the gloom beside Wendell a mountain of flesh moved slightly, a log-like arm under Wendell's back, lifting. I could see a hand the size of a prime ham sticking out from beneath his back. The mountain of flesh, the hulk, was a giant, a towering mass of blubber. The giant leaned over the Indian, gripping him, turning him like a sack of laundry, one huge leg lifted to the edge of Wendell's bunk. Except for a filthy, sagging sweatshirt, the arms cut off at the shoulders, the giant was naked and his trunk-like leg toyed with the edge of the bunk, tilting it.

Behind the giant, outlined against the light, a tall, thin man stood, dancing from foot to foot on pole-like legs, elbows flapping, his hands held up in front of him like a fighter, fingers curled, except, oddly, his palms turned forward. A stickman.

I wondered why Wendell wasn't doing anything. Why was he just lying there? What the hell was this? Wendell was an Indian—maybe this was one of his angry gods? Okay, god, whichever one you are, we won't ever drink that much again. I promise. Or do any more of that Ute shit. But, god or no god, I'm not making any promises about fucking.

Wendell brought his hands up to his throat, trying to pull the other huge hand away. Both Wendell's hands did not fit around the hand that was there, choking him, a hand that seemed to fit around Wendell's neck like my hand would fit around a broomstick. I could hear him making tiny strangling sounds.

My mind was clearing. *Wait, Wendell*, I thought. *Wait for me.*

"Stop making noise, Little Beaver, and you won't git hurt," a voice said from somewhere above the hand. I had never heard a god talk. Must be some sort of man, I thought. But, Christ, what sort of man is that big?

I was wide awake now, and I could see more clearly in spite of the ache in my head. The voice came from a puffy face that bulged as much as the hand. The face sat atop a neck that seemed to be rolls of fat stacked on top of each other, pushing up and out of the filthy cut-off sweatshirt, a shirt almost as wide as the bunk the Indian had been sleeping on. I knew I should do something, but in spite of myself I spent a long second trying to remember if I had ever seen a man this big, a mountain of fat, a hulk. I couldn't remember.

And then, turning the Indian fully on his side, the big man pulled his arm from beneath him and began to fumble with Wendell's pants, pulling at the waistband, feeling for the zipper. Wendell whipped his legs up, curling his body.

The fat man leaned forward, his face almost against the Indian's. "Goddamn it, I said don't make trouble! Jist lay still, you red asshole, and I said you won't git hurt!" The voice was jagged and grating, but with an odd cast to it that rang in my mind, an alarm, a terror. The hulk grunted the words into Wendell's ear but they forced their way into my mind. The hulk gripped Wendell harder, turning him, pressing down against him. There were months of sweat, spit, body grease and dribbled, rotted food ground into the giant's sweatshirt, and I thought I could smell his rank, green, almost-liquid breath. Wendell tried again to move, but he was held in a grip and under a weight that pressed the strength and breath out of him. He was helpless.

And then the giant's hand was inside Wendell's pants, searching, prying. Wendell rolled his legs up tighter, trying to bring his knees up as far as he could. From somewhere behind the giant I could hear a thin voice, high, nervous, and giggling.

I started to push myself up from the bunk. The giant caught my movement.

"You jist lay still, cowboy. First I git me some red, and then I git me some white. I ain't seen no blue yet, but I lay odds there's one'a them in here somewhere's, too."

"Don't hurt both of them, Ollie. Don't ream 'em out too big. Save some for me," the thin man giggled in the background, weaving, back and forth, back and forth, his voice like fingernails across a tin roof.

Holy shit, I thought, that hulk's got to be the biggest faggot I've ever seen. I had always thought of faggots as dainty, limp-wristed pussies, thin little guys who poured drug store toilet water over their asses and waggled them in the wind. Jesus, this was no pussy. This was the biggest faggot ever created, maybe the biggest anything. I was almost frozen just from the sight of the guy. Flesh hung in folds from his stomach, from his hips, from the one leg that I could see, thick creases and humps of fat that swung and bumped in the night. His lips flapped when he talked, spittle spraying from them each time they slapped together.

Somehow, the other bunks had emptied, whatever bodies sleeping in them ghosted out silently through the dirty light, down the far stairway. Wendell Klah and I were alone with a giant faggot and a stickman.

Oh, God, I thought, I think we're about to be fucked. And panic hit me.

I did my best to explode from the bunk, grabbing the edge of it as I came out and lifting my body off the floor. I rose above the Indian's bunk and drove my body straight, legs shooting out in a hammering blow in front of me. I caught the giant in the chest with my right leg, the sound of my bare foot against the compressing flesh a whacking vibration that clapped across the room. The giant moved. About an inch. He casually shifted his hold on the Indian, moved his hand to the base of Wendell's neck, and turned slightly to face me.

I dropped to the floor and brought my arms up to cover my head, expecting the stickman to be there. He wasn't. I rolled under my bunk, came up on the other side. The stickman hadn't moved; still giggling. Lets Ollie have all the fun, I thought. I jumped on the bunk and aimed another leg at the giant. The giant saw it coming and simply raised his arm, swatting me aside. I landed on the foot of the bunk and it collapsed in a screech of bending metal. I came off the mangled bed as fast as I could, but I could feel myself slowing; the last few days had left me weak. The giant's hand was back inside Wendell's jeans, still rummaging and pulling, Wendell gasping from the thick fingers at his throat.

Wendell could hardly move. The air was precious now. I knew it wouldn't be long until he passed out, but I also knew the giant didn't intend to kill him. At least not yet. The giant wanted him alive— groggy, maybe, and not in any condition to fight back, but alive.

"Ther . . ." I heard Wendell rasp.

I quickly looked around for a weapon, briefly considered the wrecked bunk, rejected it. I saw one of my boots. I grabbed the soft top and wadded it in my hand, leaping directly in front of the giant and picking my target as I moved. I swung, cracking the boot like a whip, snapping the thick Western heel straight into the center of the giant's face, watching as the giant's nose and upper lip disappeared into the mass of flesh.

The giant screamed and roared upright, his arm flailing and catching me across the chest. The impact shot me across the room past the stickman. I hit the floor and ricocheted into another bunk. The giant's huge leg came off Wendell's bunk and slammed into the floor, driving a cannon-like sound from the wood and bringing clouds of dust up from the filthy boards. In his left hand he still held the Indian by the neck, shaking him like a rabbit.

"You goddamn redneck muthafucker! That hurts! That hurts good! Good! You hear me, muthafucker? Let's hurt each other some more!"

Holy shit! I thought. *He likes it!*

"Other . . ." the Indian gurgled.

The giant started to waddle toward me, his thick gut swinging back and forth as his legs moved, each leg having to come out around the other in order to move forward, his hard dick sticking straight out and swinging from side to side, flapping with each leg movement, always in danger of being crushed between the grinding thighs. He was dragging Wendell.

I could hardly stand. I thought maybe I had enough energy for one more shot at the giant, maybe not even a good one. And I didn't know what kind of a shot to take. Fragments of memory began to glow again through the polluted haze in my mind, and I didn't like the glimpses of what I saw. I began to feel that cold weight in the pit of my stomach that always formed at times like this, a solid, freezing mass that plugged my body. Solid fear.

And then I heard the strangling voice of the Indian again, the words forced out from beneath the giant's fingers, squeezed, gagging, "other . . . faggot . . ."

Jesus, I thought, *the other faggot. The other faggot! The stickman!* I searched for the giggling man through the dirty light.

And found him.

I rushed the stickman. The giggles stopped as the man pushed a thin arm toward me. I slipped past the arm to the outside and hooked an elbow into the stickman's rib cage as I went by. I felt bone move, maybe break. There was not a sound from the stickman. I spun, intending to go for the stickman's neck, maybe a choke hold.

I never made it. The stickman was facing me and his arm shot out, a bony fist landing on my mouth, my lips splitting, teeth loosening. My head snapped back and my feet popped out in front of me. I landed on my ass on the floor. *Shit*, my mind screamed, *I thought at least this one would be a pussy!* Through the pain I heard Wendell strangling.

The stickman came in, leaning over, cocking another punch. Instead of ducking, I leaned forward, still on my ass, and grabbed the man's other arm, pulling him forward and down. I rolled backward, pulling my legs up, planting my feet in the stickman's stomach. I pulled the bony body over me and fired both legs straight up and out. And then I let go of the stickman's arm.

The jangling body rose and flew, making an odd, broken curve over a bunk and into the wall. His body hit the wall like wet paper and then collapsed almost silently into the old brick, the head finally making contact with the wall with a soft, crumpling thud. With the last of my strength, I was on the crumpled body. I grabbed it, raised it, held it in front of me, wrapped an arm around the scrawny neck, all the time screaming.

"Drop him, you fat motherfucker! Drop him now, or I'll break this faggot's neck!" I jerked my arm and the stickman's head bobbed sharply, weirdly. I thought maybe the neck was already broken.

"No, don't do it, don't hurt Stanley! No, don't!" the giant yelled, his grunting voice rising in pitch. He dropped the Indian. Wendell fell in a tangle of arms and legs, his head hitting the floor.

I backed up, dragging the stickman in front of me. The giant began to follow. I could see Wendell start to untangle himself on the floor, gagging.

"Put Stanley down, you muthafucker! You put him down right now!" The giant's voice was still rasping, but there was a pleading note in it now, almost desperate.

I turned between two bunks and backed farther toward the wall. The giant followed. I could see that Wendell was crawling now, fumbling along the floor, trying to get to his feet. The giant was between me and the light at the end of the room, blocking the way out—and I had no idea what I would do when my back finally hit the wall behind me. The giant was closer, blocking even the light now, and I couldn't see Wendell at all.

I had never heard anything to match the high-pitched sound that came from the giant. It was a scream, a pig-like squeal of pure pain and it made me blink just from the volume, the pure ripping cut of the sound. The giant's rolled lips curled and retracted, tiny rat-like teeth showing for the first time in the dank cavern of his mouth. His arms shot out to his sides and then whipped behind him, clamping tightly to his enormous ass. He spun, and then spun again, and as he turned blood squirted from between his fingers and sprayed thickly out into the room. He fell face-down across a bunk and it collapsed instantly beneath him. He didn't seem to notice. The mountainous cheeks of his ass were covered with blood and as he thrashed on the flattened bunk the blood sprayed out and over the floor.

I could see Wendell on the floor, on his knees. He must have crawled up directly behind the fat man. Wendell's head was back and his arms were held rigidly, straight out to his sides. In his right hand I could see something shiny. And blood ran from the Indian's fingers and down across his wrist.

I flung the stickman in the general direction of the giant and started for the light at the end of the room, grabbing Wendell and pulling him to his feet as I went by. Then we were down the stairs and out into the street, stumbling in another darkness in another time and in another frenzy of running away.

Running away. We were running away again. Somehow, it felt comfortable.

Later, in a darkened doorway, I wiped the blood from Wendell's arm and hand. Wendell's throat was loosening up and he could get a few words out.

"I thought you lost your knife in the whorehouse," I said.

"Did," Wendell muttered.

"Then how—"

"Belt buckle," the Indian rasped, holding up the huge, oval rodeo buckle. "One time I filed a little sharp place on the bottom edge, just in case. Worked just fine. Must'a laid his ass open a couple inches deep."

Thirteen

The Streets
San Francisco
October 1960

I got drunk in San Francisco and fucked away all my money and then the Mexican burned the police car and we lost him. None of it was very hard to do.

We didn't belong in the city. We didn't belong in a lot of places. Truth is, maybe we didn't belong anywhere.

But, what the hell, it could have been worse. Hell, I could have been back in Bean Camp, or Black Hawk Ridge. Jesus H. Christ, I could have been back in Crum.

Later, in the army, I would come to understand that, yes, it could be worse. It could be much worse.

In the alien darkness of nights in the city Wendell Klah and I walked the steep wet streets and tried to find comfort in our own company. We leaned in black doorways and blacker basement stairwells of hard-faced buildings that offered nothing more than the cold touch of brick and stone. The days brought nothing but fog and then rain and even the doorways and stairwells filled with a coldness that went straight to the bone, and to the heart. We stole ragged clothes from Salvation Army boxes and nothing fit and our steps dragged and our jeans sagged so that the cuffs wore against the grinding sidewalks, tattered, like kites left too long in the wind. In less than a week I knew that we both had assumed the anonymous and sightless attitudes of street people. Bums.

We didn't know how to make a living in a big city. We stole some more stuff to wear and then stole something to eat. We thought about begging, but there was no way either of us could do that. We'd rather steal than beg.

We knew it was only a matter of time before the systems of the city caught up with us. And then people might ask about a whorehouse and a police car and a tough Mexican with a flaming whiskey bottle and an enormous faggot with deep slashes across his ass. And we didn't want to talk about any of that.

The Indian and I walked the streets, mostly looking for the Mexican, but there was no way of finding him. We took newspapers from busted racks and read them through, but there was no mention of the police car or the Mexican. I borrowed the phone in a pizza shop and called the police, asking about the Mexican. The cop on the other end of the phone seemed more interested in finding out exactly where I was. I hung up and we walked away, quickly. But not before I stole a pizza.

Once, we came across a soup kitchen run by the Salvation Army. We went in and stood by the door for a while, just trying to get the hang of the place. The lighting in the big room was uneven, different light bulbs hanging from the electric cords. The light drained down over rows of long tables and narrow benches that sagged and tilted. Silent men moved in shuffles past large kettles where steam drifted up and washed among them, men moving through fog to the benches, hunched over their bowls.

We got in line and got our soup and sat on a bench on the far end of the room. The little man sitting next to me took his spoon and poured some hot soup down inside the front of his pants, holding his pants out from his belly and dribbling the soup in, a little at a time, letting the hot liquid splatter down inside his pants, soaking them, steaming his penis. When the spoon was empty he did it again, this time blowing on the spoonful of scalding soup before he dribbled it in.

The Indian ate his soup and did not look around.

As the little man dribbled the soup into his pants he hunched back and forth on the wooden bench, his mind not in the room. Then he made a little grunting noise, stiffened on the bench. In a few seconds he relaxed, almost folding forward onto the table. He never ate a single spoonful of the soup. He put the spoon down and left, soup dripping from inside his pants legs, the little man leaving a trail of soup out the door and onto the sidewalk.

The Indian got up and walked away. So did I. We never went back to the soup kitchen.

We were bottom feeders. We stole bread from a truck delivering early in the morning to the back door of a deli. Raided a milk truck parked behind a small hotel. Grabbed a pot of some stuff a Chinese cook set out on a rack, ran into an alley and ate it. But both of us threw up before we got out of the alley.

And then we realized that no matter what we stole, what we ate, we were still hungry. Not just hungry like when you don't have any food, when you miss a meal, but hungry as when you miss a life. Bone-deep hungry. A kind of hungry that needs more than food. A hungry that needs some vision of a future. We began to carry a gnawing that went deeper into us than we understood, that emptied out our resistance and hollowed out our eyes.

A can of sardines ended the whole thing.

We crept into the back door of a small market and lifted a case of some kind of canned stuff—we didn't even know what it was, just knew it was some sort of food. It was sardines. For two days we hung around the edge of the waterfront, our pockets stuffed with cans of sardines. Whenever we got hungry, we just opened a can. But each time Wendell pulled a can out of his pocket, he stared at it, trying to dislodge something that was stuffed deep in his mind. And then he remembered.

"Listen, white boy. I had this friend, back on the rez, name of Paladin . . ."

"Paladin?"

"Yeah. Crazy goddamn name for an Indian. Crazy goddamn Indian. Maybe the wildest Indian I ever knew. Maybe the best Indian I ever knew. Big man, could think on his feet . . ."

"So?"

"So, follow me."

We stole clean shirts from a rack outside a dry cleaner's and walked around the streets until we came to a restaurant that seemed to suit Wendell. It was one of those places that was a cut or two above a street-front joint, but not too uppity. Might have been a family place. Who knows.

Wendell took the last can of sardines out of his pocket, tore off the key and threw it away. Brilliant, I thought. Now, how do we open the can? I've tried opening sardines with a brick. It doesn't work.

We went into the restaurant.

A guy the size of a small house stepped out from behind the cash register and checked us out. In less than five seconds, he had decided. We were going to be thrown out of there, our asses dumped out on the sidewalk. And then Wendell went into his act.

"Sir," Wendell grunted, his voice low and hesitating, "my friend and me, we're from New Mexico. From the reservation."

Christ. I had never heard Wendell talk that way. He sounded like some movie Indian, getting ready to beg whiskey from John Wayne.

The guy looked at me. I was white. I just stood there, trying to look Indian. It probably wasn't working, but Wendell didn't waste any time.

"We come here to sell some jewelry we made, but some people took it from us. We hungry . . ."

We hungry? Good God. . . .

". . . and all we got is this can of fish." He held out the can of sardines. "We lost the key. Maybe you open the can for us . . . so we could eat . . . ?"

I thought the poor guy was going to cry. Before we knew it we were seated in a back booth, steaming plates of food in front of us. Wendell stopped stuffing his face with mashed potatoes and leaned over toward me. "Paladin did this in Chicago. Worked almost every time. Guy stayed up there for almost a month . . . "

A waiter came by and filled our glasses with milk. Kitchen help peeked out at us through the tiny diamond-shaped windows in the swinging doors. The big guy up front strolled by with some other people, looking at us, but not directly. Looking, but polite-like. We kept eating, wondering when it would end.

It didn't end for almost two weeks. I think we actually gained weight. Once, we lost the can of sardines and had to steal another one, but that was easy. Naturally, we never went back to the same restaurant twice, and the hard part was standing there, just inside the door, while the guy made up his mind. It was always a guy.

And then we walked through the door of another restaurant, and there stood the very first guy we had scammed. The son of a bitch had changed jobs.

Wendell and I broke for the door, but the guy was too fast. His thick body was blocking the doorway and he was yelling for help from the kitchen before we could even get turned around. We were nailed. The cops got there about a minute later.

The thing was, we hadn't broken any laws. There was no law against lying about a can of sardines, no law against accepting free food that we didn't even ask for. We were just a couple of country boys trying to stay alive in the big city—if headwaiters in mom-and-pop restaurants were dumb enough to feed us, that was *their* problem. After we got to the police station we explained all that to the cops. Actually, I did the explaining; Wendell didn't say a word, just kept looking straight ahead, doing his Indian thing.

Once the cops understood what was happening they thought the whole thing was pretty funny. They even quit shoving us around. But they didn't really know what to do with us. We were handcuffed and sitting on a wooden bench and they let us sit there for most of the night, watching the night street people come and go, dragged around by the beat cops. If I hadn't been about to piss in my pants, and if the handcuffs hadn't been cutting off the circulation in my hands, I might have found the whole thing interesting. Even funny.

It must have been about three o'clock in the morning before the desk sergeant decided that we had had enough. He was tall and rangy, with hands as big as the paper fans the ladies from West Virginia used to fan themselves with in church, his fingers spread and reaching as he pulled us up off the bench, one of us in each hand, lifting us completely off the wood. We stood there in the hard light of a police station in the middle of the night while he told us about the facts of life—if we ever came back into his police station, neither of us would recognize ourselves in the mirror ever again.

"Get out of my city, you reservation pricks."

He unlocked the cuffs and Wendell and I rubbed our wrists, the feeling gradually tingling back into our hands. We kept our mouths shut and edged toward the big swinging doors.

The doors blew open inwardly and we had to step back out of the way. Two cops stepped through, looked at us, and both of them burst out laughing.

"Jesus H. Christ, Harry, look at what we got here! We got the cowboy and the Indian!"

And then Harry hit me across the face with his nightstick.

Fourteen

Jail
San Francisco
October 1960

Night court.

We stood in front of the judge a few days later, Wendell staring straight ahead again, not looking at the judge, me with the whole left side of my face still swollen, my left eye shut.

I squinted up at the son of a bitch. He wasn't even wearing a robe. At least he could have worn a robe. I mean, we had our rights. A couple of other people were in the courtroom, but my neck hurt and I tried not to look around too much. The cop, Harry, sat in the front row. Somehow, I got the impression that Harry wasn't too interested in our rights.

"Understand you tried to run out of the police station and fell down the front steps." The judge was looking at me. His voice was flat. He wasn't being sarcastic, he wasn't being sympathetic. He wasn't being anything.

"Yes, sir. Guess I wasn't thinking too straight."

The judge looked at Wendell. "That what happened, son?"

Wendell said nothing.

"He has a little trouble with English, sir," I said. "Sometimes English words just don't sound right to him. Don't seem to add up right in his mind."

Wendell said nothing.

The judge waited, still staring at the Indian. Seems like a long time passed, maybe a year or two. Wendell stood there, not a muscle twitching in his entire body, and I knew nothing was going to get settled here.

But I was wrong.

"The court has thought this over, boys," the judge said. He shifted in his seat and did a little twisting motion, adjusting his thoughts with his ass. "You boys can pretend you're not guilty and I can send both of you off to await trial for destroying a police car—well, helping to destroy a police car—endangering police officers, paying money to a whorehouse, fucking with the police department in a dozen other ways . . . and that's going to cost the city a lot of money, and some shitty little pencil-dick lawyer will come out of some hole and try to get you off and he won't be able to and it'll take a couple of months just to ship your asses off to the pen for five years. More, if I handle the case." He paused. "And during all that time, all that time before you go to the pen, your asses will sit right in our fine jail, because you won't make bail, because you haven't got a damn dime between you."

He was seriously screwing with our lives, and he knew it. And he liked it.

"Or, you can tell me you're guilty and I can think about some other solution—just get you out of my city in the fastest possible way." He paused again. "I'll give you some time to think about it. I'll give you a whole minute."

A minute. We had a whole minute. Wendell still hadn't moved. I turned and whispered into the side of his face. "Wendell, let's get the hell out of here. They're going to cut us loose if we tell 'em what they want to hear." Wendell nodded his head without actually moving it. Or maybe I just sensed the nod.

"Your Honor, we'd like to take you up on that part about leaving town. We should'uv gone off a long time ago, but . . ."

"Did you boys do all that shit I was talking about a minute ago?"

"Uh, well, sir, I guess we was there . . ."

"Did you do it, or not?" The judge leaned forward across his

Part II

SCUMMER TRAINING

Part II

SCUMMER TRAINING

Fifteen

U.S. Army Holding Barracks
San Francisco
October 1960

Starker.

When I first laid eyes on the son of a bitch, I did not like him. Within a week I hated him. Within a month I knew that I would like very much to bust the motherfucker's head, and that I would enjoy it like nothing else in my life.

And there would come a time when I wanted to kill him.

The hallway must have been thirty yards long, wooden floors, wooden walls, wooden ceiling, naked light bulbs hanging from electrical cords that had been knotted to shorten them. Wooden benches ran down each side, young men of all sizes, shapes, and colors and wearing nothing but their shorts sitting on them ass-to-ass, staring blankly at the wooden wall on the other side, being careful not to stare at the men sitting over there. The place stank of nervous sweat and nervous farts. Somewhere far down the hallway I heard someone puke and I knew it would not be long until I smelled that, too. Strangely, the place was nearly silent. There was none of the usual bullshit, the joking, just a bunch of guys wondering what the hell was going to happen next.

Wendell Klah and I sat next to each other. We were waiting to be interviewed, tested, probed, have our balls handled, fingers stuck up our asses, and hypodermic needles jack-hammered into our shoulders.

One black guy did not have any undershorts and he sat with his legs pressed together and his hands in his lap, as though trying to protect his dick. His shoulders were wide, thick with muscle, his waist trim, his legs solid. Somewhere back there, before the army, his nose had been flattened by a fist.

Sitting next to him was a white guy, one of those guys who had almost no distinguishing characteristics. His build was slight, average weight, average height. His hair was mouse-brown and straight. His mouth was a slit across a narrow face and his nose seemed thin and fragile. A rat face. Average in every way. Except his eyes. We made eye contact, but the expression on his face did not change. His eyes were black, deep black, totally black, the total absence of light and spark, the total absence of feeling. Round pits of emptiness. There were tiny fires banked against the backs of those eyes, I thought, but those little fires would never show through. Other than me, the guy never really looked anyone in the eye. His gaze seemed to rake the hallway, the ceiling, the floor, like he was taking measurements, trying to stuff every detail of the place into his head. But me? Yeah, he looked straight at me, straight in the eyes, more than once.

A sergeant came striding down the hallway, his boots pounding on the floor like heavy drum beats, dust rising with his passing. He went a couple of steps past Wendell and me and then stopped, peering at the clipboard he had in his hand, pulling it closer to his face as though he were having trouble reading it in the bad light.

"Stone." He said the word evenly, not low, not loud. Just evenly. He never raised his eyes from the clipboard.

I started to raise my hand, but before I could I heard him say, "Klah."

I didn't move, and neither did Wendell.

"Klah?" he said again, louder this time, stomping a few steps down the hallway. "What the fuck kinda name is Klah? Klah?" the sergeant muttered, almost to himself. He raised his head and looked up and down the hallway, as though looking for some disgusting life form that did not belong in his army.

Wendell slowly raised his hand.

The sergeant looked at him. "Klah? What are you, some kinda A-rab, boy?"

Wendell put his arm down and stared straight ahead.

"He's a dog eater."

The words came out quietly. I heard the words, but they were mumbled so softly I wasn't sure if anyone else did.

It was rat-faced guy who had spoken.

Oh, shit. We were in it, now. I gathered my legs under me and stole a quick sideways glance at Wendell. When Wendell moved, I would move, and then we would be up to our noses in shit.

But Wendell sat quietly, breathing normally, not even tense.

I wondered if he had heard what the rat-faced guy had said.

The sergeant stared at Wendell for few seconds, then looked at the clipboard again.

"Stone!" he said sharply. "Which one of you dickless wonders is Stone?"

I raised my hand.

"I should have known," he said, "should have known you two jailbirds would be sitting together. What are you doing, plotting to overthrow the gov'ment?" He took a couple of steps back toward us.

Had he heard the rat-faced guy? Did he give a shit?

"That's a nice lookin' face you got there, Stone. You stick it out in front of a truck?"

I put my hand down and stared straight ahead, just like Wendell.

"Well, whatever the hell you did, or you're doing, don't you fuckin' do it on my time! Jailbirds! The army has got to stop lettin' them pussy civilian judges send us jailbirds."

He bent at the waist, shoving the clipboard in our faces.

"You think the army is better than jail, you got another think comin', dickheads. This jailbird shit is goin' to follow you through yore whole army 'career'. I'll fuckin' see to it." He said "career" like it was shit in his mouth.

We sat silently, not moving.

The sergeant finally got tired of the game. He straightened up and turned to go down the hallway. And then he saw the black guy, still sitting with his hands hiding his dick.

"Jesus Christ, you think you can walk around all day like that, trying to hide yer dick? Yore momma didn't give you no underwear? What's yore name, boy?"

The black guy's eyes did not move, his stare fixed on some unknown spot on the wall above Wendell and me.

"Murphy," he said, so softly the sergeant did not hear him.

"Cain't you talk, boy?!" The sergeant waited, but the black guy said nothing else. The sergeant snorted through his nose and started on down the hallway.

"Don't have no mama."

Again, the black guy said it softly, almost under his breath, his eyes still riveted to the wall. I heard him clearly. I thought maybe his eyes were wet. But I wasn't sure.

The sergeant stopped in his tracks. He turned slowly, looking at each of the other recruits as he came around to face back toward the black guy. He was going to enjoy this.

"What did you say, boy?" the sergeant asked, his voice low, the menace in it creeping out from underneath.

The black guy's head came around. He looked directly at the sergeant, now standing in front of him.

"He said he fucked your mother."

Guys around me who had been breathing suddenly stopped. There was not a sound, not a movement of any kind. Not even their eyes moved; no one looked at the sergeant and the black guy. I could feel Wendell stiffen on the bench, gathering his feet under him.

It was the rat-faced guy again.

I waited for the explosion, waited for the sergeant to come apart, waited for the heat of his red face to render the black guy into a pool of warm grease.

Nothing happened.

I underestimated the sergeant.

The sergeant did not look at the rat-faced guy. He looked at the black guy.

"Stand up, recruit." He said it almost casually.

The black guy stood up and looked the sergeant full in the face.

"Is that what you said, recruit?"

The black guy said nothing.

The sergeant looked around, but not at the rat-faced guy. "Is that what he said?" He was asking everyone, but no one in particular. And then he looked at me.

"How about you, jailbird? That what he said?"

"Man can answer for himself," I said, trying to keep my voice from shaking.

"*Goddamn it! I'm asking you! Is that what he said?!*"

I felt Wendell gather himself. I knew he was going to come up off the bench, but I didn't know who he was going after. And I knew it would be a righteous shit-storm. I put my hand on his arm and gripped it.

"No. He did not say that," I said. I turned my head toward the rat-faced guy. "That motherfucker said it, and that motherfucker is lying through his teeth." And then I stood up.

"Easy, recruit," the sergeant said, raising his hand toward me. He turned back toward the black guy, his arm still out toward me.

"Just what the hell *did* you say?"

"I said I ain't got no mama," the black guy said, his voice steady. "And I ain't. My mama died last week."

The sergeant stood for a long moment, looking at the black guy. And then he turned toward rat-face.

"What's yore name, recruit?'

"My name is Starker, sergeant. What's yours?"

I thought I saw the flicker of a smile at the corner of the sergeant's mouth. But maybe it was a sneer.

"Starker? You're Starker?" The sergeant was looking at his clipboard, a puzzled expression on his face. He raised his head. "Recruit Starker, you will follow me. Now." And he turned and walked back down the long hallway.

For a few steps Starker watched him go, then rose from the bench and started casually after him. Then he stopped and looked back at me. I had never seen a face like that.

"Nigger lover," he said casually. Then he walked away.

Sixteen

Fort Ord, California
October 1960

Fort Ord, California. U.S. Army Basic Infantry Training.

I don't really have to explain basic training. If you ever saw Tab Hunter in the movie *Battle Cry* you get the idea. Sure, Tab was in the Marines and I was in the army, but it was all the same. Same bullshit, different uniform. Actually, I liked that movie. I liked Tab Hunter. Hell, I even like him now. Way to go, Tab.

The walls of the three-story barracks building were raw cinder block, covered with some sort of white coating that crumbled and flaked in the dim sunlight of winter on the California coast. Inside, on the third floor, in the huge room that served as squad bay for our training platoon, the light played softly off the polished tile floor, bouncing along the edges of the two rows of double-decker metal bunks set perfectly aligned along each wall.

I sat on my bunk, eyes fixed on the window and the gray clouds that hung on the horizon, over the rooftops and beyond the limits of the huge army base. I could smell the salt in the air from the ocean. I remembered the smell of salt air. It was the same air I had smelled back in South Carolina, back on a beach where the girls came down to sit in the sun, Kleenex stuffed down into the tops of their bathing suits, under their tits.

The room was empty, as it almost always was when I was there. Which fit with everything I had seen of the army so far. From the very first, from the way they treated me, spoke to me—when they absolutely had to speak to me—the army made it clear that it knew how I got there, made it clear that it didn't particularly like guys who had been sentenced to service in the army, made it clear that I was nothing, that I would never be more than nothing. Made it clear that, at the first opportunity, they would cleanse the army of my presence. They had a simple way of showing their dislike, one that every other soldier would recognize—they kept me on KP and on other jobs that were called "shit details"

Other than the Indian, I paid little attention to anyone in basic training. They were faces, numbers, carriers of rifles, shiners of boots, kissers of asses. I didn't know them when I came in and I didn't want to know them when I went out.

The Indian? For some reason, while the army kept kicking my ass all the time, it paid little or no attention to the Indian. He was just there. Somewhere.

Usually, they kept me and the Indian apart. We had been sentenced to the army together, and the army seemed afraid of that. In the squad bay, my bunk was on one side of the room, Wendell's on the other. But I could see him in the weak light of California nights. In the hard hours of early morning we would leave our bunks and sit together against the wall and talk, and plan, and dream. Or at least talk as much as I could get Wendell to talk.

And then there was Starker.

Yeah, Starker. The asshole from the holding barracks. He had shown up in our training company during the first week. I was surprised to see him, thinking maybe the army had decided to dump the lying son of a bitch. No such luck. He was here, and they put him in our platoon. And I could see the pale remains of old, large bruises across his face.

Starker never spoke to me. In fact, I never saw him speak to anyone. In the holding barracks he had made it clear how he felt about me, Wendell, and other races in general. But now he said nothing, not to anybody.

But I could tell he was watching me, trying to see what made me go, what made me stop. The bastard was studying me.

When I eased out of my bunk in the middle of the night to sit with Wendell and talk, I had to move past Starker's bunk. He lay on the bunk on his back, his arms down at his sides, stiffly, as though he were told to "lie at attention." I never saw him in any other position.

How can anybody sleep like that, I wondered.

Simple. He wasn't asleep.

Even though I knew he was watching me, I rarely saw him look at me. But I looked at him. The bastard was smiling. Only it was not a smile, it was some sort of facial twitch, a grimace, an expression that would stick in my mind. . . . Jesus, I can see it now.

Usually, Starker did little that was obvious, always operating in his own way and, seemingly, on his own time. He paid little or no attention to the army, and the things the army did. He was a flat cold, flat eyed, nearly silent ghost who seemed to drift in and out of the barracks, and in and out of training, on his own schedule, on his own time.

But everywhere I went, every time I looked up, Starker was there.

The Indian and I would sit, talking in the darkness, only to discover that Starker was there, somewhere, never in the same place, silent, listening, hearing everything. Wendell would turn and face him and Starker would slide away as though he were on his way to somewhere. Only he never really was.

"Maybe he's just a harmless bigot asshole," I whispered to Wendell, "all mouth and nothing to back it up."

"Harmless? You think he's harmless?"

I thought about it. I knew the answer. "No."

I finished KP and left the mess hall late one night, dragging myself back to the squad bay long after lights-out. As I eased myself into my bunk I noticed that Starker's bunk was empty. I lay quietly, surveying the room in the dim light of a full moon. I finally saw Starker, sitting with his back against the wall, slowly running a rag up and down something thin, something that caught stray bits of light and kicked them back into the room. Several minutes went by before I realized that it was a bayonet—not the short, stubby one we had been issued, but a long, narrow one, from far back, World War I, maybe.

As he worked on the bayonet, Starker was looking at me. Even in the dark, I could see that.

My God, I wondered, *where the hell did he get that thing? And where the hell does he keep it?*

But I didn't really want answers. I just wanted away from Starker. I slipped out of my bunk and took a blanket with me. I went out the door and down the stairway to the first landing, sat down, wrapped the blanket around myself, and stayed there until daylight.

And I wondered which one of us would break first.

Basic training went on. It was nothing to me; growing up in the mountains and life and work on the ranch had been harder. And it was nothing at all to Wendell Klah; daily existence for him on the reservation had been a type of training that the army could never match.

But the army tried to make it hard. Our training company was somehow considered special, or at least different. Physically different.

We always moved on foot. Where other training companies rode in trucks, we walked. Where other companies walked, we ran. Where other companies ran, we ran there also, and then ran back again. It was the part of training that I hated most, and the part the Indian loved. If he could run, even carrying all his equipment, he seemed happy, seemed alive. But the running always ended and then the Indian seemed to retreat again, into himself. Gone.

The light was fading and we were running again, coming out of the desert and heading generally west, double-timing in formation, sweating, racing the night that pushed at our backs, trying to get to the barracks before thick darkness fell along the coast. We were in full field gear—heavy packs, helmets, rifles carried at port arms as we ran relentlessly through the sucking sand.

We caught up to another training company going in the same direction, only they were walking, strolling, out of step, rifles slung on their shoulders, heads down. When we saw soldiers like these, humping along at the end of the day, we took some sort of perverse pride in our own company's hard-nosed approach to training. In-evitably, our heads came up, our steps were a little sharper, lines straighter, rifles at the proper angle. As we ran past the other guys we tried not to breathe hard, tried not to gag and cough and puke from exhaustion and the constant cloud of talcum-like dust that rose every time we veered from sand onto loose earth.

I tried not to care about that sort of army rah-rah bullshit. But ev-ery time it happened I got caught up in it, my own step sharpening with the others, my own breathing more under control.

That's what we did now, sharpening up our whole outfit as we went pounding by the other grunts. We looked straight ahead, pre-tending they weren't even there. Gloating in our misery.

Except that I sneaked a look to the side and that's when I saw the

Mexican. At least I thought it was the Mexican. I wasn't really sure. I went past him quickly and I'm not sure we even made eye contact but there was something so familiar about the shape, the form of the man, the energy that seemed to leap at me through the heat. But we were past them in seconds and there was nothing I could do about it.

Later, at the barracks, I stood by Wendell's bunk. "You see Caton? In that other bunch we went by."

"No," he said.

I started back toward my bunk, my shoulders sagging.

"I felt him," Wendell said behind me, his voice soft and distant.

The Mexican. The Mexican was in the army.

Starker tried to become part of me, a Siamese twin, joined at the brain.

Whenever we got to sit for a few minutes while on a training exercise, Starker was there. Not really close to me, but not really far away. Just close enough to observe, to stay in touch. I began to expect it. It made me nervous. And I began to hate it.

The army noticed, and it mattered to them. It mattered to them that a man like Starker seemed to orbit around me. It mattered to them that, when Starker was near me, he seemed less threatening, somehow. Less tense. It mattered to them that I didn't like it, and that made them happy.

Our basic training company officers had one goal where Starker was concerned: keep the lid on him until they could ship him out. Keep him settled down. Keep him quiet. They knew, as surely as they knew anything, that Starker was probably crazy. And so, at every opportunity, they kept him near me. After all, maybe they could solve two problems at the same time; put the crazy guy with the criminal. No problem. No problem at all.

I agreed with the army. Starker was crazy. But I knew, I was sure, that he was something far worse than that.

I was pretty sure the army did not know about the bayonet.

And I was damned sure the army knew something about Starker that I did not know.

Seventeen

Fort Ord, California
October 1960

The air was close with dampness and chill. We were not far from the beach and fog had come in, turning everything to a misty gray that took away our energy, made us want to find a cave to huddle in, build a fire, roast a chunk of mammoth while we dozed.

We huddled under some low, spiny growth, waiting our turn in the grenade pits. The pits were shallow trenches wide enough to crouch in, to throw grenades from, warfare ideas left over from World War I. Above the pits were roofs of ancient, loose planking, enough space between the roof and the front of the pit for a man to heave a grenade out into the scrubby growth toward fake machine-gun emplacements.

Fake machine-gun emplacements, fake grenades.

The training grenades looked and felt like the real thing, miniature pineapples with a ring through the top. They were packed with enough powder to make a loud noise, enough to raise clouds of sand downrange, enough to rattle the planks over our heads. They were training grenades, but no one wanted to be around one when it went off.

We crouched in the pits, clutching our grenades, waiting for the command to throw from the noncoms standing up on the ground behind us. We had to throw in a prescribed way, no deviations, no baseball pitches, no copying Tab Hunter. When a noncom gave the order, we pulled the pins, extended our arms, and made a looping throwing motion, being careful not to throw the damned grenades into the planking above us. Once the grenade was away, we were supposed to flatten ourselves on the bottom of the pit and wait the few seconds until the damned thing exploded.

Just like real war.

I was into it. Hey, this was fun.

When my turn came I climbed down into the far left end of the pit, dirt walls on three sides of me. I picked out one of the emplacements about mid-way downrange, thought I might as well see if I could actually hit it. I got into position. When I heard the command to throw I pulled the pin and looped the grenade as far out as I could.

I was on the floor of the pit before my grenade even reached its target, my chin digging into the dirt, my helmet pushed back against my forehead, looking at a grenade that was lying in the dirt not more than a foot from my face. It didn't take a genius to realize the pin had been pulled.

I rolled onto my left side and frantically threw my head back, ramming my knees up into my stomach, twisting, violently thrashing to swap ends in a too-small space, trying to get my face away from the grenade. I was still trying when the son of a bitch exploded.

I felt a burning on my thighs and shins and through the ringing in my ears I could faintly hear men shouting.

How could I have done this? How could I have thrown the damned grenade into the roof, had it bounce back into the pit? How could I have damned near blown my face off?

Hands dragged me up and out of the pit, soldiers gathering around, everybody talking at once. I was propped up under a small tree and I heard someone yelling for a medic. The legs of my fatigue pants were smoking and one of my boots was charred. They cut the laces off my boots and pulled them off, then cut the legs off my fatigue pants, checking my feet, legs and then my face. My right leg seemed to have taken the worst of it. A large hole had been burned in my pants leg and the skin of my right shin was glowing red. All in all, it seemed to be nothing much. Except for the fact that I could not hear for shit, I seemed to be okay. But I wondered what my face would have looked like if I had not seen the grenade in time.

I was glad that I couldn't hear very well. I didn't want to hear what the noncoms and officers were going to say to me. I could hear some people yelling. I looked up, ready to take whatever was coming.

But they were not yelling at me. They were yelling at Starker, who was looking at me, that crooked slit-smile on his rat face.

When the grenade went off in the pit, I thought it was my grenade. But it wasn't. It was Starker's.

Starker had been a few positions down the pit from me. When the command came to throw, he had simply turned and softly lobbed his grenade in my direction. I didn't see it coming.

When they dragged me out of the pit, Starker climbed out. Didn't understand the order, he said. Got mixed up. Was turning to ask what he was supposed to do when his grenade slipped.

The soldiers, the medics, the noncoms, the officers all just stood there, surrounding us, most of them looking at Starker, wondering how any ordinary man could make such a mistake.

Starker was not an ordinary man.

And it was not a mistake.

I was trying to get to my feet.

It was time to kill Starker.

And then Wendall Klah stepped out of the crowd and stood facing Starker. I saw Wendell rise on his toes a little, balance himself, his hands coming up slightly.

"Didn't get confused," Wendell said, one of his arms coming up, his finger pointing straight into Starker's face. "Mutherfucker knew exactly what he was doin'."

And then Wendell hit Starker so hard in the face that Starker's helmet flew off. His body hit the ground, flopped once in the dirt, and rolled into the grenade trench.

They kept Starker out of the training platoon for three days. I don't know where he was during that time.

They did nothing to Wendell, just sent us all back to the barracks.

When Starker came back, the side of his face was still swollen.

For days, he did not look at Wendell, or at me.

Somehow, I really liked the idea of Starker with a swollen face. At least it gave him some personality.

But Starker knew, and I knew, that one of us would not walk away from the army.

Eighteen

Fort Ord, California
November 1960

I have always liked birds. On Black Hawk Ridge the birds brought
the daylight over the tops of the ridges and spread it over the trees,
pulling the light with song. Most of the time I never saw them, only
heard them, took them for granted. But I always liked them.

In the last near-dark hour before we were supposed to drag our
asses out of our bunks, I saw Wendell get out of his bunk and step
quietly to the last window in the squad bay, the window farthest
from the bay doors. The window was open and Wendell put his arm
through and seemed to place something on the narrow ledge outside.

Later that morning, when the men were struggling with their
clothes, running back and forth to the showers and the latrine, the
noise level rising, I sneaked a look out the window to see what Wendell had put out there.

Tiny pieces of dried bread.

Wendell was feeding the birds.

The only birds I had noticed were seagulls that circled overhead,
never really coming down, never really going away. And a few pi-
geons. There were other birds, but I never really paid any attention.

But now I paid attention. I wanted to see what Wendell was doing. At the same time each morning he would go to the window,
check around to see if anyone were awake and watching, then put
his arm through the open window. As time went on, he seemed to
leave his arm out the window for longer periods of time. I could hear

some sort of bird noises out there, but I could not really see what was going on.

Wendell knew I was watching. And he knew I would never interfere.

After that, I started bringing small scraps of food from the mess hall and leaving them on Wendell's bunk.

And then, one gray morning, the mist from the ocean rolling through the company streets, spreading a chill that layered on top of yesterday's heat until you didn't know what the hell the temperature was . . . one gray morning, Wendell carefully, slowly, brought his arm back inside the window. He held a bird in his hand.

I couldn't tell what sort of bird it was, but it was big, a gull, maybe a pigeon. Wendell's fingers wrapped around the bird, tenderly, lovingly, I thought. He held the bird for only a moment, then put it carefully back through the window. I knew the bird had flown.

Wendell had found a way, even here, even in a training barracks, to reconnect with something wild.

Wendell was on KP. He was up early, in the mess hall, scrubbing floors.

And yet, there was a form at the far window, an arm reaching through the opening.

What the hell was the Indian doing here? If they noticed that he was gone from KP, he was in deep shit.

But it was not Wendell.

It was Starker, with his arm through the window.

And then Starker looked directly at me. And I realized that, all along, all those mornings in the early mist, he, too, had been watching.

He brought his arm slowly back inside. He had a bird in his hand.

He stood straight, very soldier-like, his face expressionless in the weak light. He held the bird out in front of him, in his left hand, pushing it carefully toward me in some sort of offering. I knew exactly what I was going to do—nothing, absolutely nothing.

I sat on the edge of my bunk, my eyes locked on Starker and the bird, Starker's eyes locked on me. The squad bay was silent. Even the guys who snored were not making any noise.

And then Starker reached behind him, drew the long bayonet out of the back of his pants, and sliced the head off the bird.

Nineteen

Fort Ord, California
November 1960

I lost the Indian shortly after that.

I awoke in the cold and silence just beyond midnight and rolled over, facing in the Indian's direction. A single, bare bulb burned all night in the latrine down the hall and reflected its dull, yellow light through the tiny glass panels of the swinging doors and into our platoon bay. I could see the silhouette of the Indian, sitting in the center of his bunk, arms and legs folded. Doing his Indian thing again, I thought.

It had been a hard day in the army and the exhausted, sleeping bodies on the other bunks did not move. I eased out from beneath my blanket and padded my way silently around the end of Starker's bunk to Wendell's bed. As I passed Starker, I noticed he was still sleeping flat on his back, his arms straight down along his sides, as though laid out for burial.

Stands to reason, I thought.

I could not tell if he were actually asleep.

The Indian sat motionless. His eyes were open, staring straight ahead, but they weren't really seeing anything, I thought, not vitally seeing, not anything. The lids drooped slightly, and the Indian's breathing was slow and shallow.

"Wendell," I whispered, lightly touching the Indian's arm. "Wendell, what's the matter? You okay?"

The Indian did not move and made no sign that he knew I was there. I stayed where I was, not knowing what to do. Once, I gripped the Indian's arm, hard, but it brought no reaction that I could see in the dim light. Finally, I sat on the floor, leaned back against Wendell's bunk, and waited. I dozed, and each time I awoke I checked on the Indian.

An hour later the Indian moved his arm. I saw the slight motion and got off the floor, swung my leg across Wendell's bunk and sat down facing him.

"Wendell, can you hear me? Wendell, what the hell are you doing?"

"I've been away, Jesse," the Indian answered softly, in his rich, smooth, almost-gone voice. "It is the best place to be—away. You must learn how to go away, Jesse, or you will never survive in this army. Going away is the one thing they can not control, not ever control. You must learn how to go away."

"What the hell are you talking about, Wendell? Look, I know you've been . . . away . . . been somewhere, but how did you do it by yourself. Did you use anything? I mean, man, if they catch you with that stuff there's no telling what—"

"No, Jesse, that's part of the greatness of being able to escape, to go away. You don't need anything to help you. It helps to be an Indian—we're very strange, you know—but even some white boys can learn to do it. You can learn to do it, Jesse. Your skin is white, but, I think, in your heart, you are really an Indian.

"And Jesse, you must understand. I want to kill him. Starker. I have never really wanted to kill another human. But I want to kill him. See, Jesse, he's like that bad dog back on the rez. Leavin' him alone ain't enough for him. He really don't want to be left alone. He'll keep after the chickens, sneakin' up, killing your sheep. And that still ain't enough. Sooner or later he will come after you. And that's when you know you have to kill him.

"So I have to go before I do that. Kill him. See, Jesse, if I kill him and then run away, the army will look hard for me, and for a very long time. They will never give up. But if I *don't* kill him, and I just go away, the army will look for me, but not very hard. I'll just be another AWOL Indian."

Somewhere in the huge barracks room a body twisted in its bunk and coughed, accentuating the stillness.

Starker. Wendell had thought about killing Starker. And so had I. But with me, it was a fantasy, something to hang onto that focused my anger at the army. But it was not a fantasy with Wendell.

I put my head in my hands.

"I know what you're thinking, Jesse," Wendell said, "you want to hurt him, too, hurt him bad. But don't do it. Not right now. It ain't the time. Wait for a bigger reason. Wait for a time when the Earth is turned in a direction only you can see."

I did not know what to say to Wendell. Maybe there was nothing to say. Maybe what he had been thinking about was as natural as killing a rat. There were people on this planet that did not belong here and one of these days they would just stand up in the line of fire . . . .

But if Wendell was leaving, where did that leave me?

Deep within my mind the misty concept of escape, of freedom, began to form. Freedom. I had to get out of here, out of this place, out of the army. But I couldn't bring the foggy ideas into focus, couldn't get them clear. I sat on the Indian's bunk, trying to concentrate on the ideas running around in my head. Trying *hard*. The darkness of the room wrapped itself around me, held me tight in a California night near a beach in a building where I never wanted to be. The darkness helped.

But what the hell was the problem, I wondered? I could do this army shit all day long, standing on my head. Hell, I had even considered volunteering for airborne training, but I couldn't get Wendell to agree to go along with me.

And, seen in the right light, the army was pretty funny. And, in the right light, I was pretty funny. So what was the problem? Why was I in such a hurry to get out?

Maybe it was because I did not *choose* the fucking army. It was not my idea.

Finally, I decided that *why* was not important. It was only important that I wanted to go on to something else, go on to some other place. It was my pattern.

Going away. It was what I did. Just like Wendell. We just did it in different ways.

And the army would not let me do that.

Gradually, my ideas came clear. Sometime, I thought, when the time was right, when I had stuck with it about as far as I could go, when the shit was a little too thin to walk on, when the army wasn't funny anymore, I would just go. I would take a trip. Like the Indian, except for real. And the army would never see me again. Maybe nobody would ever see me again. Well, maybe except for the Indian. And the Mexican. Maybe. If I could find the little bastard.

But I would never be safe if the army would not leave the Indian alone.

I took a deep breath and pulled my legs up in front of me.

"Wendell," I said softly, "you're right. Leave the prick alone. He isn't worth killing."

But when the time comes, I thought, *that'll be my job.*

A few days later I again awakened in the silence and heavy darkness of the small hours after midnight. It took me a while to figure out why, and then I felt the Indian's presence beside me. Wendell was squatting, motionless, beside my bunk, his face only inches away. I started to say something, but the Indian held up his hand, motioning me to silence. He slowly raised his other hand and extended it, palm up, directly in front of my face. Weak light from somewhere outside the barracks crawled into the room and I could see in his hand a small stone that had been neatly split in half. It was not a straight split. Some of the edges curved slightly, tucking themselves around corners in a pattern that caused the two halves to fit together in only one way. I sat up and pulled the Indian's hand closer to my face. Even in the dim light I could see the polish of the pieces, the deep, glowing sheen of a stone that had been much-handled.

With his fingers, Wendell Klah carefully pushed the two pieces of stone together in their perfect fit. But it was not a perfect fit. There was still a piece missing, and it was not in Wendell's hand.

I was fascinated. What the hell was Wendell doing?

I whispered to him, "Where's the other piece?"

"Caton has it," he said, again in his almost-gone voice. "I gave it to him long before you came to Crested Butte. But there has to be three, Jesse. Not two. Not four. Three. I was waiting for someone else to give the other piece to. And then you come along. I've been waiting ever since for the good time to give part of the stone to you. It's turquoise, Jesse. Very precious."

He dropped a piece of the stone in my hand.

"One day, Jesse, we will put the stone back together. All of it."

He reached down to his side and came up with a small leather pouch that had been tied by a thong through an empty belt loop. He turned the pouch slowly. It was plain, not a mark on it, but Wendell fingered it as though it were special, very special. He dropped the other half into the pouch.

"Wendell, you can't wear shit like that on your uniform. They . . ."

It was only then I noticed that Wendell was stripped to the waist, wearing only a pair of fatigue pants, no shoes.

We sat in silence for a long moment, staring at each other in the darkness.

"Wendell, sometimes I don't understand the way your fuckin' mind works. How will I know when it's time . . . how will I know *where*—?"

Wendell held up his hand, stopping me.

"You will know."

Fucking Indian.

And then he turned and without hesitating walked silently and quickly down the aisle between the rows of bunks, past the glowing light from the latrine, and disappeared into the darkness of the stairs beyond.

I could only watch him go. It was mid-winter on the Central California coast and the Indian was going out into the night, half naked, on his way to some place the army never heard of. Some place no one ever heard of.

I did not know where the Mexican was. He might have been in some building not far from my own, lying silently, eyes wide open, on his narrow army bunk. But I wanted to think that he was somewhere south, maybe on the Yucatan coast, catching big fish and selling them to gringos to take back to Texas and brag about. But I knew he was not.

And then there's me, I thought. Goddamn, this is getting less funny by the minute.

I sat on my bunk, gripping the turquoise tightly, feeling my mind slipping into escape. There must be a way, I thought. There must be some way. My mind began to grow light and soft, wandering from the present into a place that had no time, no restriction.

The army never saw the Indian again.

Twenty

Fort Ord, California
December 1960

We stood in silent formation in the damp winter of the California coast, rows of dark green uniforms jutting up from the street in front of the barracks building. We stood as quietly as we could, waiting for our last inspection as basic infantry trainees. Within twenty-four hours we would be gone, all of us, shipped to advanced training posts across the country.

I hadn't really expected to be there, standing in formation, waiting to be shipped out. I thought they would punish me, hold me over, put me back in another training platoon, make me do it all over again . . . punish me somehow because the Indian was gone. But, apparently, they were as tired of me as I was of them. They were going to ship me out.

It was almost Christmas and the dampness from the ocean seemed heavier than usual. I shifted my weight carefully from foot to foot, trying not to shiver, trying not to sway the upper part of my body and cause any commotion in the formation. I eased my head forward a little, to see if Starker was standing in formation. I hadn't seen the bastard when we were running from the barracks to the street, and I had an uneasy feeling that he was not there.

Starker. At least when they shipped me out I would be rid of the son of a bitch.

We stood in the street facing the building. In front of us a narrow strip of grass, brown and fragile, ran from the edge of the street to the building. In the center of the building a short flight of concrete steps led up to a small deck. The heavy door on the far side of the deck jerked open and the company commanding officer, a captain, a man we had seen only once or twice during our time there, strode stiffly to the front of the deck. His head was back and his back was straight. He wanted us to know that he was a soldier, and we were not. He wanted us to know that he was in command, and we were not. He wanted to send us away with a vision of the army. His vision. His army.

You're too goddamn late, I thought. *I already got my vision.*

The captain intended to make a short speech. I thought he had probably done this many times and was proud of his speeches, proud of his job. He opened his mouth and the words began to roll. He kept his voice heavy, his inflections military, his bearing military, his message military. He thought he was good at this, and he was. As he talked, he loosened a little, once even raising his arms to emphasize a point. It was then, with his arms raised, with another fine military point caught on the end of his tongue, that a single, green, very familiar piece of paper, tumbling like a falling leaf, dancing in the heavy air, drifted down from an upstairs window and fluttered directly in front of the captain's face.

The captain's mouth snapped shut and his arms dropped to his side. He bent forward slightly, looking at the green paper lying on the steps in front of him. For a few seconds he did nothing, then slowly bent and picked up the paper. As he straightened, he held it in front of him, staring intently, his face a classic mask of puzzlement.

In the front rank, a soldier couldn't help himself. He didn't mean to speak, but he did. "My gawd," he said in a hoarse and excited whisper, "it's a twenty dollar bill!"

A metallic rasping sound grated through the silence. On the upper floor of the barracks building a window was pushed further open and a green-uniformed arm appeared. At the end of the arm a hand opened and another piece of paper fluttered downward. The soldier who had spoken took a quick step forward.

A sergeant stepped from the side of the formation. "You're at attention, mister!" the sergeant bellowed, and the soldier recovered and stepped back into formation. But it was too late. The other trainees, now freely turning their heads to watch the action, saw clearly that more money was coming from the window.

Above, the arm withdrew and then appeared again, this time launching several bills into the gray afternoon sky above the formation. A slight breeze caught them and they spread, drifting a little along the building.

The formation broke.

Soldiers rushed forward to grab at the bills, leaping to try to catch them before they hit the ground, an entire company of fresh infantry troops in dark green winter uniforms pushing, shoving, yelling, wrestling, punching—a green-clad mass of arms and legs flailing in the cloudy light. As more money came down from the sky the flailing grew more intense, soldiers shoving harder, diving at the fragile pieces of money, wrestling in the dead grass and dirt, a cloud of dust rising lowly in the damp air.

And then, of course, it happened. Two soldiers grabbed for the same fluttering bill; one of them got it, the other didn't. The guy with the bill held it over his head in triumph, and the other guy drove a fist straight into his face. You could hear the sound of flesh striking flesh, even above the dull grunts of the wrestling money-grabbers.

For a second or so, there was near silence, a false calm in what had been a softly roiling storm. Soldiers stood looking at each other, and at the scraps of money they held in their hands. And then the guy who had been punched, punched back, and the calm disappeared in the blink of a swollen eye. Fists, feet and elbows, drove out and back in a rage of motion as an entire platoon brawled in the middle of the company street.

Someone hit me from behind and I went down, rolled onto my stomach and crawled up on the dry, brown grass, just trying to get out of the way.

Above the roar I could hear the officers and sergeants yelling for attention. No one, not one single soldier, paid any attention at all.

And Starker continued to throw money from the barracks window.

The captain, still standing on the steps of the barracks, was waving his arm at a small, wiry sergeant that I did not know.

"Sergeant Willard," the captain screamed, "take two men and get up there and secure that squad bay! On the double!"

The sergeant pointed to two men. The three of them broke into a run up the steps of the barracks.

"No!" the captain screamed again. He pointed at one of the men with the sergeant.

"You stay!"

The captain whirled toward me; he knew exactly where I was.

"You, Stone! You go! You go *now*, mister!"

The three of us stood outside the big swinging doors of the squad bay. I was not going into that room. *I was not going in.*

The sergeant looked at me.

"Peek through the glass and see what he's doing."

"No thanks, sergeant. I know what he's doing. He's getting ready to fuck with somebody."

"I'm not asking you, Stone. I know about you, and about that asshole in there. I'm ordering you—peek through the glass and see what he's doing!"

Fuck it. I turned, bent my knees, slid carefully beneath one of the tiny glass panels, and slowly raised myself to where I could see into the room.

Then that good soldier, Sergeant Willard, slammed his body hard into me from behind, blasting me through the doors and into the room where I fell flat on my face.

Twenty-One

Fort Gordon, Georgia
January 1961

Somewhere along the way—I thought it was just after basic training—Christmas had come and gone. They did not let me go home during the holidays; I was one of the few who did not get Christmas leave. I needed the additional training, they said, and so I heard Christmas carols played over the scratchy public address systems of Fort Ord, California.

I painted part of a colonel's house, repaired two vintage motorcycles owned by a major, and then spent a week-and-a-half on KP. But it was okay, I told myself. I wouldn't have gone home, anyway. Besides, where the hell was home? If they had turned me loose, where would I have gone?

Anywhere. Anywhere at all.

Once, and only once, did they give me a day pass to go off the post. I went into town and found a small jewelry store.

I knew the army blamed me for the Indian's disappearance. I tried to explain that no one had to help Wendell Klah disappear, that the Indian could disappear whenever he damn well felt like it, mentally and physically. The army didn't buy it. They were sure that, somehow, I had been in on it, only they couldn't figure out how. In the end, they didn't care. They couldn't court martial me—there was absolutely no evidence that I had done anything wrong. But I was beginning to realize there were worse things in the army than court martial.

Yes, there was.

In a classic piece of irony, especially for the army, they told me they were sending me to Fort Gordon, Georgia. U.S. Army Military Police Training School.

I laughed for ten minutes straight. The sergeant who handed me the orders tried to get me straightened up, shouted at me, ordered me, but nothing worked. I fell on the floor, rolled over, gripped my sides. My God, I thought, the army has one messed up sense of humor.

Still, I really couldn't figure out why they were sending me to MP school. I thought maybe MPs, as a group, were probably hated by all the other branches of the army, and maybe the worst thing the army could do to someone it didn't like—and it sure as hell didn't like me—was to make an MP of him. But maybe it wasn't the worst thing the army could do. Maybe it was just the funniest thing.

So, for whatever reason, they shipped me to Fort Gordon. I didn't go with other graduating recruits. All the others going to Gordon had been sent home for Christmas and would go to Georgia when their Christmas leave was over. I traveled alone. But it didn't matter. At least I was away from Starker.

Actually, that was my one regret. After Starker ripped me with the training grenade, I spent days toying with different ideas on how to get payback. It couldn't be just any old way—I couldn't just walk up to him and kick him down the stairs. Too simple. Too easy. No real creativity. Or so I thought.

Finally, I just got tired of trying to figure it out. One morning, on the way out of the squad bay, I saw Starker in front of me.

"Hey, asshole."

Starker turned to face me—and I raised my leg and kicked the son of a bitch backward down the stairs. He tumbled, elbows, knees, feet, head all smacking into the hard surfaces.

For a moment, no one moved. And then I heard the slow, rhythmic sound of forty men, clapping in unison.

My reputation preceded me. Some sergeant at Fort Ord knew some sergeant at Fort Gordon, and I was marked for shit details from the first day I arrived in Georgia. During my first four days at Gordon I was kept on KP eighteen hours a day.

And then the army seemed to forget about me. I sat for two days in an empty barracks building, waiting to be assigned to a training company.

As far as I had been able to tell, all the barracks buildings in the entire training area were the same: thin, frail, wooden, and built before World War II. The planks didn't fit and the windows hung loose in their frames, rattling in the cold night winds of January in Georgia. The creaking buildings sat on concrete pilings, the floors almost three feet off the damp ground. The wind sang between the planks, dove underneath the floors and drove chill and dampness through the gaping cracks, stealing large gulps of heat from the buildings and from the bodies of the men inside them.

Sitting in my lonely, frigid, empty barracks, I began to shiver. A row of metal double-decker bunks lined each side of the building, each with its thin mattress rolled tightly to the head. I pulled two mattresses from the nearest bunks and threw them in a corner. I sat on one, then wrapped the other around me, Indian-style. I looked stupid, but I was warm. Wendell Klah would laugh his ass off if he could see me now, I thought.

During my second day in the groaning building, at about four o'clock in the afternoon, the door opened and another trainee was shoved through, followed by two MPs. The trainee's back was to me, but even without seeing the guy's face I began to get an uncomfortable feeling in my stomach, a tenseness, a slight twinge of something I couldn't identify but which I did not like.

The MPs waited as the trainee walked directly to the far wall and stood there, still not turning around. The smaller of the two MPs put his hand on the club hanging at his belt and started to take a step toward the man at the wall.

"Nah," the other MP said. "Not now. There'll be plenty of time later." The MPs edged back out through the door, never turning their backs.

When they were gone, the man turned slowly and looked directly at me.

Starker.

"Hello, Stone," he said, his voice level and low, flat, a voice like preachers have when the body is lying in the box in front of them. "I told them we were friends. I told them that's why I didn't fuck with you when that sergeant kicked your ass into our squad bay back at Ord. They're going to put us in the same training company. Ain't that nice?"

I knew he was telling the truth. It was just too ironic to be a lie . . . *the same goddamn training company.*

"Starker, you motherfucker, how do you get away with this shit?"

"Because my . . . because they can't figure me out. Because I'm different, and they don't have a handle on that. Nobody's supposed to be 'different' in the army. So I just give them an idea and they go for it."

"And you know something? You're just the same, only you don't know it yet. You're just like me."

"The hell I am," I mumbled, my voice shaking a little. The bastard had never spoken this many words to me. I hated the whining sound of his voice.

"You are, Stone. You fucking are. Why do you think they sent me to MP school? And put us in the same company? Just so it'll take fewer people to watch us. And all of those faggots will be carrying side arms. See? It's simple."

Starker. He was a walking, breathing bomb. I swear to God, if you listened carefully, you could hear him ticking.

But why me? Why the hell did he want to stick to me?

I had spent a lot of time thinking about it since the last time I had seen Starker at Ord and I never really figured it out. Maybe, I thought, it was the game, the contest, the back-and-forth that he created between the two of us. Maybe there was nothing else in his life to occupy his time, his mind. Maybe I was a 'worthy opponent'. He hadn't killed me back there at Ord because it would have been too soon; the game would have been over.

Maybe he was just goddamn crazy.

God only knew what made Starker move from day to day, what made him breathe, what made him live. No, forget that. Whatever it was that had created Starker, God had had no hand in it. In fact, I was goddamned sure that God didn't know Starker existed.

But the army knew, and a certain captain back at Fort Ord knew, and a bunch of recruits who had fought over a green snowfall of money knew. Murphy knew. And Wendell Klah knew.

They all knew that Starker existed.

And I knew.

When that asshole, Sgt. Willard, shoved me through the doors of the squad bay I was already out of control and all I could do was throw my arms out in front of me and hope to break the fall. It almost worked. Still, my head snapped down and my nose flattened on the tile and I knew it was going to bleed.

I didn't know where Starker was. I rolled over on my right side, pulled my legs up into my gut and brought my arms up to cover my head. I thought if Starker didn't hit me quickly I might be able to bounce up . . .

Nothing happened.

I rolled over again and ducked down behind a bunk, looking for Starker . . . and felt the sharp point of something poking into my neck.

I didn't think he was going to kill me. If he were going to kill me, I already would be dead, the bayonet driven through my neck. I slowly stood up, blood from my nose running down the front of my uniform, more blood seeping down the side of my neck. I could hear his breathing. I could hear my breathing. And I still could hear the last few shouts coming from the street below.

"Why don't you just get it over with," I said. It wasn't a question.

Starker did not make a sound, just increased the force on the bayonet. He seemed to be twisting it a little.

I tried to remember what I had read in the self-defense books, what I had done in Judo training back in Wyoming.

"Okay, Starker, you're in control here. What do we do now?"

I heard—felt—his breathing move more closely to my ear.

"You always act like you are in charge, Stone. Just like the army, always thinking the *army* is in charge. And it was, for a while—all those soldiers standing in their little formation down there, and all it took to fuck it up was a few twenty-dollar bills. Some goddamn army."

I said nothing. If he wanted to talk more about the army, that was fine with me.

But he didn't.

"I'm not supposed to be here, Stone. I was sent here, against my will, just like you. And I hated the fucking army—at first. Now I'm beginning to kind of like it, especially since the dog eater is gone. 'Cause that just leaves you and me, Stone."

I heard him suck in a breath.

"When I want you dead, Stone, *really* want you dead, you will be just that. Dead. But not yet, Stone. This is just too much fucking fun."

He stepped back and to the side, just out of reach, the bayonet out in front of him.

"They know I have this, Stone. But they've never been able to find it. That's why they sent you up here, boy. They sent you up here to get cut. They didn't want to send a nigger or one of those greasers—look too much like prej-u-dice," he said, drawing the word out slowly. "And the dog eater is gone. So that just leaves you. You should have known it would be you—you hillbilly shitheads just never learn, do you."

And then he turned and walked calmly out through the doors of the squad bay, still holding the bayonet.

Twenty-Two

Fort Gordon, Georgia
January 1961

The door opened, a little bit at a time, and a scrawny, nervous lieutenant eased through the opening. The two MPs were with him.

"Tench-Hut!" one of the MPs snapped. I got slowly to my feet. Starker, still standing, did not move.

"Stone?" the lieutenant said, looking from one of us to the other.

"Lieutenant," I answered softly.

"Starker?" the lieutenant said, looking at the dark shape still standing partially in the shadows.

Starker had been looking at me. He kept looking, deliberately not facing the lieutenant.

The two MPs split up, each moving out to the side of the lieutenant.

I let my eyes rove over the officer. I had been in the army long enough to recognize the type. He was a first lieutenant, too old for his rank. If he had been any good he would have been a major by now, I thought, or at least a captain. He was probably an ROTC puke who had never made the grade as a real officer. He had gone as high as he was ever going to go, getting stuck as a first louie and assigned to obscure training duty until the army could get rid of him in some quiet, bureaucratic way.

The officer seemed to know exactly what I was thinking.

"Keep your goddamn eyes to the front, private!" he snapped. I riveted my eyes to the far wall.

"My name is Lt. Swink. I'm the commanding officer of your training company. I want to tell you that I am not any happier to see you than you are to see me. I didn't want you. The army just gave you to me. The army didn't see fit to ask me about it. You understand? So let's try not to get too used to each other, because you're not going to be around long enough to make it worthwhile. The sooner I get your asses shipped out of here, the happier I'll be." He seemed to wind down, drawing in a deep breath.

"Now," he snapped, "you men fall outside and get in the truck."

A warped smile played briefly across Starker's face. He hesitated, took a single step toward the door, spun on the ball of his foot and drove his fist into the face of one of the MPs. The other MP made a single, swift motion with his club and the heavy stick caught Starker across the small of his back. His body arched and he began to sink slowly to the floor, his knees buckling under him.

I knew what was coming. I spun and tried to cover myself but I was too late. The club of the other MP caught me in the side and my guts seemed to tangle instantly, choking off my blood. I hit the floor, my arms wrapped around my ribs.

Starker had known we would never walk out of the room. And he didn't really give a shit. All he wanted was to put me in the middle of it.

Ten minutes later we stood again in front of Swink, who sat behind a bare metal desk in a twelve-by-twelve room in another wooden barracks building that served as headquarters for the training company. It was difficult for us to stand up straight, but Swink kept us at attention. The room smelled of cigarette smoke and gun oil and shoe polish, the lingering stink of the military.

"You men listen up," Swink said, measuring his words like a fencer measures his target. "It is unfortunate that you've had an accident, falling down the barracks steps like that. I've asked the two men who witnessed your accident to write complete reports. Those reports will be on file here if you ever want to read them." He paused, making sure we knew exactly what he was saying.

"I know what sort of men you are. I know that you are dickheads who don't really belong in this man's army. And I don't want you here, sure as hell I don't, but I don't have any choice. I don't get to pick who I train and who I don't. As long as you don't cause me any trouble I won't cause you any trouble. This is Bravo Company, Military Police Training School. You've been assigned to the fourth platoon, barracks building thirteen."

He took a deep breath.

"One more thing. I'm dammed sure you want to get out of here just as much as I want you out of here. Well, there's only one way you're going to manage that—you'll have to graduate with a military police training company. If you fail to do that, you'll be recycled—put back through another training company. And if you fuck up that one, you'll be put back in another one, recycled again and again until you finally make it, or until somebody runs over your ass with a Jeep to put an end to it. In any case, you probably won't be in my company any more after the first time around, so I don't really give a shit. Do you understand?"

"Yes, sir," I said automatically. Starker did not move, did not respond.

Swink got up and walked out and left us standing there, at attention.

Two rows of the frail barracks buildings that were assigned to Bravo Company faced each other across a barren-clay parade ground. The wind blew constantly between the buildings and across the open field. The barren ground and the faded wooden buildings gave the place an air of desolation. It was a look of poverty, a place starving for some touch of hope, some last vestige of humanness. I held my stomach and hunched my shoulders against the cold as we started across to the other side.

"Goddamn," I muttered, "goddamn, goddamn."

Starker stopped and looked directly at me. "You know what your trouble is, Stone? You're just not in control of yourself. That's why you're here. You're here by mistake. You're here because some judge said for you to be here." I couldn't help it; I stopped and stared at him.

"Me?" Starker muttered, "I'm not here by mistake, at least not my mistake. Only I know how to get out of here, Stone. And so do you. Only you don't have the balls for it, boy."

Starker's voice was flat, cold, like a chill wind crawling under a door. His face, like his voice, seemed devoid of emotion. Screw him. I turned my back and started across the parade ground.

"And don't worry about that asshole lieutenant; don't worry about him at all. He can't keep me from graduating. He knows better."

Starker's voice trailed off in the wind. I turned but he was already moving away, at a trot.

I stood there, my brain rushing toward overload. It didn't make any sense, I thought. None of it. Not the army, not the MPs, not Starker. And, sure as hell, not about Starker knowing how to get the hell out of the army. I mean, if Starker knew how to get out, why did he hang around and fuck with "them" every time he got the chance?

There really were only two ways out. You could go AWOL, or they could throw you out because you were crazy.

Or maybe there was some other way I did not know about, had not seen.

This would not end well. Starker. And me.

It would not end well.

Twenty-Three

Fort Gordon, Georgia
February 1961

The wind blew steadily into February. It blew over the hard red clay and through the cracks in the windows. It blew up through the gaps in the floors and ate its way under our blankets and into the far corners of the latrines. It brought a heavy dampness into the barracks buildings for a few days, and then switched to dust. The dust came off the barren parade ground in thick clouds that penetrated every corner of the buildings and then settled onto clothes, floors and bodies. It was impossible to get rid of it.

It was cold and damp, and then cold and dry and dusty, and once, for a few hours, some snow fell and then melted and the training turned from exercises in military police procedures to exercises in surviving the thick Georgia mud.

For the most part, I was indifferent to the training. I did not care what constituted a crime according to the military; I had no intention of driving a Jeep in hot pursuit of anyone; I had little interest in the various types of riot formations . . . but I did like throwing smoke grenades.

And I liked the weapons training. I became an expert in the use of a .45 cal. pistol, riot-type shotgun and a piece of .45 cal. metal trash that we called a grease gun.

And I loved the Judo training.

I knew most of the Judo they were trying to teach, so they put me into advanced classes at night, before they put me on KP. Eventually, they allowed me to teach some of the other trainees, and, briefly, fleetingly, I had thoughts of staying there, at Fort Gordon, learning more Judo. Maybe even getting on the Judo team. I even talked to the training sergeant about it.

Think about it, I had said. This might be my rehabilitation. Make a real soldier out of me.

The sergeant talked to Swink.

No way, Swink had said. I would not stay at Fort Gordon. Not under any circumstances. They took me out of the advanced classes. In fact, they took me out of Judo training; my Judo days were over.

I tried to think of things to do to relieve the boredom; I decided to go into business. Often, when I was on KP, the mess sergeant would assign me to the clean-up window, a hole in the barracks wall where each soldier dumped the scraps from his tray. I stood behind a counter at the hole and collected the trays, dumping the colorless food-muck into huge garbage cans and stacking trays and cutlery in bins, or dumping them into drums of scalding water. It was a sweating, messy, stinking job, the worst job they could give you. Which was why they gave it to me.

But I noticed that all the MPs who smoked were lighting cigarettes by the time they got to the window, most of them with packs still in their hands.

"Got a cigarette?" I said one night to the first MP who showed up at the window. He didn't know I didn't smoke. The MPs usually felt sorry for the guy working the clean-up window, so this MP dug one out of the pack and handed it to me. I held it until he walked away, then dropped it into an empty coffee can under the counter. By the end of the night, I had the equivalent of several packs of cigarettes. I kept it up, every night I was on KP. I separated the cigarettes by brand, put them into small plastic bags and sold them to MPs in other training companies. I was saving the money—sooner or later I would be some place where I could buy beer.

The blowing dust invaded a small group of soldiers huddled at the end of one of the long buildings, forcing them to turn their backs on it and curse whatever gods they thought had brought them there, to Fort Gordon, Georgia, on a near-dark evening in bitter winter.

I was making my way against the wind toward the same building, Barracks Building #13, where there was a hot shower and a bunk and maybe a little relief from the presence of fools. I was tired, weaving on sore legs as I shuffled across the rutted parade ground. I had been on KP since 4:00 a.m. and my mind was numb from the clatter of pots and metal trays, the smell of spattering grease and the stinking steam that rose from countless tubs of boiling, filthy water. My head was down against the wind and I didn't see the little group of men until it was too late.

"Stone! Where the hell you been? Goddamn it, I've got a job for you, mister! Now get your ass to attention!"

Swink was nearly screaming, his face puffed with anger, his skinny body trembling. Standing next to him was a sergeant. Three other MPs hung on the fringes, their heads hunched into their shoulders against the cutting wind. They were all wearing pistols.

I stopped and straightened out, not quite at attention.

"You know damn well where I've been, lieutenant. I've been the same place I've always been as long as you've had anything to do with it."

"Watch your mouth, Stone," the officer muttered.

"Look . . . sir . . . you've have had my ass in a wringer ever since I came to this place . . ."

The corporal made a move toward me.

"Hold it, corporal," Swink said, raising his hand.

I tried not to notice the corporal's movement.

"Stone," the lieutenant said, "we've got a little problem with Starker."

They all just stood there, waiting for me to say something, waiting for me to ask what the job was. Hell, I didn't want to know what the job was, and I wasn't going to ask.

"Sorry . . . sir. No way. I don't want to do it—whatever it is. And I don't want to know what it is. If you don't mind, lieutenant, I'll just pass this one up."

"Like hell you will, Stone. You and Starker came in here together and you are going out together. I'm not asking your goddamn cooperation, private, I'm ordering you, goddamn it! You may be the only dickhead who can pull this off without getting killed, and if you do get killed, well, that's one less problem for me to worry about."

I heard a small laugh from the sergeant.

The wind began to die a little and Swink lowered his voice.

"Now look, Stone, I don't want Starker to hear us out here—"

"Jesus Christ, lieutenant," I broke in, "do you really think he doesn't know we're out here?"

"I'm going to explain this only once," Swink continued, "so you listen carefully, mister. He's got a .45 in there. The last we saw of it, he put it under his pillow. Under his goddamn pillow! The fucker's been sleeping on it. He thinks it's a goddamn Teddy bear, for Christ sake! God knows how long he's had it in there, or where the hell he got it."

I knew about the gun. Yeah, just like I knew about the bayonet back at Fort Ord. I didn't know where Starker got the bayonet or where he hid it. I didn't know where he got the gun. Trainees weren't supposed to have any personal gear of any kind on the post—just like in basic training—and especially not a gun. The army wanted to teach you how to kill, but only with *their* guns. Having your own gun in a training camp was an ultimate sin. And for Starker to have a gun, any gun, was terrifying.

A week ago I had finished KP and come stumbling through the night and into the barracks, dropping onto my bunk like a dead man. Starker's bunk was next to mine, but he was not in it. I rose on my elbow and looked around through the gloom and dim light from the naked bulb in the latrine at the end of the room. Starker was sitting on the floor at the back end of his bunk, leaning against the wall. He was wiping down something heavy, and shiny. He held it up into a shaft of light and turned it so I could see every angle of it. It was a .45 Colt semi-automatic, match grade, with custom sights and walnut handles. Damn gun was so shiny it must have been nickel-plated. But when he turned the gun in his hands, I could see there was no magazine in the handle. The gun was empty. Wherever he had picked up the pistol, he hadn't picked up any ammo. No ammo— that was the only good thing about that week I could remember.

And the army didn't give Starker any ammo, either. Not for any-thing. In fact, I had never known the army to give Starker live am-munition for any gun it had issued to him. Starker had not been given ammo to qualify with a rifle in basic training, and he certainly hadn't been given any ammo for the army-issue .45 that he used in MP training. The army would just mark a scorecard for Starker and send him on through his training. Sometimes the army was smart.

But why the hell did the army do that?

"Maybe he got it the same place he got the hand grenade," the corporal said, taking a few steps toward me.

Hand grenade? I didn't know anything about any goddamn grenade.

The sergeant spoke with an accent, probably Puerto Rican, maybe Mexican, I thought. I had never seen the man before, but I remem-bered that some MPs, led by a corporal with a Spanish accent, had locked the entire platoon out of the barracks one day while they tore the place apart looking for something Starker was supposed to have stashed somewhere. They never found it.

A grenade.

"We've talked long enough, Stone," the lieutenant said, doing his best to make a growl out of his thin voice. "There's no one in the barracks but Starker. I want that weapon, mister. Now get your ass in there and bring it out. He's your buddy."

"Goddamn it, lieutenant, *he's not my buddy*! His name is Starker. My name is Stone! It's just a fucking alphabetical coincidence! The goddamn army makes us stand next to each other, sit next to each other, sleep next to each other, and whack off next to each other! But that doesn't mean he likes me any better than he likes anybody else—*and he doesn't like anybody else!*"

"Now hear this, Stone! I don't give a damn whether he likes you or not! All I want to do is get that whacked-out piece of crap out of my training company and off this post! I'm not going to risk my training record on a dickhead like that! Now get in there and get that weapon! That's an order!" Swink tried to control his voice, but it cracked, grinding on the near edge of hysteria.

I looked at the outlines of the men, half-concealed by the blowing dust. Even through the gloom I could see the shine on the tiny crossed pistols on the lieutenant's collar, the insignia of the Military Police Corps. The little pistols glittered, tiny brass weapons that seemed to generate light from within. I stared at them, feeling my mind start to slip, a gentle move toward that far and deep place within me where only I could go. Like Wendell taught me.

The lieutenant's voice snapped me back. "Stone!"

I looked closely at the man's face, a face too old to be only a first lieutenant, the face of a career soldier whose career was going nowhere. It was the face of a man who could not afford a mistake, who could not afford to have anything blow apart in his training company. It was the face of a man who could not afford Starker. Or me.

"Hey," I said suddenly, "what about the other guys? There's supposed to be a bunch of men sleeping in that building."

None of the men would look at me, not even Swink.

"We cleared them out—" Swink started to say.

"Nobody will go into the building as long as Starker's in there with the gun," the sergeant said, not looking at Swink.

I waited, but no one said anything.

"Has he got ammo?" I had almost forgotten to ask about ammo.

There was a long pause. "No. Not that we know of," the lieutenant said. But he would not look at me.

I stepped in front of the barracks door, then turned and looked directly at the officer. "Lieutenant, maybe he doesn't have ammo, but he's probably still got the grenade. And that's Starker you're dealing with in there—to him, a grenade is only good if its pin is pulled."

The lieutenant turned pale, a small choking noise gathering in his throat.

"That's enough of this shit."

It was the sergeant talking, and he was talking while he was drawing his pistol. And pointing it at me.

I stepped inside the barracks.

Twenty-Four

Fort Gordon, Georgia
February 1961

Barracks Building #13 was like all the rest of them, one large, oblong room with a row of double-decker bunks down each side. The bunks were carefully aligned, precisely, absolutely. Each morning before leaving the building, two men in each barracks building took a piece of string and held it taut down the inner end of the bunks, a third man making any minor adjustments necessary. The blankets on each bunk were pulled taut, flat brown surfaces without a wrinkle or a bump. The tautness of the blankets was tested by dropping a quarter in the center of the bunk. If the quarter bounced, the bunk was tight enough.

A single, naked light bulb burned in the exact center of the ceiling. At the far end of the building Starker lay on his bunk, his head toward the wall, arms placed carefully at his side.

If he's asleep, I thought, *I'll kiss the lieutenant's ass.*

I walked slowly down the center aisle to my own bunk, next to Starker's. I walked solidly, wanting Starker to know I was coming. My footsteps made a dull, heavy, drumming sound on the thick wooden floor.

All too quickly I was at my own bunk. I threw my cap on the pillow and sat down, starting to unlace my greasy boots. On the next bunk Starker moved his right arm, very carefully. There was no sign of the gun.

"You alone?" Starker asked.

"You know fucking well I'm alone," I said angrily. "You think any of those other assholes are going to come in here?"

I thought I saw a hint of a smile on Starker's face. It seemed to me that Starker never smiled. If he had smiled, if he had let some expression free across his face, he might have looked almost human. He never did that. His black eyes kept his face in a permanent expression of crazy.

But more than anything else, there was not a spark of fear in Starker. No fear, no respect, none of those feelings that, in the long run, provide caution, judgment—maybe even wisdom. Where those feelings should have been in Starker, there was only blank space. Black space.

"Starker, you doing it again?"

Starker didn't move.

"C'mon, Starker, you doing it again? You driving them crazy again? Every time you do something like this they send me in here to deal with you. Christ, man, I don't want to be in here messing with you. I just want to get some sleep. Why don't you give me the gun, or the grenade, or the howitzer, or whatever the hell it is—or give it to them, or throw the fucking thing out the window? You know they'll keep at you until they get it, whatever the hell it is."

"It's a gun, Jesse, a very good gun," Starker said slowly, no hint of emotion showing in the voice. It was the first time he had ever called me anything but Stone. "I've had it for almost a month. Bought it in town on my first weekend pass. It's been right here all that time. Isn't that something?"

He was lying and I knew it. Neither of us had had a pass since we arrived at Gordon. But the lie really didn't matter.

From outside the window at the end of our bunks I could hear some thumping and some scratching sounds. I knew Starker must have heard them, but he paid no attention. I decided I had better keep an eye on the window.

And then I thought, the hell it, it was the army's problem, not mine. Let the army figure out what to do with him. I fell back on my bunk, stretching my aching legs and arching my back. "Christ, Starker, just do me a favor, will you? When they finally get up the guts to come charging in here with fixed bayonets and riot guns to get that fucking .45, try not to let 'em step on me, will you?"

"Don't worry about that, Jesse. If they do that, you will already be dead."

That was the second time he had ever put it that way. Directly. No hesitation. And I couldn't figure out why it didn't really bother me this time. Was I getting used to Starker? Jesus H. Christ.

There was no more noise from outside the window but I glanced over that way, anyway. It was dark outside now, but through the thin pane of glass the faint glow of the lieutenant's face shone in the weak light of the naked bulb, a pale expression of fear hanging in the night.

Starker opened his eyes, carefully put his legs over the side of the bunk and stood up. The wind gusted and sand rattled against the side of the barracks. Outside, the lieutenant must have shifted his weight on whatever he was standing on; I heard a slight creaking sound.

"They are not going to come in here, Jesse. The lieutenant isn't going to let them. That's why I can do this. That's why I can do these things." The pistol appeared in Starker's hand, a shiny, heavy, beautiful weapon that glistened in the light of the single bulb. I turned my head to look at Starker and my breathing went shallow. I expected to see the gun, but I didn't expect to see the magazine in Starker's other hand. And I didn't expect to see the round hardball nose of the bullet that peeked out of the top of it. Ammo. Live ammo. The magazine was stuffed full of it.

Starker slipped the magazine into the butt of the pistol and rammed it home with the heel of his hand. He grabbed the slide and jacked it back, then let it slam forward. The sound of a weapon being jacked, any weapon, was one of the first sounds you learned in the army, and you never, ever, forgot it.

The lieutenant's face disappeared below the window sill.

That son of a bitch, I said to myself, *he knew Starker had the ammo. He knew it all the time.*

Starker dropped his arm and let the gun dangle down at his side, casually, a toy.

The wind paused and I could hear creaking sounds from whatever the lieutenant was standing on outside the window. I hoped Starker didn't notice.

"Look, Starker, this isn't my job. I'm not going to play their game any more, you understand? And I'm not going to play your game, either. If you want to blow somebody away, help yourself. I don't give a shit." I tried to be casual about it, stretching on my bunk and even closing my eyes. But, involuntarily, I stiffened, and I knew Starker could see that. I opened my eyes again.

Starker looked blankly at my tense form. He shifted his fingers on the gun, balancing it carefully, gripping it, fingering it, ready. The safety was off. The hammer was cocked. Neither of us moved and in the silence I could hear my own breathing as the air escaped from my chest in bursts harder than I wanted. I began to sweat.

"Don't worry, Stone. I'm going to give them the gun."

I let my eyes slide toward the window. The lieutenant's eyes had edged just above the sill again, two dark spots reflecting nothing.

Starker snapped his arm toward the window and leaped directly for the glass, plunging the pistol and half his arm through the thin pane. The shattering glass sounded like a thousand bottles breaking.

Through it wood and falling bodies crashed outside the building.

I don't know if the pistol hit the lieutenant in the face. I never did find out. But I heard him scream as he fell, *"Don't shoot! Oh Jesus God don't shoot!"*

Starker stood there, his arm rammed out into the night. He slowly opened his fingers and let the pistol fall into the darkness. He never pulled the trigger.

Starker carefully pulled his arm back through the broken glass. It wasn't even scratched.

In slow jerky movements I sat up on the edge of my bunk.

"Starker, one of these days you're going to get us both snuffed, you know that? You're going to get us into something we can't get out of. There's going to be a better man than Swink out there waiting for us, and he's going to blow our asses off."

"Don't think so, Jesse. Just don't think so. And, anyway, maybe that's the way it ought to be, you know? Just a couple of old gun runners getting snuffed."

Gun runners? Just when the hell did I become a gun runner?

Starker sat down on his bunk, looking at me. "You know, Jesse, we're tied together, you and me. We're tied together. Isn't that magnificent?"

The lieutenant lay with his face grinding into the hard Georgia clay, his arms twisted beneath him. Empty ammunition cases lay scattered around him; he had stacked them up to climb on, to get up to where he could see through the window. An MP shined a light on his face. Tears formed in his clamped-shut eyes. His body shook slightly, even though we could tell he was trying not to move, one arm holding the other clamped tightly to his body. And when he finally opened his eyes he saw the pistol lying directly in front of his face, so close he could smell the gun oil. His stomach knotted and began to heave. He tried to hold it back, but it was out of his control. He vomited on the pistol.

The MPs handcuffed us, and led us away.

Twenty-Five

Fort Gordon, Georgia
March 1961

The early morning light had barely hit the tops of the barracks buildings but we already sat on the bus, more than twenty of us, waiting. Our stay at Military Police Training School was over. We were leaving. Even I was leaving. Swink had seen to that.

The bus reminded me of the buses I once rode to high school, except that this one was painted olive drab. I sat at the very back. I hated buses, but if I had to ride one, I didn't want anyone behind me. There was one consolation to being on the bus—Starker wasn't there.

In fact, I hadn't seen Starker for a while. After that business with the pistol they had kept us locked up in an empty barracks building for a couple of days, then put me back in training as though nothing had happened. A few days after that, Starker's uniforms were gone, and the mattress on his bunk had been rolled. He had simply disappeared from the barracks, just dropped out of sight. Those last couple of weeks were the only good ones I ever had at Fort Gordon, Georgia. Or any other place in the goddamn army.

The bus was parked in front of the training company headquarters, another old barracks building propped up off the ground by ancient concrete blocks. We were waiting for Swink to come aboard and give his goodbye speech. Officers at training companies always had goodbye speeches. It was cold gray early morning and the sweat and warm breath of the men had already fogged up the windows. I took mental inventory of the men who sprawled in the seats. With one or two exceptions I thought they were the scum of the training company graduating class, myself included. They were a total collection of misfits—too small, too thin, too fat, or too stupid to be real MPs. This was actually interesting, I thought. If these guys can't be real MPs, what the hell can they be? I knew the whole bunch was headed to North Depot Activity, some lonely little storage depot in Upstate New York. Jesus, I wondered, what the hell kind of place is North Depot Activity, that it can make use of this bunch of total jerk-offs?

Including me.

But there were a couple of exceptions on the bus, men who could be real soldiers, real MPs. The only one I knew personally was Hays Tucker. They called him "Kansas." He was handsome, serious, stood well over six feet, had the build of a linebacker, and carried himself with pride and dignity. He had been in a different platoon during training, but I spent so much time on KP I had gotten to know some of the other men. Tucker was one of the best men in the training company, always standing first in the classes, always prepared. He seemed to be the ideal career soldier, and he looked the part. He obviously liked the training, liked the work, liked the discipline.

In spite of myself, I thought I might like Tucker. But how the hell did Tucker end up here, on this bus, with the sorriest bunch of newly minted MPs in the history of the army? It made no sense at all.

I slid over to my right and wiped the window off with my sleeve. There was no one outside the bus, no one to see us off. The training company area was empty and silent. And then I saw Swink come out of the headquarters building. Behind him, two MPs were leading Starker to the bus.

Shit, I said to myself. *Shitshitshit. How the hell does he do it? How the hell does he pull this shit on the army, time after time, and they still leave him in? It just doesn't figure. Who the hell is this guy?*

The doors of the bus pushed open and Swink got on, standing at the head of the aisle. No one spoke. Swink stood there for a moment, staring in my general direction. His right arm hung angled in a cast, the plaster reaching from his fingertips to his shoulder. The cast had appeared the morning after he did the swan dive from the pile of ammo boxes. Arm was broken in four places, so we heard in the mess hall.

Swink was wearing his pistol on his left side, butt forward. Some of the men had seen him practice drawing the weapon, awkwardly hauling the fat iron out of the leather in unfamiliar motion.

Swink let his left hand hang there, his arm swinging slightly back and forth, brushing the butt of the pistol.

"As you men know," Swink began, his voice low and controlled, "your permanent duty station will be North Depot Activity. You will begin your transfer of duty stations by bus, then by plane, then back to another bus for your final leg of the trip. You are not to leave the group at any time. Private Tucker has all the travel orders and he will be in charge. If you have any questions, save them until you arrive at the depot."

He paused. For effect, I thought. I'll bet he's got a parting shot.

"Stone . . . and Starker," he said, flicking a look over his shoulder, "I've taken the responsibility of notifying your new commanding officer of your . . . personalities and . . . special abilities. I trust that he will respond to you accordingly." The lieutenant's face broke into a sneering smile.

"That's all," he said. He stood slightly aside, his hand on the butt of his pistol, and nodded his head, motioning Starker forward. Starker stepped up on the bus. He paused, his hands awkwardly close together in front of him. He looked at no one, raising his hands slowly. He was wearing handcuffs. Then without hesitation he walked straight to the rear of the bus and sat down in front of me. Swink backed off the bus and turned toward the company headquarters building, no more than fifteen feet from the side of the bus. He disappeared inside, slamming the door behind him, never taking his hand from the butt of his pistol.

The son of a bitch! I thought. *The son of a bitch!* North Depot Activity—whatever the hell that is—is going to be just like Gordon! It's going to be tough shit all over again from the very first day I get there. And I still have a year-and-a-half left on my "enlistment." Except that I did not "enlist."

And how could they possibly send Starker to a permanent duty station?

The driver started the engine and began to clank around in the transmission. We were about to say goodbye to Fort Gordon, Georgia.

At least things had to get better, I thought.

Sometimes I just don't think straight.

The drab buildings began to fade back into the weak light. And then, somewhere back there in the general direction of the training company, a plume of thick, dirty, gray smoke was rolling straight up into the cold air of the frigid Georgia morning, a plume of such intensity that it was nearly black. It puffed and grew, spreading against the heavy air. I stared in utter disbelief. A fire. A fire in our training company, a fire on the morning when we were leaving.

I couldn't hear them, but I knew that by now there were Fort Gordon fire brigades on the way or already there, men running, sirens screaming, hoses being pulled, water pouring into whatever buildings were burning.

Beside me, I felt the presence of Starker. "It's not a fire," he whispered. "Smoke grenade. I put it under Swink's office." I expected to hear him laugh, or at least chuckle. But Starker never did those things.

The company headquarters building. The fire brigade would be pouring water into Swink's office.

And somewhere along the way they would discover what it really was, that it was only a smoke grenade, and some senior officer would be very, very angry and would want to talk to Swink.

Goddamn, I was almost happy about that.

Part III

THE SCUMMERS

Twenty-Six

North Depot Activity
Romulus, New York
March 1961

I didn't wake until the bus stopped. As long as there had been movement I had slept, but when the movement stopped I woke up instantly, wondering immediately where Starker was.

Not to worry, I thought. *He's there, a few seats in front of me.*

The windows were tightly closed against the cold. The heavy smells of diesel fumes, stale bodies, vomit, shit, and other assorted body odors were trapped inside, all of them pressing against my face. I wiped my sleeve across the frosted glass. There was a harsh, glaring light flooding the outside of the bus and I could see that it was snowing hard, the late-winter flakes layering on top of other snow that looked gray and old, a thick, graceless mass.

The bus was not moving but the engine was still running, driving the heater at full blast against the cold. From somewhere there was a hard freezing wind, and I realized the door of the bus was standing open. The glaring light gave the inside of the bus a garish cast, exaggerated shadows streaming from one side to the other.

"Private Tucker, front and center!"

The voice was crisp, efficient. Not angry, but not all that pleased to be addressing new arrivals. Some of the men stirred in their seats, pretending to be asleep, content to let the army order them to make any necessary movement. Somewhere up in front of me Hays Tucker pulled his huge frame from his seat and moved toward the front of the bus. He carried a thick manila envelope; the traveling orders.

I was still trying to clear sleep from my head. I could hear Tucker talking to someone at the front of the bus, their voices only dull mumblings in the distance.

"Stone! Private Stone! Fall out!" the voice yelled from the front of the bus.

Fall out? Fall out into what? I wondered. Fall out into the snow? But I thought I had better not screw around. Not yet. I got on my feet and staggered quickly down the aisle. Tucker was still at the front of the bus, but the other man was gone. I stepped off the bus.

The first thing I saw was the fence.

I was groggy from the polluted air of the bus, from the long ride in the dark in the middle of a near-Canadian winter, from crawling off the bus at three o'clock in the morning. But the fence cut into my consciousness, a jagged weaving of hateful wire drawn across the naked bone of my mind.

A couple of moments went by while I stared at the fence—before I realized I was standing in snow up to my crotch. The bus had come down a narrow road in the snow-filled dark, turned into an empty parking area and plowed a deep, wide furrow, piling snow up to the sides and in front. If the bus had not stopped, the snow would have stopped it.

The fence glittered. At intervals, some of the metal poles were higher and topped with floodlights, jutting far above the fence, their brilliance angled down and carefully directed, flooding every foot of the running wire and the reaching crown of metal thorns probing off into the light. The lights from one pole overlapped the next, the unbroken brilliance running with the fence until they both made turns and disappeared behind darkly shimmering masses of buildings in the distance. The heavy chain link was ten feet high, topped by a V-shaped wedge of barbed wire that stabbed out at an angle on both sides of the fence, adding another two feet to the height. And every razored barb, every bend, every thick metal post, every tiny angle between the mad race and flow of the wire as it warped itself into the distance of the lights and the snow and the frigid air, every single aspect of the fence glittered and danced through the veil of the falling snow, alive with crystals of ice.

A crystal fence. Glistening. Deadly.

In the glaring light of the floods I saw the silhouette of a fat man, his feet spread, his chest pulled up in a useless attempt to make him look taller. His back was to the floodlights and he stood with hands on hips, short enough that the snow rose almost to his waist. He was wearing full winter field gear—bulky woolen pants and a parka with a fur fringe around a hood that was pulled tightly around a shapeless pile hat that covered what looked to be a ball-like head. He looked like a small, dark green blimp anchored to the snow. Around the bicep of his left arm was a dark strip of cloth, the bright, white letters "MP" standing out in the light.

He did not speak for the first minute I stood there, but I knew he was angry.

Screw it, I thought, *these guys are always angry.*

"You better get your ass to attention and listen good, Stone! This ain't no goddamn training camp—you ain't gonna be leavin' here in a few weeks. This is the real army, your permanent duty station. And if you don't listen good, real good, it may become more permanent than you ever bargained for!"

The fat bastard turned his head slightly toward the bus, but never really took his eyes from me.

"Tucker!" he yelled, "close that damn bus door and stay put! I'll call for the rest of your asses when I want 'em!" He turned and plowed through the snow in the direction of a small building about the size of a comfortable outhouse, his plump ass waddling through the drifts like a small fleshy bulldozer. He glanced over his shoulder and noticed that I was not following.

"Well, follow me, Stone! What the hell do you want, a kick in the ass? A fucking formal invitation?"

There were no lights inside the tiny building. There was only one room, and there were two men already inside, leaving barely enough space for me and the other man to enter. Large glass windows looked out on the road—or where the road was supposed to be. Other windows looked down the fence line that stretched away from both sides of the building. Leaning against one of the windows was a tall lanky MP, casually running his eyes from my boots to my cap.

Backed into a corner, a short, squat MP stood, his frame almost a square. He looked solid and his arms seemed too large for the rest of his body. His hands twitched nervously, swinging at the tops of short, bowed legs that he now spread apart. He began to finger the pistol hanging from his belt. I could hardly see his eyes but they were the sort of eyes you didn't really have to see to know that they glowed.

Jesus, I thought, *wait till Starker gets a load of this guy.*

The little fat man stood in the center of the room. Even under the melting snow his boots had the gleam of high polish. The legs of his thick field pants were turned up and inside at the top his boots, ballooned out over the boot-tops by thick elastic bands hidden under the folds. There were creases sewn into the heavy pants and they, like his jacket, were pressed to razor sharpness, or as close to sharpness as heavy wool ever got.

Regular army, I thought. *Career man. No doubt.*

The fat man turned and stepped closer to me. "Private Stone, I'm Staff Sergeant Kraus, platoon sergeant for the third MP platoon of this security company. You and some of the men on that bus are going to be assigned to the third platoon, my platoon. That means you and me will have to live together as long as we are here on this post. Do you understand?"

"Yes, sergeant," I said steadily. *Don't let this bag of meat get too far ahead of me,* I thought. *At least not until I find out what the hell is going on here.* But I thought I already knew.

Kraus turned toward the other men. "Bannerman, Sabolino, get on the bus and check things out. Tell the driver that he can't bring that vehicle on this post. And get those men ready to march to the barracks."

"Excuse me, sergeant," the tall guy, Bannerman, said, "but you know we can't leave this post, this *guard* post. It's against orders, particularly when we would have to leave an unauthorized person in here . . . alone . . . with the sergeant. If Lt. Ringer should come along—"

"Goddamn it, Bannerman, do like I said! I know where Ringer is, and that asshole ain't gonna to be in this area all night."

That wasn't good enough for Bannerman. "Listen, sergeant, you know damn well that if we leave this post, even under your orders, that Ringer could—"

"*Bannerman!*" the sergeant shouted, his voice rising to a squeal and screeching out of his fat neck in short bursts. "Get your ass out there! Now!"

Bannerman did not move. I had no idea what the regulations really were, whether Bannerman was in the right, or whether he was just trying to mess with Kraus's head.

Sabolino edged forward slightly, his body seemingly in a permanent crouch, hands dangling at his sides. *Jesus,* I thought, *the little guy is going to take him, he's going to take the sergeant!*

"Sabo," Bannerman said quietly, without actually looking at the little man, "let's go check the bus. I'm sure the sergeant can handle things here. And," he added, facing the sergeant squarely, "I'm sure that the sergeant will see to it that his order is properly mentioned in the daily report."

I glanced at Kraus, noticing that he had taken a step backward, away from Sabolino. Beyond Kraus, Sabolino seemed to uncoil a little, relaxing his hands. Bannerman and Sabolino moved to the door. Just before they stepped out into the snow, Sabolino turned and looked carefully at Kraus, measuring him. Then the door swung slowly shut behind them.

Kraus is not sure of Sabolino, I thought. *He really isn't sure. Jesus, what am I into here?*

Kraus turned to face me. "Stone, there's a couple of things I want to say to you in private, right now, before we go any further, before you even set foot on this post. I want you to know that I won't put up with any of your bullshit. I want you to know that I don't care how you got into this man's army, or what you think of it. You're here, and, goddamn it, you're going to stay here until you finish out your tour. Now, you and some of them other assholes are going to be in my platoon. And I know all about that dickhead named Starker. So let's you and me get one thing straight—if I have any trouble with that asshole, Starker, I'm going to have *your* ass up before the company commander quicker'n you can get your pants down. You hear me? I'll kick your ass all the way to Fort Jay—and that's where you'll spend the rest of your time in the army, Stone, at Fort Jay! In the stockade! You got that?"

"Yeah, sergeant, I got that," I said evenly. "But what the hell is this all about? I haven't even set foot on this post yet. I haven't done anything here. And I am not responsible for Starker, anyway. We all just got here, for Christ's sake." I stared at the fat man's face and kept my eyes level, not flinching. I noticed that Kraus was sweating, his jowls glistening in the reflected glare. *Good God*, I thought, *he's afraid. Afraid of what? Something's shaking him, right now, right here, right in the middle of the damn night.*

"Stone," Kraus said, trying to keep his voice low and mean, "you and me's got to have an understanding about Starker."

Oh, shit, I thought, so that's it.

"I heard about you and Starker, heard about how you take care of him when he gets out of line. And you're both goin' to be in my fuckin' platoon.

"Well, now hear this, trooper—I don't want either of you here! Most of all, I don't want you in my platoon. But you *are* here, and there ain't shit I can do about it. Except this—if there's any trouble with Starker, I'm going to come lookin' for *you*. If Starker's in trouble, you're in trouble. That's the way I work things, Stone. That's the way I get what I want. And that's what you're going to have to live with as long as you're here. You got that?"

"Sergeant, I think you've got this all wrong—"

"Don't tell me what the fuck I got wrong! I know what happened all the way back to Ord. I know what happened at Gordon. I know about the gun. I know what happened the day you left. And I know that the people at Gordon can't prove a thing, not a goddamn thing—them people at Gordon just wanted you two the fuck out'a there. And that's the only reason you and Starker ain't bustin' rocks some place!

"You're dog meat, Stone, and Starker's dog meat—first chance I get." His voice had dropped to a low growl.

Outside, Bannerman and Sabolino got off the bus and started toward the guard post.

"You just remember what I said," Kraus muttered, glancing

through the window at the two men wading through the snow.

Fuck you, I thought. *Fuck your fat ass, you simple son of a bitch. I'm not going to take this shit this time. I'm not going to do it, and I may as well start pushing now.*

And I thought he was afraid of the little guy.

I lowered my voice and spoke softly, wanting him to have to strain to hear me.

"I'm sick of this shit, sergeant. I'm not responsible for Starker, and I don't intend to spend my time here in the mess hall on KP, or scrubbing floors in some fucking officer's quarters, or carrying out your garbage." Kraus snapped his head back toward me, eyes wide, not used to being talked to this way.

"You see that short guy on his way in here, sergeant? You think he's tough shit? You haven't seen anything, sergeant. That guy is a pussy, an honest-to-God pussy. The real tough shit, the real crazy, is out there, on that bus, and his name is Starker. And, sergeant, it isn't going to take any effort at all for Starker to figure out what the hell's going on here—" The door opened and I shut my mouth, hoping I was right about Kraus being afraid of the little guy. If he's afraid of the little guy, I thought, he should be downright paralyzed about Starker.

Bannerman came through the door first. "Well, sergeant, I've seen some scummers come on this depot before, but they must have had to dig those fuckers up from someplace really special. Jesus Christ, you should see 'em," Bannerman said, thin laughter creeping into his voice.

"Bannerman, I've told you enough times that no one on this post is to be called a scummer!" Kraus screamed. "Now, are those people ready to go to the barracks?"

Bannerman ignored him.

"Yeah, sergeant, they're ready," Sabolino said, moving in front of Kraus, "only there's one of 'em that got a little excited about bein' in the army, and all. Pissed in his seat. Don't know which one it is, but you can smell it all over the bus—"

Kraus bolted out the door, charging toward the bus. He slammed the bus doors open and disappeared inside. I stood in the guard post, silently weighing what I had heard Kraus say; Kraus, a fat, angry sergeant, who had the power of life and death over me. I didn't know if the bluff about Starker had any effect, but I knew that Kraus could be scared, and I sure as hell had tried to scare him. Maybe it had been a mistake. I would find out soon enough.

Bannerman and Sabolino stood looking at me.

"On Kraus's shit list already, huh?" Bannerman said. "You don't waste any time, trooper."

"Name's Stone."

"Yeah," Sabolino said, "we heard."

Through the falling snow they could hear Kraus, screaming at the men on the bus.

"Welcome to the inside, scummer," Bannerman said.

Twenty-Seven

North Depot Activity
Romulus, New York
March 1961

There were eighteen of us, all that had been on the bus, and we stood in the basement of the concrete-block, three-story barracks building. It must have been what standing in the basement of the Great Pyramid felt like—a room hidden from all time and reason, built to hold the secrets of gods. Kraus tried to march us to the building through the heavy, clinging snow. As we pushed the snow up to our knees and then to our waists, Kraus had more trouble than any of us and he fell behind. When that happened the men straggled out and then settled into a single line, beating a deep path to the building. Kraus was the last man to get there.

The basement room was brilliant with lights set flush into the ceiling, lights hidden behind thick panes of glass and bracketed with heavy metal frames. We stood in loose rank-and-file formation, steam rising from our wet uniforms, waiting for someone to tell us what to do. I stood in the front rank, Tucker next to me, the thick envelope of travel orders in his hand. Somewhere in a rank behind me, Starker stood, motionless and silent. The other men shuffled and coughed, stretched, blinked their eyes in the bright lights, and generally tried to warm themselves after the short march through the drifting snow. None of us had winter gear; we all wore the light field jackets that we had been issued in basic training and had worn all through MP School at Fort Gordon.

We faced a window in the far wall, a window not covered with glass, but with wire mesh, a window that didn't open to the outside, but opened into another room that stretched away into the darkness at its far end. Through the window we could see rifles, carbines, machine guns, shotguns, pistols, ammunition and other items of fire and destruction stacked and racked in neat rows.

Behind us a door opened and the sound of heavy, crackling treads came to the front of the room. A huge black man stopped in front of us, smacking his heels smartly against the hard, shiny tiles of the floor. He must have had metal caps on the heels of his boots; when he walked the metallic crackling sounds gave out an air of absolute authority. I couldn't help but steal a glance at those boots. I had never seen any boots like them. They were just the ordinary, high, black, military boots, just like those every one of us was wearing. But this guy's boots shone as though they were lit by a black light from the inside, the toes glistening like none I had ever seen—the boots of a career soldier who wanted you to know he was a career soldier. In the time I spent in the army, I never saw another pair of boots like those.

"At ease," the man said, his voice rumbling, rich, amplified by the hard walls of the room. The men stopped their muttering and shuffling. He was the most soldier-like man I had ever seen. His uniform, even in those dark hours of early morning, was crisp, the creases sharp. His boots shone like patent leather and the brass of his belt buckle and MP insignia on his collar reflected like small golden mirrors. His back was straight and his arms hung at his sides, his hands never moving from the side-seams of his pants. I thought maybe he was the first real no-bullshit career soldier . . . Jesus Christ, everything about this guy was something I had never seen.

In the far corner of the room Kraus stood with his thumbs hooked loosely into the front of his belt, his hat shoved slightly back on his head, a stance of insolence. He stared at the black man.

"My name is Sergeant Major Murphy. I am the ranking noncom of this MP company. In case you men don't know what that means, it means, on behalf of the company commander, I run this company."

Murphy. Another black man named Murphy. What the hell?

"I want to welcome you men to North Depot Activity and tell you that your stay here can be as pleasant . . ." He paused. There wasn't a sound in the room. " . . . or as difficult as you want to make it. I also want to tell you that everything that goes right in this unit will go right in front of me. And that everything that goes wrong will go wrong in front of me. And I get very angry when things go wrong.

"I realize that you men have never been on this kind of post before, and you must learn that things are different here. You will be given a written list of this post's security regulations. Learn these regulations within the first twenty-four hours after you receive them. After that, there will be no excuse for violating any regulation of this post.

"You will find that our regulations are different. This is a maximum security post." He paused again, letting the words sink in. "Violation of this post's security regulations will be dealt with quickly and severely. You men are MPs—you are supposed to *enforce* our regulations, and therefore protect the mission of this post. Any violation of regulations by an MP will be looked upon as a violation of your own mission, and the punishment will be harsh."

Kraus was looking my way. And smiling.

Murphy turned and walked along the front line of men, stopping in front of Tucker.

"Private Tucker, you got the orders for these men?"

"Yes, sergeant," Tucker said clearly, handing over the envelope. I searched Murphy's face for some sign of what was to happen next, but saw nothing.

"Men," Murphy said, "you are standing in the guard mount room. This room is used to form the guard for duty when the weather prevents us from standing outside for prolonged periods. The walls of this room are six feet thick and made of steel-reinforced concrete. Behind you is a sliding door, solid steel, to be opened or closed only by the officer or NCO in charge, or at his command. We may enter and leave this room only through that door.

"Through that wire mesh back there," he pointed over his own shoulder, "is the armory. You are to go in there only when the armorer tells you to do so, and he probably never will."

Murphy's voice began to drone and my mind wandered along the line of men, the most recent collection of fuck-ups from Fort Gordon, wondering which of them would be the first to make something go wrong, which of them would be the first to end up in front of Murphy. Murphy, I knew, would not be the one to mete out the official punishment. That would be done by the commanding officer of the company. But Murphy would be the one to tell the CO what to do, to whom, when, and how much. And Murphy was probably one tough son of a bitch.

" . . . and Starker, Third Platoon, room 318. Stone and Tucker, Third Platoon, room 320 . . ." My attention jumped back to Murphy, who was reading off platoon and room assignments. For the first time in months, I felt a slight twinge of relief. Starker and I were not going to be in the same room.

"Although you men are assigned to different platoons," Murphy continued, "you will be in close contact with each other. You will, in fact, be serving together for as long as you are here at NDA. I am sure you are all happy about that."

Murphy paused, his eyes wandering from man to man. I could see that he was reading the name tags on the front of each man's uniform. Murphy's eyes found the tag he was looking for and he moved casually along the line of men until he was standing directly in front of Starker. He stopped there, staring directly into Starker's face. There was neither respect nor fear in Murphy's eyes. Only curiosity. Unblinking, Starker stared back, his face expressionless.

Murphy stepped back.

"Guard Platoon—tench-HUT!" We jammed our boot heels together and straightened our bodies, arms and hands rigidly at our sides. "You men have your platoon assignments. When you fall out, pick up your bedding, find your rooms and make up your bunks. Then get some sleep.

"And one more thing. Yesterday was the last day of the month. Payday. Some of the other men probably went into town tonight, and may not be back yet. When they do come in, they may be a little noisy. I'm telling you this because I don't want any trouble. . . . Privates Tucker and Stone—fall out and stay behind. The rest of you men—fall out!"

The formation broke up and the men began to file from the room, picking up their bedding and disappearing down the hallway. Kraus had already gone.

Murphy waited until the others were gone, then turned to Tucker and me. "Normally, your platoon sergeant takes care of this sort of thing, but I thought I should . . . lend a hand." Murphy looked around the empty room. Probably looking for Kraus, I thought.

We listened carefully, intently, as Murphy talked.

"I've put you two in the same platoon," Murphy continued, "just because I thought it might be a little better that way. I've seen your test scores and I know that both of you are smart men.

"But that's not really why I did it. I did it because I want you to straighten out, Stone. I want you to soldier like I know Tucker here can. You men should stick together. I've heard about you, Stone. You're supposed to be some kind of lightning rod, draw shit down on yourself. Well, this may be the last chance you ever get to lose that reputation."

Straighten out, I thought. *Straighten out. The army screws with me for months, and now its telling me to straighten out.*

"And one more thing—both of you—don't bring me no transfer requests. Usually the smart ones bring me a transfer request right away. Want me to take it to the captain. Well, I don't take nothin' to the captain that I don't have to, and I don't take him no transfer requests.

"For your information, there's four ways off this post. *One,* you can finish your tour here in an honorable manner. *Two,* you can extend your enlistment for one year and volunteer for Ranger training and you might, just maybe, be transferred out.

"The other two ways are a little different . . . *three,* you can go AWOL, and then Ruker or one of his men will find your ass and bring you back, and no one can guarantee the condition you will be in. *Four,* you can die. And between you and me, I might pick dying before I let Ruker find me." He laughed to himself.

"That's all. Go find your room." And he turned and started to leave, the metal-capped heels of his boots smacking into the tiled floor.

I stopped him. "Sergeant Murphy?"

"You goin' to ask the question now, right Stone?" Murphy said quietly as he stopped and turned in the doorway.

"The question? Well, sergeant, I don't know. I mean, I want to know— "

"Get on with it, private."

"Okay, sergeant. Just one thing. You going to hold me responsible for Starker? I'm not responsible for him, sergeant. No way."

"Yeah, in a pig's ass," Murphy muttered.

"That's right, sergeant, in a pig's ass. And I think I know who the pig is. Look, sergeant, you know too much to have learned it through official channels. Now why don't you tell me what's comin' down, and where it's comin' down from." I tried to keep my voice even. I wanted to yell at Murphy, but knew that would be the first real mistake I would make on this post. Maybe the last.

Murphy stepped closer to us, then turned his head and glanced down the hallway. There was no one else in sight.

"Okay, that's the question I thought you would ask, Stone. Now listen up, because I'm only going to say this once. I spent three years in Korea with Swink, but he ain't no fuckin' friend of mine, you understand? He just thinks I am. He called me. Told me a lot of shit about you and Starker. Says Starker's crazy and that you ain't far behind. Says to look out for you two, don't turn my back and all that shit. Well, I don't have to look out for nobody—you got that, Stone? Not nobody. You know why? Because you're on NDA, that's why. And on NDA, I got everybody where I want 'em. Nobody on this damn post gets away clean if I don't want 'em to. Sooner or later, everybody fucks up—busts a security regulation—and then the army has its way." He paused, but I said nothing. Tucker looked stricken.

"Look around you, for Christ's sake, you two. Look who got off that bus with you. A bunch of thumb-sucking, mouth-breathing scummers. There's Tucker, here, and then there's you, Stone. And then there's the rest of them. Oh, I know you graduated at the bottom of your MP class, Stone, but I also know you're smart—I've seen your test scores from basic training. You and Tucker, you're both too smart for this place . . . " He paused again. I was beginning to hate his pauses. " . . . and the smart ones always screw up first.

"I mean, just think about it, Stone. Every man on that bus has got an IQ of about the speed limit. IQs of maybe half of what yours is. You ever think about that on the way up here? You ever wonder about that?"

I had, in fact, wondered about that. I didn't wonder so much about myself, just thought it was the army's little way of telling me they loved me. But I wondered about Tucker, and a couple of the others. Tucker, who had graduated at the top of his MP training class. Tucker, who probably could be the best MP the army had ever had. What the hell was Tucker doing here at NDA?

"It's simple, Stone. Just think about it. And I'm telling you this so maybe you'll keep your head down around here. And if you keep yours, maybe some of the others will keep theirs. Me? I just want to do my hitch and then get the fuck off this place, you understand? So listen up. The army, in its fucked up wisdom, needs men to guard places like this, maximum security places, places with electric fences around 'em, places designed to keep people out. The army uses MPs, always MPs. They take the bottom of the barrel, the lowest guys in the graduating class of a training platoon, the guys who will never make it as real MPs, the guys who are too short, too fat, too fucked up, guys they just can't send anywhere else, and they send them up here. Guys they need to keep an eye on, guys who need a keeper. But they know that them scummers will blow the lid off this place if they're left to themselves, so they send a few 'keepers' along with them, MPs with good test scores, MPs at the top of the class. MPs like Tucker, here.

"You think I'm shittin' you, Stone? Just think about it. You're here to take care of Starker—two scummers who deserve each other. They want Tucker, here, to take care of everybody else. Only I don't think Tucker is going to make it." Tucker was standing in a slouch, the weight of what he had just heard draining the blood from his face.

"Jesus H. Christ," I muttered.

"That's right, kid. Jesus H. Christ has sent you to the zoo. 'Cause there is one little thing about a place that's designed to keep people out, and that's the fact that it's also got to *keep people in*. And you're on the inside, with the rest of the animals."

I felt my stomach sag into my bowels, felt the energy drain from me. I looked at Tucker, who was standing straighter now, almost at attention, legs locked, his face a mask of disbelief, the dead weight of desperation dragging at him.

"Christ almighty, sergeant, what the hell do we do?" Tucker mumbled.

"Do? You do nothin', private, except what you're told to do. You stay straight, you hear me? You *soldier*. And you watch yourself . . . Kraus is a cheese-eatin' asshole. He's made sure that a bunch of people never got off this post in an honorable manner." Murphy stood watching us, rocking slowly back and forth on his heels.

"Oh, and one more thing, private," Murphy said softly, "just while I'm thinking about it. Starker still got that cannon?"

I hesitated, holding my mind carefully in place. The last time I had admitted to anyone that Starker had a gun, they had made me go and get it, ordered me to go get it. And besides, the gun was back at Gordon. I kept my mouth shut.

"Forget it, Stone," Murphy laughed, "I know he's got it. And I know about the last time you had to go get it. And I know that it disappeared the morning you men got on the bus and that chicken-fuckin' Swink at Gordon couldn't find it."

Murphy chuckled. Maybe it was a chuckle. Maybe it was something else.

Starker had the pistol. He must have the pistol. Was carrying it to his room right now, right as we were standing here in the guard mount room, just talking, just waiting for Starker to haul the piece out of his bag. How did Starker do that shit?

"And hear this, Stone. Every time Starker gets out of line, Kraus is going to send you after him. *Every* time. Kraus don't take no chances with his own ass—just like Swink."

Kraus held up his hand before I could say anything. He knew what I was going to say, anyway. And, frankly, my dear, he didn't give a damn.

Murphy turned and stepped toward the hallway.

"Sergeant Major," I said softly. He stopped, but did not turn back. "You got any relatives in California?"

Murphy stood for a moment, then walked smartly down the hallway, the heavy clicking of his tread echoing through the building.

Tucker still had not moved, his big frame towering beside me. Only his fingers moved, slowly opening and closing, absently searching for a throat.

I'm not going to make it here, I thought.

"I'll make it if I have to break every one of these dickheads," Tucker said.

"That include me?"

Tucker looked at me, then walked away.

Twenty-Eight

North Depot Activity
Romulus, New York
March 1961

The room was small, barely large enough to keep two men from falling over each other. The floor was tile, polished to a high shine. The walls were concrete block, covered with one layer of white paint. There were two GI cots and, just inside the door, a large, upright, metal double-locker, a heavy gray cabinet designed to hold everything that the army allowed to be kept in the room. And that was all. Nothing else. A bare, hard room in the middle of a bare, hard building in the middle of a frozen, hard piece of country.

Tucker and I tossed our bedding on the cots and sat down, making no attempt to prepare the cots for sleeping.

"I never asked you before, Hays, but what the hell are you doing here?"

Tucker shifted his weight and the cot springs squeaked. "Well, I guess I just got tired of cowboying in Kansas. Didn't seem like I was getting anywhere. Been out of school for four years, and still ridin' a horse for a living. Army seemed like a good idea—at the time."

"You volunteer?"

"Yeah. Just went into Wichita one day and signed up. You?"

"You wouldn't believe it. Was working on a ranch near Gunnison. Couple of friends and I pulled into San Francisco one day, in the rain—"

I was cut short by a hollow, booming sound from down the hallway, a heavy sound that crashed along the hard walls and forced its way into the room.

"Christ," I hissed, "what the hell was that?" Instinctively I leaped to the wall and snapped off the lights. I heard Tucker get up from the cot and knew that he had moved into a corner, probably crouching.

The booming sound thundered again, closer this time. And then again, closer still.

Tucker crept through the darkness to the edge of the locker, its mass protecting him from the door. "Better have a look," he said.

"I'll do it," I said, "you're too fuckin' big." I edged to the door and slowly pulled it inward until, by pressing my face against the frame, I could see into the hallway, only partially lighted at night by a single bulb about halfway down the corridor—and the faint glow spilled into the room. The booming sound came again, this time almost on top of me. I couldn't believe my eyes.

"Hays," I whispered, "there's some big son of a bitch out there in the hallway—*kicking in doors*! No shit! He's staggering down the hallway, picking out doors and kicking them in. And the bastard is big! Jesus H. Christ, Hays, he's twice as big as you are!" My voice was coming in a hoarse whisper. The last thing I wanted was for the big man in the hallway to hear me. Strangely, no one else was visible. No one seemed to be trying to stop the kicking of the doors.

"Goddamn, Stoney, we just got here. If that big fucker kicks in our door, we're in trouble before we even get started!"

"Okay, look, I'm watching him," I muttered. "I think he's pretty drunk. He stops in front of a door, plants himself, lines himself up, raises his leg and lets go with everything he's got. His leg's like a goddamn' silo!

"Listen, if he stops in front of this door, I'm going to whip it open. Okay?"

"Okay, Stoney. You want to take it out there, or bring it in here?"

"In here. Better off if he doesn't have room to move that big goddamn body around."

Another door, the room next to ours, crashed in. The doors were thin hollow-cores and when the big man's heavy leg hit them they splintered, chunks of wood flying into the rooms. But no one appeared in the hallway.

"Get ready, cowboy, here he comes," I whispered.

For a few seconds, everything was quiet, Tucker frozen behind the locker, me with my face pressed against the doorframe, watching. The only movement was me, carefully removing my belt and letting it dangle in a loop from my right hand.

We heard shuffling footsteps from outside the door and I tensed, trying to time my move. I waited . . . in an explosion of motion I leaped away from the door, pulling hard on the handle. Light from the hallway silhouetted the flying form of a huge man, caught in suspense, trying to kick in a door that suddenly wasn't there, his violent motion carrying him into the room. I began to coil, aiming a kick of my own at the middle of the huge man. In mid-air he sensed the movement and twisted, blocking the kick. Christ, I thought, this guy is good. I felt a numbness and tingling mix inside my leg and I thought it was broken. A fist crashed against my chest and drove me back against the wall, the huge body following. The pain in my chest matched the pain in my leg and in spite of the dim light the room turned red and seemed to glow within my mind. I forced my thoughts to focus and I brought the belt up, searching. Grappling with the thick shoulders I managed to get the belt over his huge head, whipping it tight in one smooth motion. The huge body jerked upright and I knew the man's hands were at his throat, trying to find the belt. I stepped in beside him, planted myself against the wall and shoved, driving across the room toward the locker, whipping hard on the belt. When I hit the end of the belt I felt the man jerk forward, maybe almost leave the floor, his balance broken. He slammed into the locker, head first. I hit the floor.

The wrenching of metal was deafening as the locker caved inward. The big man slid to the floor and lay still, the crushed locker tilting precariously against the wall. I rolled across the floor and was crouching again, waiting. The big man did not move.

"Goddamn, Stoney, that was pretty good. No wonder they send you after Starker all the time," Tucker said quietly. And with an almost lazy movement, he reached forward and gently pulled the top of the heavy locker away from the wall, smiling as the huge metal box crashed down on the body on the floor.

"Yeah, damn, Stoney, you did that real good," he said again, laughing now, but not taking his eyes from the locker on the floor.

The lights in the room suddenly came on, bringing the room to a brilliance that was painful in its detail. Kraus was there, his hand still on the light switch. On the floor, only an arm was visible beneath the lockers, an arm twisted at an odd angle, an arm maybe broken, an arm wearing the three stripes of a buck sergeant.

Twenty-Nine

North Depot Activity
Romulus, New York
March 1961

Tucker and I stood at attention in Murphy's office on the first floor of the MP company building, my leg throbbing—not broken, but pain-raging. Outside the single window I could see that the snow had stopped falling but the sky was still overcast and there was flat, dull light bouncing into the room, loading the office with misery and apprehension. Murphy sat behind his desk, rigid. Kraus stood off to the side.

The buck sergeant, a guy named Olsen, was in the infirmary in the HQ building, nursing a concussion, a swollen larynx, a long cut over his eye, a dislocation of his left shoulder, a possible arm fracture, and a hangover the size of Seneca Lake.

Kraus ranted and Murphy talked, but it all came down to this: last night—payday night—was to have been Olsen's last night on NDA. He was a career soldier and he had put in his two years on the post. He was going to a new duty station, somewhere in Europe. He had gone into town, gotten drunk, and had celebrated his departure from NDA by bashing in a few doors. Seems it wasn't the first time.

Murphy looked at Tucker. "Why didn't you stop this, private?"

Tucker opened his mouth, started to say something. "Sergeant Major . . ."

"He didn't have time," I butted in. "I saw the asshole in the hallway, saw what he was doing. I invited him into the room. Tucker had nothing to do with it."

Behind me, I heard the office door open, someone move into the room. Whoever it was stood against the back wall, not moving, not speaking. There was a subtle emotional shift in the room. Out of the corner of my eye I could see Kraus stiffen, stand a little straighter. But he was looking at me, not at the guy who had come into the room. I noticed something in Murphy, even. Not fear, but something that changed him a little, put him on guard.

Whoever had come in did not say a word, and no one said a word to him.

"So you 'invited' Sergeant Olsen into the room." Murphy paused. "So you're taking the rap for Tucker, is that it?"

"No, Sergeant Major, I wouldn't take the rap for. anybody. Fuck 'em. Truth is, Tucker had nothing to do with it."

Murphy stood up behind his desk. "That right, Tucker?"

Don't fuck up! Goddamn it, Tucker, don't fuck up! Don't let 'em get both of us! The words streaked through my mind.

Tucker seemed to be thinking it over. He cleared his throat. "Sergeant Major, whatever Private Stone says will be the truth."

The room was silent. I could hear Murphy breathing. I could hear Tucker's heart beat.

Murphy looked directly at Tucker. "Get the fuck out of my office."

Tucker spun an about-face and started toward the door.

"And, Tucker," Murphy said, softly, "you ever lie to me again and I'll hang your ass."

I could hear Tucker hesitating. But then the door opened and Tucker moved his ass through it, quickly.

I did not see who opened the door.

And there I stood.

For long minutes, no one spoke.

Then, Murphy leaned forward on his desk, his hands balled into fists.

"Sergeant Olsen has already paid for the doors," Murphy said quietly, "so that leaves two issues to settle. First, there's disorderly conduct on the part of Olsen. Then, there's the striking of a noncommissioned offer by a suck-egg private. A private I believe I warned about such things."

And that is when Kraus decided that he should get into the game. He moved away from the wall and stomped his way directly in front of me.

"And just which one of these offenses do you think is more serious, private?"

He was standing so close that spittle sprayed out between his flabby lips. Some of it landed on my chin. The bastard really pissed me off. I could not help myself—I opened my mouth, and that, of course, has always been one of my many problems.

"Is that a rhetorical question, Sergeant?"

"Is that a rhet . . . rhet . . . what?" Kraus could not pronounce the word. He didn't know what it meant.

From behind me I heard someone make a snorting noise.

"A rhetorical question. Sergeant," I said, "the word means—"

"I KNOW WHAT THE FUCK IT MEANS, PRIVATE!" Kraus balled up his fists and raised his arms. I thought the fat little shit was going to hit me. "IT MEANS YOU ARE GOING TO THE GODDAMN STOCKADE!"

Murphy started around the end of his desk.

"I'd like a word with the private."

The voice came from behind me. It was a voice made by dragging lumber over gravel, a voice from somewhere that voices should not live. It sent shivers down my back.

Murphy looked past me. Kraus seemed to deflate, his short body crumpling. He stepped back toward the wall.

I was still standing at attention, so I could not turn my head, but I heard heavy steps behind me and then a huge shape seemed to appear on my right. And stopped.

"Sergeant Major," the gravel voice said, "I would appreciate a few minutes alone with the private."

Kraus headed quickly for the door. But Murphy did not move. Kraus was about to shit his pants, but Murphy, I thought, was only curious.

"You can use my office," Murphy said. "I'll be right outside."

A threat. Murphy had issued a threat. What the hell, was he trying to protect me from something?

Murphy walked slowly out of the room and closed the door behind him.

I had not moved.

The shape moved to the end of Murphy's desk. "At ease, private," the voice said.

I relaxed—not much, but a little—put my hands behind me and turned my head toward the big man.

He was the ugliest man I had ever seen in my life.

He was at least six-feet-five, maybe taller, with heavy shoulders, thick arms, massive hands that looked like they could close around your throat with killing room to spare, his body so thick that he seemed barely able to fit inside the small office. His face was craggy, split by a large nose that had been broken in some long-ago bar fight. He tried to smile, but he didn't make it. His mouth did not turn up; the smile was just a jagged slot across his ugly face and, for a moment, made me forget that he really was not trying to smile at all. He was wearing a civilian suit, the coat cut large enough to hide a howitzer, a white shirt and black tie, tied haphazardly, as though he did not really give a shit and did not care who knew it.

"My name is Ruker," he said. He pronounced it 'Roo-ker'. He did not offer his hand. I was grateful.

"I heard what went down last night. Olsen's a stupid fuck. Been in the army sixteen years and only a buck sergeant." He waited for some reaction from me. I didn't give him one. He didn't seem to care.

"Read your file. You're smart. But still graduated at the bottom of your class at Gordon."

I kept my mouth shut.

"You really take a pistol away from a whacko down at Gordon?"

I did not know where this was going. I did not know who Ruker was, or what the hell he wanted. I did not know anything.

"I had no choice," I said. "I was ordered to do it."

"But you did it."

"No, not exactly. He threw it out a window."

"Yeah, I heard about that, too."

"And that whacko is now here, on this post, sir."

"Yeah, I know. I've seen him. Even talked with him."

"If I might ask, sir, did you learn anything? About him, I mean."

"Yeah, I learned what you already know."

I knew exactly what he was talking about.

Ruker stared at me for a long moment. "But there's something I think you do not know. That whacko was 'sentenced' to the army, just like you."

I did not know how to react, so I just stood there.

"He won't toss out the pistol the next time, Stone. You'll have to take it," Ruker said.

"There won't be a next time, sir. I'm not responsible for Starker."

"That's what you *think*, private. You've made that clear. But that's not what the army thinks, and it isn't what Private Starker thinks. You are responsible, all right. Yes, you are."

There was no use arguing. The goddamn army could think anything it wanted to, but I wasn't going to take responsibility for Starker, even if it was unofficial.

"You going to kill him?" Ruker asked.

"*What?*" Jesus Christ, what was happening here?

"He's a whacko. Certifiable. But the army has no choice but to try to deal with him. That's the way it's been set up. Seems to me he's going to kill *somebody*. If he kills you, Stone, the army will just put him in a mental hospital. But you'll be dead." He waited, building the drama. "But if you kill him, I have to come after you. And the hospital you go to won't be mental. You understand?"

I couldn't speak. I just nodded.

The room seemed so very small, so dark. There was not enough air—Ruker seemed to suck the atmosphere out of the space I was standing in. I tried to control my breathing, tried not to let Ruker know how goddamn scared I was. But he knew anyway.

Ruker moved next to me, so close I could feel his chest move when he breathed.

"Stand at attention, private."

I snapped to.

"Now listen carefully. They have to punish you in some way for what you did to Olsen, but they won't do anything serious to you. I'll see to that. But this isn't the end of it. I may need you one of these days. And when I do, you *will* be available. You hear me, private?"

I heard every word. I nodded again.

Ruker stepped behind me. I couldn't see him.

"One more thing, private," he said. "Don't ever call me 'sir', not ever again."

And then Ruker was gone. I never even heard the door open.

In the end, they did nothing to Olsen, just shipped him off the post a day or two later. It was the easiest solution, especially, they said, since he was a career soldier. No sense messing up a man's career over a few cheap-shit doors and a cheap-shit, fuck-up MP. Me.

I took the whole rap. I told Murphy that I jerked open the door, that I hit Olsen, that I had used the belt. All of which was true. For a split second, I thought I saw the flicker of a smile across Murphy's mouth. I was probably wrong.

In the end, they did nothing to Tucker. Apparently they needed someone with a brain to make noncom in due time, and it sure as hell wasn't going to be me. But they moved Tucker out of my room, transferred him to another MP platoon. After that, the only time I saw Tucker was in the chow hall, usually when we were carrying our trays to a table. We would make eye contact, Tucker would nod and keep on walking. He never sat with me.

They confined me to the post for thirty days.

Kraus was boiling. I found out later he wanted me court-martialed. But he never said a word to Murphy. And he sure as hell did not say anything to Ruker.

All Kraus did, from that moment forward, was try to turn my life to shit.

I had news for him. It already was. Shit, that is.

Maybe Kraus could have done a better job of that, of turning my life to shit, except for one thing. After the Olsen incident, everybody seemed to think I worked for Ruker, that maybe I was some sort of "plant" in the MP company, a spy, Ruker's spy. Ruker's toady.

Some of the men hated me for that, some of them were afraid of me, some of them, like Bannerman, just didn't give a shit. Me? I knew I didn't work for Ruker, but I never figured out how to prove that I didn't. So screw it, what the hell could Ruker do to me?

It would take a while for me to find out.

Thirty

Confined to the post, to North Depot Activity, Romulus, New York, a place where there was no post exchange, no theatre, no gymnasium, no recreational facilities of any kind and, as far as I could tell, no town named "Romulus." North Depot Activity, the entire place under a crust of hard-frozen snow so old and dirty it had begun to look like the crusts of ice that froze on the street signs in Laramie. Once the snow fell in the early winter, one of the MPs told me, it stayed, compacting, freezing, slushing, and then freezing again. Until spring.

Confined to the post. Big fucking deal. When I was not on guard duty I sat in my room and wrote in my composition books. I had a lot of catching up to do.

What the hell was I doing there?

Always the same question.

This place was not where I was headed. I was headed west, not east. What the hell was I doing in New York State?

I was leaving. I was getting out. It was just a matter of time, and not the army's time.

What went wrong?

I was born on Black Hawk Ridge, deep into the Appalachian Mountains in West Virginia. Black Hawk Ridge—a loose collection of mountain cabins, slab-plank barns, cows with their ribs showing, hard-scrabble plots of scratched earth.

There were no schools on Black Hawk, just my cousin Minnie, who taught me and three or four other kids until we were old enough to be sent away to high school. They sent me to Crum, a blight on the landscape on the edge of the Tug River. And to Crum High School, a place I could not have imagined, even though I had read every book Cousin Minnie had ever given me. But I found a girl there, a girl who would be in my mind for years, only I didn't know it at the time. But I lost her.

A girl who is still in my mind. Yvonne. I did not know it then, but not a day would go by for the rest of my life when she would not be in my mind.

I actually graduated from Crum High School, then escaped from Crum and Black Hawk Ridge. Made it all the way to Myrtle Beach, in Horry County, South Carolina. I didn't know shit, about anything, and that got me in trouble. In the middle of all that, I found the girl again. And then lost her again, and then those wonderful folks in Horry County decided there were other places I should be, and they made sure I headed in that direction. Any direction.

There was water to the east. It was called the Atlantic Ocean.

There was West Virginia to the north. No way was I going there.

To the south were more assholes, like the guys who had run me out of Horry County.

I picked west. At least, if there were assholes there, maybe I was one of them. I needed to be one of something. I needed, well. . .

I had no idea what the hell I needed.

But it sure as hell was not North Depot Activity.

North Depot Activity. It didn't even have a real army name. We weren't a fort, or a post, or a camp. We were a damned "depot," a place everyone called NDA, a few hundred acres of fenced and guarded real estate, an island of paranoia lying smack in the gut of middle class America vacation land.

NDA was a U.S. Army maximum security storage depot, and the army was deadly serious about protecting what it was storing. A storage depot stored weapons. Not rifles. Not pistols. *Weapons.* But the army never called them weapons—it called them "items." Just what sort of items, we were never really told. But we knew, and it scared most of us shitless. After all, it took one hell of an item to have to be delivered on a rail car, or a flatbed semi-trailer, one item to a truck, and then lowering it several stories underground, never to be actually seen by the likes of us lowly MPs. Us scummers.

We must have been driving our olive drab pickup trucks over the tops of some of the biggest nuclear warheads this country ever produced. And I doubt if any of the nearby civilian population knew what the hell was going on.

NDA was about eight or nine miles south of Geneva just off a narrow two-lane highway. A curving, two-lane access road, thickly lined with trees and brush, ran east from the highway to the guard post at the main gate, the only gate, into NDA. The access road was curved so cars passing on the highway could not see straight down the road, could not see the main gate, could not see NDA. There were no turn-offs or parking areas along the access road. Inside the depot, a narrow strip of two-lane blacktop ran from deep out of the inner security area, through the center of the depot, divided at the gate into enter and exit lanes, than joined again and ran another half-mile—the access road to the main highway. Fifty yards before the road reached the gate, the trees and brush ended. The highest thing that grew in that fifty yards was grass. A bare, clear area; an "effective field of fire," the army called it.

There were two fenced areas that made up NDA: the "outer

compound," and the "inner compound," reached only by going through another gate that made the outer compound's main gate seem like a toy.

The outer compound had only a single fence around it, and it wasn't electrified. The outer compound held the MP and ordinance barracks, the depot headquarters building and the mess hall, all arranged around a square parade ground on which there never was a parade—everyone on the depot simply called it the "rectangle." The headquarters building, called HQ, was on the north side of the Rectangle, an enormous water tower just to the east of it. In one of those wondrous touches the army used to let you know you were really in the army, a small cannon was permanently mounted on a concrete pad out in front of HQ. The cannon was pointed up and over the rectangle and in the general direction of the mess hall, to the south. A detail of MPs fired the damned thing every evening, using some sort of heavy blank shell stuffed with powder, enough to rattle the windows in the barracks.

Eventually, I discovered there were four MPs who were never on the cannon detail: Starker, Sabolino, Bannerman—and me.

The MP barracks was on the west, nearest the depot's main gate. That left the east side for the ordinance barracks, nearest the inner compound, nearest the semi-buried buildings. Nearest the items.

MPs and ordinance pukes. The only two types of soldiers on the depot.

The road that came through the main gate ran straight past HQ, past the cannon, to the gate that guarded the depot's inner compound, the main security area of the post, larger, more heavily guarded, surrounded by the three concentric fences running around the perimeter, the middle fence electrified, hot enough to melt a freight train.

There was only one other gate into NDA. On the far southeast corner of the inner compound, railroad tracks slipped through the trees and heavy undergrowth and into a hidden siding deep within the depot. "Items" were supposed to come and go on the train, but in the time I was there I never saw a train on those tracks. It was simpler to ship the items in and out of NDA on semi-trucks, their trailers covered with huge layers of olive-drab canvas that covered the things, the items, the size of small silos lying on their sides—trucks that drove straight through the city hearts of Geneva, Syracuse, Albany, and points south.

The inner compound was dotted with humps of earth that covered enormous buried buildings, warehouses for the items. Trees and underbrush grew everywhere, the underbrush sometimes cut in lanes so MPs could see across the patrol areas. Half-buried deep inside the compound was the guard house. It held the body of all MP operations on the post—the nerves, the blood, the muscles, the guns. It was the only location called a "house"; all the other guard posts were called "shacks" by the MPs.

Back out the access road and across the highway and then across some fields and through a few lonesome stands of timber was Seneca Lake, a deep, stone-frozen gash in the center of a rising plain that held the depot and the lake up high and clear, fatally in front of the winters. The thick cold seemed to come to rest directly and permanently on the lake. Once it settled in, it never moved. From here at North Depot Activity, as far as I was concerned, the world was frozen all the way to the North Pole.

On the ground floor of the barracks building there was one room called a "day room." It was where MPs could go, sit, relax, have a cup of coffee, read a magazine, watch television. On the first day of my confinement I went to the day room after morning chow. There was only one magazine, a year-old copy of Playboy, all the good pictures torn out. There was no coffee. And two days before we had arrived at NDA someone had stolen the television set.

I couldn't leave the depot but I could go anywhere else on the post that wasn't a secured area. Big fucking deal. That left only the mess hall. I could walk from the barracks to the mess hall, and back, in less than five minutes.

A week into my confinement to post I sat with Bannerman in the mess hall. It was the first time Bannerman had actually sat and talked with me. Usually, he was in another world all his own, not really caring what was going on around him. But that day, he seemed to want to talk. He had heard about the fight with Olsen and I think maybe he thought we had something in common. Maybe we did.

"They goin' to be watchin' you like hawks over a dead rat."

"The way I hear it, they watch everybody," I said.

"Not like they gonna be watchin' you. You already earned a special place in their hearts."

"They got hearts? I thought the bastards just had big holes in their chests."

Bannerman smiled.

Sabolino came through the big doors and went to the chow line.

I waited until Bannerman looked at me. "How come you talk like some street guy? You don't seem like the type."

He did not answer immediately, as though he were trying to make up his mind about something. And then, "Look, Stone, you and I are going to be spending a lot of time together. My guess is, at Post No. 1, the main gate. They will put us there because it is a very, very easy place to fuck up, and that is what they want. I use street language, especially with them, to keep them off balance. If they think I am smart, they will try to give me more responsibility, and I do not wish to acquire more responsibility. Responsibility is the harbinger of failure, and I wish to be seen as having already failed."

He smiled at me. In the time I knew Bannerman, it was maybe the longest speech he ever made. And it was perfect.

We sat and watched Sabolino work his way slowly down the chow line, then find a seat at a table in a far corner, where he could survey the entire hall.

Bannerman told me he usually worked with Sabolino because 'they' knew he did not give a shit what Sabolino did, or when he did it. And, besides, most of the other men were scared shitless to spend a guard shift with Sabolino on some lonely post.

"We came here to the depot at the same time," Bannerman said. "We usually go down the chow line together, but in all the time we've been here he has never sat down with me. In fact, I've never seen him sit and eat with anybody."

Sabolino was a private, no stripes, a "slick sleeve," the lowest rank on the army. Just like me.

"Why is he still a private?" I asked Bannerman. "He's been here long enough to make some other grade."

"Because he's crazy. You know the drill—they keep the crazies here . . ."

We sat and watched Sabolino. The stocky man ate slowly, his eyes constantly sweeping the mess hall.

"Look," Bannerman said, nodding toward the door.

Starker came in and went straight to the chow line. He took little, mostly just looking at the chow, seeming to hesitate, and then passing it by. When he was finished, he held his tray in front of him and stood surveying the room. He looked at Bannerman and me and started toward our table. But I knew damned well that he would not stop and sit with us. He kept right on going—to Sabolino's table. And sat down.

Sabolino kept eating, not looking at Starker.

Starker did not eat at all, just sat there, his eyes wandering around the room.

And then Sabolino got up, picked up his tray and walked away, all the way across the chow hall to another table.

Starker did not follow. And he did not eat. After a few minutes he got up and strolled out the huge double doors that faced the rectangle. He left his chow sitting on the table.

Starker turned slowly and looked at me. Expressionless.

"Oh, fuck," Bannerman mumbled under is breath.

"What?" I whispered.

"That was a challenge," Bannerman said, "a challenge. And nobody challenges Sabo."

Bannerman took several deep breaths. "This is going to be fucking great . . ."

I waited. But Bannerman never finished the sentence.

I looked over at Sabolino. He was not eating. He held something in front of his face, staring at it. It looked like some sort of cylinder, maybe metal, but it was hard to tell from where I was sitting.

"What the hell is that?" I nodded toward Sabolino.

Bannerman looked.

"Oh, fuck," Bannerman said again.

Confined to the post.

It can't get any more boring than this.

At least I thought so, until the next evening.

Thirty-One

North Depot Activity
Romulus, New York
March 1961

It was incoming. Some sort of ball-like object blew out a single pane of glass in one of the big north windows of the mess hall, caromed off the hard surface of a dining table, thunked into a shiny metal milk dispenser and disappeared over the serving line and back into the bowels of the kitchen. We heard it bong off a couple of other metal things back there, and then there was total silence—for an instant.

We didn't know what it was; we never really saw it; it never touched anybody.

It was almost dark. There were only a couple of dozen MPs and a handful of ordinance GIs in the mess hall, guys who had missed the regular evening meal for some reason, the MPs and ordinance guys in their own little groups, scattered around the mess hall, talking.

I was sitting alone at the side of the room, day-dreaming about ranching and horses and sleeping in the cold, dreaming about anything but NDA. I saw Tucker sitting a few tables away, but he kept looking down at his food.

I heard "Taps" playing over the loud speakers at the end of the Rectangle and I waited for the boom of the retreat cannon. And then I heard it.

And then there was something slamming around inside the mess hall.

When the thing came through the window the mess hall snapped into silence, as though someone had flicked a switch and cut off all the sound. I heard it thunk off the milk dispenser. We never actually saw it, but from the sounds back in the kitchen, we knew where it went.

Oberhaus, the mess sergeant, exploded through the swinging doors that led from the kitchen. Oberhaus weighed maybe 300 pounds and he ran straight through the center of the mess hall, his fat clenched fists pumping over his head, knocking over tables as he ran. And he was screaming, his heavy voice rolling out across the tables . . .

"GRENADE! GRENDADE!"

In the split second it takes to think about such things, I thought maybe it wasn't a grenade—would a grenade bounce around like that?—but, considering the circumstances, I did what everyone else in the mess hall did at the time—I got the hell out of there.

The fastest way out was through the big front doors that led to the Rectangle and I was through and down the short flight of steps and out onto the grass running hard and then I felt bad because I had left Tucker sitting there, the huge bulk of him just waiting for the grenade. Only, when I looked around, there was Tucker, ten yards ahead of me.

Out in the middle of the rectangle we waited, MPs and ordinance guys hunkered down on their heels, watching the empty mess hall. There was no explosion.

Bannerman came strolling down the sidewalk, in no particular hurry, casually heading for the mess hall.

He grinned as he went by.

A week went by before we found out that it wasn't a grenade. It was an 8-ball. Fired out of the canon.

Thirty-Two

North Depot Activity
Romulus, New York
May 1961

For me, there was nothing left to do but settle into the routine of maximum security guard duty.

But I did not count on standing guard duty with Bannerman. Or Sabolino.

Hays Tucker had told me that Bannerman and Sabolino always stood guard duty together. That way, it was easier for Kraus to keep an eye on them. It must have been Kraus's idea of a joke—putting me on duty with one of them—it didn't matter which one, maybe pissing off the other one in the process, maybe, that way, putting both of them on my ass as well as Starker.

And that's what Bannerman had said would happen.

But whatever it was, there I was, inside the tiny guard shack at the main gate, Post No. 1, in the dark, in the cold, in the dirty, crusted remnants of old snow. With Bannerman.

It was Hank Bannerman's sworn personal duty to fuck with the army in any way he could.

Bannerman was a draftee. He did not want to be at NDA, did not want to be in the army, did not want to be anywhere but back in his hometown, somewhere in Minnesota. I asked him once what the name of the town was, and where it was in Minnesota. He would not tell me. He would not tell anybody.

"If I tell you, you fuckin' guys will try to look me up, one day. Fuck that."

For a moment it pissed me off. But then I thought about it. Hell, I sure as hell did not want these guys looking me up, either. But then, that really would not be a problem.

I did not have a hometown.

After a few hours I had to bring it up. "Hank, tell me about the eight-ball."

"What eight-ball?" And he never said another word about it.

Bannerman and I huddled inside the guard shack, the six-by-six concrete building stuck just in front of the high chain-link fence topped with two arms of V-shaped barbed wire and floodlights—the building where Kraus had taken me the first night I had gotten off the bus. An electrically operated gate on each side of the building allowed traffic to enter and leave, all traffic checked and controlled by MPs. The road was knee deep in snow and no car had passed either way in more than an hour.

The shack had foot-thick walls, two metal doors, and heavy glass windows on all sides. The windows weren't bullet proof, but they would make a lot of noise if they ever got hit by bullets, heavy glass shards flying everywhere, cutting the MPs to ribbons. But then, that was the whole idea. The glass, and the MPs, were expendable.

Everybody on the depot—*everybody*—wore a badge with his ID on it. If you were on the depot and did not have your badge in plain sight, it was a security violation and some tight-ass noncom would have you standing in front of the company commander within minutes. And the badges were issued by the badge office.

The badge office was the only building that had a door that opened to the outside of the fence. If you were a visitor to the depot, you had to go to the badge office; you had to have a visitor's badge. The thing was the size of a playing card, a piece of paper with your picture, name, an identification number and some other letters and numbers the meaning of which was known only to the security people in the badge office. The badge was laminated in plastic and you wore it clipped to your shirt pocket.

The badge was a part of some of NDA's strictest security regulations. When on the depot, you wore the badge at all times. The very second you left NDA, you were supposed to take the badge off and keep it out of sight. Failure to do either could get you arrested. "Apprehended," the army called it.

Visitors without badges who drove up to the main gate were immediately sent to the badge office, a one-story building along the fence line a few yards from the gate. The badge office was home to Master Sergeant James Heffner, the man who controlled and issued all the badges on NDA. If you got a badge from Heffner, you could enter the depot. If Heffner chose not to issue a badge to you, you turned around and went home. It didn't make a damn who you were.

On the night I had arrived at NDA, they took us into the badge office in the middle of the night and issued temporary badges, taking us into the office two or three at a time, the rest of us standing in the freezing dark, in the snow. Even though we had our orders in our hands, were wearing uniforms, were tired, stank, had come off a chartered bus and could only have come from MP School at Fort Gordon, we still could not get on NDA without a badge.

MPs at NDA were taught to identify everyone by their badges. While you were on guard duty you were required to check the badge of everyone who approached you. Everyone. It didn't matter if the guy was your roommate and you had borrowed ten bucks from him the night before. Didn't matter. If he didn't have his badge, or if something about the badge didn't look right, you held him there, at gunpoint if necessary, until the officer in charge came and took him away.

The badge office. I did not know it at the time, but the badge office was also the office of the Criminal Investigation Division—the CID. And the CID was Ruker, and his partner, a guy named Garcia. I had seen Ruker only once. I had never seen Garcia.

I was not sure if I ever wanted to see Ruker again.

We had hidden the radio in the wastebasket to keep it out of sight. The guard shack was so damned small that we couldn't put it anywhere else. We couldn't put it on the narrow shelf where we wrote our guard duty reports. In the dead of night, like now, the bright lights of cars passing our guard post would shine through the windows and scatter across the shelf. Officers could see the shelf as they drove by, and military policemen weren't supposed to have a radio, or anything else, at the guard post. And officers, any officers, were always looking for something about MPs, any MPs, they could report to Captain Arnold. Arnold, our company commander, as mean a little son of a bitch as ever got passed over for promotion.

So the radio was in the metal wastebasket, the hardcore country music rising and falling. The wailing voices rose out of the wastebasket like screams from an amplified tin megaphone, and drilled straight into my head.

My head was aching and my legs were on the verge of cramping. There were no chairs in the room—MPs weren't supposed to sit while on duty—so I leaned against the heavy glass at the front of the building, trying to find a remotely comfortable position. The temperature inside the room was barely above freezing, a light, cold, spring rain falling, but I was sweating inside my field jacket. The sweat was partly from the clothing and partly from a hangover that had pounded me for almost twenty-four hours. Bannerman had brought some vodka onto the depot a couple of days ago, and we took turns going out to his car, sitting in the dark and cold, and drinking. I'm not even sure we wanted to get drunk; it was just another way to do something the army didn't want us to do.

The drinking did not seem to bother Bannerman at all.

I was trying to figure out a way to silence the radio without pissing off Bannerman.

"Give me a break, Hank," I muttered, my hands at the sides of my head, "I'm a sick man. Turn that thing off."

"Up yours, Stone," he growled, striking a gunfighter pose and letting his hand drift down to his pistol belt, caressing the holster that held the heavy pistol. "Sick isn't good enough. You're only hangover-sick, and that doesn't count. And besides, it was my vodka."

"Okay, see if this is good enough—because if you don't turn it off I'm going to go over there and shit in that wastebasket, right on top of that radio. And then you'll shoot me, even before I have a chance to pull my pants up. And then I'll bleed all over the fucking guard post. And then you'll have to explain the naked body with its pants down, the bullet hole, the blood, the bucket of shit, the radio, and the spent round. And you'll be in big fucking trouble over that spent round."

Bannerman laughed and reached into the wastebasket. He didn't turn the radio off, but he turned it down. I turned my aching body back toward the glass, grateful for small victories.

Outside the window the tiny drops of rain seemed frozen in descent, moving in slow motion to land silently against the building. The glare of the floodlights reflected from the rain, shortening our vision into the empty space beyond and, I knew, shortening our effective field of fire. I didn't really give a damn about effective fields of fire. No one did, except maybe Sabolino. And Starker. Yeah, I thought, Starker cared about fields of fire.

I stood there with Bannerman, staring through the glass, saying nothing. Any creative limits of our conversation had long ago been reached. I knew we would go through identical nights many more times, and the long blackness would rapidly consume any intelligent words that might possibly pass between us.

Outside the guard shack the fall of the rain kept pace with the fall of my mood.

"Damn, the whole access road is running with water. Temperature's dropping. Keeps this up, its going to be a bitch at guard mount in the morning," I grunted.

"Yeah. Maybe some bastard will freeze to death and then we'll get to have a military funeral. Like when that asshole colonel died. Or like that funeral last September when Higgins shot himself." Bannerman laughed. "Shit, wish he'd of asked me. I'd of done it for him."

Bannerman said that Higgins, an MP, had climbed to the top of the NDA water tower, a round, menacing mallet in the sky that loomed high over the depot's headquarters building. He stood on the narrow catwalk that ran around the enormous tank and blew his brains out with his army-issue forty-five. But he didn't fall off the tower. His body jerked backward and hit the side of the tank, then slid down and caught on the railing, dangling, head down, half off the catwalk. He hung there in the late September sun and no one knew where he was until the depot commanding officer, Col. Rice, went out to his car, and Higgins' blood had changed the car's paint job from oyster white to spattered death red.

I looked at Bannerman through the near darkness of the inside of the building. The reflection of the lights gave his narrow face a sinister exaggeration, like the lights on faces in old Boris Karloff movies. I wondered where Hank's mind was. I watched him move nervously, shifting on his long legs, his face a concentrating mask as he listened to the music from the wastebasket.

The music faded away and Bannerman went to the wastebasket to see what else he could tune in. But there was only static.

And we were out of vodka.

It was going to be a long night.

Thirty-Three

North Depot Activity
Romulus, New York
May 1961

There were four platoons in the MP company and we pulled guard duty every four days, twenty-fours at a time. After our shift, we had twenty-four hours off; then a day of detail duty, usually shit details, picking up cigarette butts from the compound, painting, cleaning—always cleaning—then a day of training; and then another day of guard duty. Each platoon followed the same routine, but on different days, so there was always a platoon on guard, a platoon screwing off, a platoon cleaning, and a platoon learning to ferret Communists out from under rocks.

In other words, there was never a time, ever, when the depot was unguarded.

Mounting of the guard was carefully controlled, carefully done. The new platoon coming on duty "fell out" into the guard mount room, or, in warm weather, outside on the parking lot beside the barracks. The platoon officer and platoon sergeant would inspect the platoon, walking the rank and file, looking for something to rag your ass about, usually finding it.

When inspection was over, the MPs were taken to the various guard posts around the depot, relieving the old guard. By the security regulations of the post, no MP could leave his guard post until he was properly relieved, even if the poor scummer had to stand there for days. He could die there, but he could not just walk off.

Guys who were not assigned to a specific post were assigned to the riot squad, a bunch of leftover troopers who hung out in the guard house, fully dressed, weapons at hand—ready to go as a group to quell riots, defend NDA, kill Communists. Whatever.

The guard house. Everybody not standing guard—the extra MPs, officers, noncoms, guys assigned to the riot squad—all went to the guard house inside the inner compound.

Twenty-four hours later, it all happened again.

And again and again and again.

And that is how I spent my thirty days, confined to a routine that would stun a musk ox. And I had read about musk oxen back in the outhouse-sized library at Crum High School.

In general, my entire life on the depot was limited to my platoon. We hardly ever saw the men in the other platoons. The rotating work schedule kept each platoon on a separate schedule and now and then we would run into an MP we had never seen before—and learn that he had been on the depot longer than any of us.

It didn't take very long to figure out that our platoon was the dog platoon of the MP company, and that all the other platoons knew it.

The platoon leader, Lt. Thurman Ringer, was one round short of a full clip, a half-educated ROTC puke who had been a cheerleader at West Virginia University. I was careful, very careful, to never let him know I was from West Virginia. Ringer wanted desperately to be accepted by the other officers in the MP company and his way to acceptance, he figured, was to make life for his own men as hellish as possible. Ringer lived for the day he could bust one of his own troopers on a security violation—or bust them for anything. Fortunately, he was too stupid to be really dangerous. Mostly, he was just funny. But funny men can get you killed, too.

Ringer had a willing accomplice in Staff Sgt. Leonard Kraus, our platoon sergeant. The two men despised each other, but their mutual dislike was tempered by their dislike, and constant harassment, of the men who served under them. Kraus had made a career out of hiding out in the military. He avoided going to combat areas in Korea by driving his car into a ditch, feigning a leg injury, and then limping around on some sort of rehab duty until the army forgot about him. He had been in the army a long time; NDA was to be his last active duty before retirement.

Within the platoon the people I really paid any attention to were the men in my squad, eight other men and me, men who worked together, trained together, pulled the same guard posts, showered together, went into town together, drank together, played poker in the parking lot together, and tried to fuck the army together.

And, for the most part, we didn't even like each other.

Some of them stood out, usually for the wrong reasons.

Vincent Sabolino, from Rahway, New Jersey. Before the army he had lived with his aunt in an apartment in sight of Rahway Prison. His aunt was in love with one of the prisoners and would pick up prison guards in local bars, bring them home and fuck them in exchange for favors for her boyfriend.

Sean Dugan, an Irish kid from the Bronx, whose mother made him take ballet lessons all his life. Sean could kick your hat off without touching your hair, and when he found out that feet were stronger and more effective than fists, he became one of the most feared men in the MP company.

Henry Bannerman, lanky, cool, maybe the smartest man in the platoon. Free spirit. Hard drinker. And he absolutely did not give a shit—about anything.

And Harvey Melton—they called him "Melt Down"—the only black man in our platoon. Melt Down existed on another plane, in another time. He played the army like a busted fiddle, never quite in tune, never quite on the beat, but still making motion, making sound.

And Fleet and Milken, two guys who hung around together, both of them sort of frail and quiet.

And there was me.

And, goddamnit, there was Starker.

I thought maybe every man in my squad was a member of the walking wounded, only they weren't wounded. Battle fatigued, except they had never been in battle. Borderline crazy, except they weren't borderline. Mental cases, except they weren't cases. Men in their late teens and early twenties, men who had been trained to use guns and drive trucks with machine gun mounts and throw hand grenades and choke the life out of you with a stick.

In a movie, if any of these guys had ended up in a mental institution, he would never have gotten out. The audience just wouldn't have accepted it.

But this wasn't a movie.

This was the real thing, flesh and blood men with warped intelligences and twisted outlooks on life, men with short attention spans and even shorter fuses, men who wanted to be MPs in Berlin or Paris or Panama, men so fucked up that even the army could see the problem with their being in the army in the first place. Men who were sent to NDA, where they could be kept inside the fence.

Men who were easily bored, doing jobs where boredom was the central facet of every creeping minute.

Strangely, with the exception of Harvey Melton, who always looked as though his uniform were going to disintegrate and fall off his body like dandruff, the men in the squad looked "sharp," the army's official word for looking good—starched uniforms, razor creases, shiny brass, mirrored boots, white tee shirts worn backwards so the white showed more brightly above the collar of your fatigue shirt.

And, stranger still, one of the sharpest of the sharp was Starker. Which is what got him assigned to funeral detail.

Thirty-Four

North Depot Activity
Romulus, New York
June 1961

A flicker of light slipped across the rear window of the guard shack.

Somewhere inside NDA a pair of headlights turned off a side road and headed for the main gate, where I was pulling guard duty with Sabolino.

It was three o'clock in the morning on a wet night of early summer. We were guarding the main gate on the graveyard shift, two MPs stuck in some of the most God-forsaken MP duty in the world—and we weren't even out of the United States. We just stood there, staring out through the glass at the rain falling in a thick mist, glittering inside the flaring lights mounted above the fence.

On the floor in front of us, next to a wastebasket, a tiny electric heater buzzed uselessly from beneath a small shelf that held a single clipboard and a telephone. The phone was a direct link to the main guard house inside the security area.

We had hidden Bannerman's little transistor radio in the wastebasket. Sabolino was listening to a religious program, some screaming preacher who bounced into our tiny radio on a skip-distance station out of West Virginia. The preacher's voice twanged out of the radio and then scratched out of the metal wastebasket like a demented cat in a rain barrel. A wastebasket. Where that shit belonged, I thought.

Sabolino loved the radio, loved the preaching, his thick arms working slowly underneath his clothing, his short, stump-like body swaying in the thin reflected light from the floods, his bow-legs somehow supporting his heavy chest. If ever I saw a man built like Popeye, it was Sabolino. But no one ever called him Popeye.

"Sonabitch, Stone, just listen to that bastard scream. It's enough to make me fill my pants. Damn, I love that shit."

Sabolino bounced up and down in rhythm with the preacher's wailing delivery. I was a head taller than Sabolino but his thick upper body always made him seem larger, stronger. I had seen him pick up a much larger man than I and throw the poor bastard down a flight of stairs.

Sabolino rocked back and forth on the balls of his feet, shoulders hunched, chin tucked, a fighter with no one to fight. Except maybe me. His arms were jammed underneath the folds of his field jacket, his hands shoved deep into the front of his pants. I knew he was playing with himself. And I knew he didn't care that I knew. Every now and then his arm would stop moving and he would stare intently out into the light that gave way at the edge of the woods. He seemed to be looking for something out there. Or, maybe he was just doing what MPs were supposed to do—look for something out there.

"Car comin'," Sabolino muttered. "Too damn late for a civilian to be comin' out. Probably an ordinance puke."

Sabolino smiled. He didn't laugh, but he smiled. It was a crooked gash across his mouth that he was never comfortable with, opening on slightly crooked teeth, a smile that didn't belong. Throughout the night he would look at his reflection in the window, trying out smiles—or what the thought were smiles—maybe trying to come up with a smile he liked. But he couldn't. Finally, realizing that he and I were going to be pulling a lot of guard duty together and that he would have to put up with me, he even asked me about how those movie stars always had those perfect smiles. He was sure they weren't born with them, but he didn't know how they got them. I told him they clamped a long stick between their teeth until their lips took a permanent set. For about a week after that Sabolino walked around with a pencil sticking out of both sides of his mouth. Everybody laughed, but not where he could hear them. He finally figured that maybe I was bullshitting him. He was almost sure of it. But not quite sure enough to kill me. So he decided there weren't any smiles he liked; not his, not anyone's.

I never really messed with his mind again. Eventually, I would learn for myself, first hand, that Sabolino really was stone-cold crazy. Not inwardly crazy like Starker—not cold and calm and bottled up inside—but outwardly, plainly crazy. A crazy who talked all the time of killing and guns, of ambushes and fragging officers, of death. But he hadn't killed anybody yet, so the army didn't care.

There was a psychology professor, a guy named Longfellow, back there somewhere in the college I went to. I remember him saying, "It's not what a person really is, or even what he says he is, that counts. It's what he *does*. So, it's perfectly okay to be a pathological killer—just as long as you don't actually kill anyone."

That guy Longfellow, maybe he was right. But he never met Sabolino, who had not actually killed anyone. Yet.

Sometimes it was the things that Sabolino did *not* do that scared the hell out of me.

We stood by the door, relaxed but alert, waiting for the car.

The car pulled to a stop at the gate. The gate could only be opened by an MP on the inside of the shack, and Sabolino was at the button, waiting.

I stepped outside, leaving the shack's door open. Oddly, the car's windshield wipers were off, even in the rain. I could barely see through the frosted window and I waited for the driver to roll down the glass. And I waited, standing in the falling rain. And waited.

"Sabo, we got some shit going on here," I said over my shoulder. "Watch your ass."

I popped open the cover on my holster, fingered the heavy butt of the forty-five, then reached behind my back and slid my flashlight off my belt. I flicked the switch and pointed the light toward the glass. With my other hand I rapped gently and politely on the car door. Slowly, the glass came down.

The big gate in front of the car started to slide open. Out of the corner of my eye I saw Sabolino appear in the doorway.

"Oh, gee, an MP!" The voice was syrupy with feigned politeness, almost sticky.

I shined the light inside and saw two enlisted men from the ordinance company. Ordinance pukes. The guy in the passenger's seat was staring straight ahead, his eyes wide, his face lit by the heavy reflection of the lights of the guard post.

"Badges," I said evenly.

Both men inside the car went through elaborate motions of trying to find their identification badges, which both knew, and I knew, should have been clipped to their coats.

"Gee . . . uh . . . I can't find . . ." the voice said, sounding confused now. "I really don't mean to keep you standing out there . . . Jesus, is it raining?"

I thought the ordinance puke was joking. I leaned in for a closer look. He was staring at the rain on his windshield. He wasn't joking—he had just discovered that it was raining. The guy on the other side did not move.

I hated these pukes, and I didn't even know them. Ordinance

people hated the MPs, and the MPs hated the ordinance people. That was the natural way of things. It was the only thing that kept life interesting at NDA.

Sabolino was suddenly, and silently, by my side. "Yer fuckin' badges," he said, the words crawling heavily through his lips.

Two badges magically appeared in the light. I leaned down, checked the badges.

"Ordinance puke," I growled at the driver. He did not react. I leaned in closer. "MOVE IT, ASSHOLE!"

The car's engine revved, but the wheels spun on the wet pavement and the car lurched forward. As it jerked away from the guard shack the man on the rider's side stuck his head out his window. He was puking.

Sabolino was still standing in the road. He took a deep breath, then unzipped his pants and pissed in the general direction of the car.

When he came inside I was already fiddling with the radio that was hidden in the wastebasket.

"Fuckin' junkies," Sabo said. "Blowed out'a their fuckin' minds."

Junkies. On a maximum security post.

I was still thinking about the junkies when I caught a movement at the far edge of the parking lot, where the light barely reached. It was the sort of movement that did not want to be seen, furtive, and quickly gone.

To Sabolino, "You see that?"

"Yeah, been waitin' on the little motherfucker," Sabo said, moving toward the door. "Won' be gone more'n a minute." And he was out into the rain.

It was hard to see Sabo in the bad light and the misting rain. I watched his dim form move steadily toward the edge of the woods on the far side of the parking lot. When he moved he always bounced, sort of, as though he were trying to make up for the short length and stunted shape of his body; a small circus clown in an MP's uniform. When he got to the trees he stood, motionless, for what seemed like minutes, his hand in his coat pocket.

And then I saw the movement again at the edge of the trees, something coming out of the undergrowth. An animal.

Sabolino did not move.

A dog. It was a dog, hunkered down and slinking, creeping toward Sabo in some sort of dog slow motion. It stopped a few feet from Sabo, both of them motionless now, just looking at each other. Sabolino's hand came slowly out of his pocket. I thought he had something in his hand, but I couldn't be sure. He bent toward the dog and put something on the ground, then backed up a few steps. The dog crept slowly forward and picked up whatever Sabolino had put on the ground, and then, in a flash, was gone back into the woods.

Sabolino came back to the guard shack.

"Fuckin' dog," he muttered. "Fuckin' dog won't leave me alone." He pulled a handkerchief from his pocket and started wiping his hand. I could see grease shining on his skin.

I did not say a word, not one goddamn word.

I was learning.

I wished I had a drink. There were lots of times I wished I had a drink, but the worst were these early morning hours when my legs ached from standing in the heavy cold that flowed across the concrete floor and my head began to get that fuzzy, packed feeling that always came with lack of sleep.

We stared in silence, trying our eyes against the reflected glare. The black road disappeared, unmarked and empty, into the darkness.

"Hey Sabo," I said, "how do they pick the guys who go on funeral detail?"

Thirty-Five

Cemetery
Geneva, New York
July 1961

Funeral detail.

Maybe that was my way off the post, at least for the day.

The MPs always pulled funeral detail, honor guard, a bunch of guys looking sharp in dress uniforms, going into Geneva or Seneca Falls, standing beside the grave of some guy they had not known, trying hard to be respectful. Sometimes actually being, well . . . respectful. Looking stern and sober. Sometimes they actually were . . . sober.

Firing blanks from M1 Garands. That was the fun part.

A couple of days earlier some guy committed suicide inside one of the storage structures. Hanged himself with a bra the size of a hammock. We never really found out if he was a soldier or a civilian. And no one ever found out where the bra came from. All we knew was that there would be a funeral detail.

And MPs would do almost anything to get out of funeral detail.

Except for me. After all, I really had nothing else to do, so I would do anything to get off the damned depot, to go somewhere, anywhere. I volunteered.

And, Jesus H. Christ, they picked Starker.

I stood right next to Starker, beside the grave.

It was a Hitchcock movie.

The graveyard was old and tightly packed. It had rained the night before and oversized headstones loomed in a heavy mist. No room to move around, to stand back at a respectful distance. But the lack of room did not matter. There was practically no one else there.

The preacher said some things that I did not really hear and then looked at the widow, a great-looking woman who stood expressionless in the mist, and who did not have a tear in her eye. She did not move, and said nothing.

For some reason, the funeral guys had already lowered the coffin into the ground and a man took the widow's arm and tried to get her to look into the hole, but she would not, staring straight ahead across the hole, staring through us as though we were panes of colored glass tinting her view of her future.

There was nothing else to do but to get on with it.

The preacher looked at the sergeant, who was in command of the funeral detail. The sergeant brought us to attention and started through the commands that would end with "FIRE!", and we would duly, in unison, fire off our blanks.

On the first order to "FIRE," I pulled the trigger and felt the rifle buck against my shoulder. And then I noticed that Starker had taken his left hand from his rifle and dropped it to his crotch, where he carefully squeezed his dick while looking at the widow.

The widow did not notice.

The sergeant did, but the sergeant did not know what to do.

The sergeant brought us to "FIRE!" again.

We fired again.

Starker grabbed his dick again.

This time, the widow noticed and promptly fainted. She hit the ground, sliding on her ass toward the grave on the slick layer of fake grass that covered the raw dirt at the edge of the hole. Her legs dropped into the grave. As her body moved forward her skirt slid up to her thighs, and then above her hips. She was wearing dark nylons and a garter belt. She wasn't wearing any underpants.

Only a quick grab by the preacher kept her from falling in on top of her husband's casket. And then he didn't seem to want to let her go.

A couple of other guys grabbed her and while they were hauling her limp body away from the grave, Starker dropped the muzzle of the rifle toward the coffin and fired off another round, point blank into the shiny coffin lid.

The sound of the shot froze everyone in motionless silence. Starker's back was to me and I could not see the expression on his face. But I knew what was there. Nothing. Absolutely nothing.

I edged forward until I could look into the grave. I was curious to see if the fire and powder from the blank had done any damage.

And that's when Starker kicked my ass over the edge and face down onto the top of the coffin.

Thirty-Six

North Depot Activity
Romulus, New York
July 1961

Once, back on Black Hawk Ridge in West Virginia, I had stood at the edge of a grave dug in the raw dirt of a small ridge-top cemetery and watched my relatives bury my cousin Elijah. It had been raining then, too, and the water had caused the edges of the grave to crumble and slide back into the hole, a runny black soup with a wooden box floating in the center of it. Men had trouble keeping their footing and they were using their shovels to keep themselves upright as they staggered around the edge of the grave, mud up to their ankles, trying to get into position to shovel more mud down onto Elijah's pine-box coffin.

And that's when Cousin Innis fell into the grave. He fell smack on top of the coffin and started screaming and we didn't know what he was screaming about until he got out. He said he screamed because he could see the devil down there.

It was pretty funny. At the time.

I could not see the devil down there. The devil—that fucking Starker. In fact, I could not see anything. My ass had hit the edge of the fake grass and I flipped face-down onto the casket. The casket was made of some sort of metal and when my face hit it I thought it made a drum-like sound. It was odd that I thought I could hear that through the pain of my nose flattening out against the top of the coffin.

I'm not sure if I passed out. I don't think I did, at least not all the way out, but my head was screwed up and I had trouble thinking straight. But at least I was beginning to see a little.

I felt around for something to hang onto but there was only the coffin. I brought my knees up under me and tried to stand, but the coffin was wet-metal-slick and I flopped back down, on my back this time. The mist was still hanging in the air but, even so, I was sure I could see Starker up there, calmly looking down into the grave. And then he snapped back out of sight, as though someone had grabbed him.

None of the other MPs wanted to get into the hole. Finally, my hand hit one of the lowering straps that went down into the grave and underneath the casket.

I scrambled the hell out of there.

I don't know whatever happened to the rifle.

The funeral detail went back to the depot, but Starker was not with us.

I went to the barracks and took a shower, put on some fresh fatigues, grabbed a baton and went to Starker's room.

The time had finally come—the time to kill Starker. I would beat the son of a bitch to death.

He was not there.

I went downstairs and poked my head into the empty day room.

In less than a minute I was at the mess hall. There were only a few MPs there and they had already heard what had happened to the funeral detail. One of them—some guy I did not know—started to say something, but then saw the baton that I was gripping so hard my knuckles were white. He shut his mouth.

I went back to the barracks and strolled by Murphy's office. Starker was not in there. Starker was nowhere.

I went back to my room and sat on my bunk, the baton on my lap. I would wait. He would come back. He always came back. And then

I would beat the son of a bitch to death.

A few minutes later I heard footsteps in the hallway. Fleet poked his narrow, wan face through the open doorway.

"Some guy named Ruker at the badge office wants to see you." And then Fleet disappeared.

The metal door had no nameplate or number, but it was the only door that didn't, so I knocked on it. There was no response from inside the room so I knocked again. Nothing. I turned the knob and pushed the door open.

The room did not look like an office. It looked like an interrogation room.

Ruker was sitting, slouched, on the corner of an old wooden desk, which seemed about to crumble under his huge body. He was still wearing that dark, rumpled suit and the tie that was slightly off center. I did not know it then, but there would be only one time in my life when I would see him wearing anything else.

Another guy sat behind another old desk. He was sitting straight up, his hands folded in front of him. I knew Ruker had a partner, a guy named Garcia, but I had never seen him until now. At least, I thought this guy was Ruker's partner. Ruker was incredibly ugly and Garcia was, well, handsome; he was as graceful, even sitting, as Ruker was crude, slender where Ruker was thick. Where Ruker was tall, Garcia was medium height; Ruker wore rumpled civilian clothes. Garcia was the kind of guy who tailored his uniforms, his tie tucked carefully into his shirt. The uniform was starched, the creases sharp. It fit perfectly on his perfect body. His hair was combed and his face was slick and shiny, as though he had just finished shaving. But I knew he hadn't. His complexion looked like he had been lying on the beach, tanning slightly under a gentle sun, the type of complexion a lot of white guys try to get most of their lives, and never do. On his collar were the round pieces of brass with the crossed pistols, the insignia of a Military Police Corps enlisted man. There was nothing else on his uniform, no name plate, no rank, nothing.

"You don't give a shit, do you." It was not a question. Ruker just rumbled it out into the room as a description of me.

I said nothing.

"Where's the baton?" Ruker asked.

How the hell did he know I had been looking for Starker? "I left it in my room, si—" I saw Ruker's bushy eyebrows rise slightly and I clamped my mouth shut on the "sir" that I was about to say.

For a long moment there was silence in the room. There was a single window covered with heavy grillwork, the glass so thick that light had to fight its way inside.

"I'm going to ask you to do something that you might find hard to do," Ruker said, "and I want you to listen carefully when I ask it."

I said nothing. I thought I knew what he was going to ask me.

"I want you to leave Starker alone . . ."

I was right.

" . . . at least for a while."

"Fuck that."

Ruker's big body seemed to float up from the desk, filling the space in front of me, filling the room. I thought he was going to hit me.

"I don't get it," I said quickly, trying to cover my ass. "Any other soldier pulled the shit that Starker does, he wouldn't walk away from it."

"You aren't listening. I said 'at least for a while,' and that's what I meant." He was still standing there, but he seemed almost relaxed. "We have some serious shit to take care of here. Starker is just an irritant. But if you fuck him up, he'll become something more, and I don't want that.

"And one more thing—if you fuck with Starker, it will be the second time in your very short stay at this depot that you have screwed up. And I don't want you to do that. *For a while!*

"Were you listening to what I said, back there in Murphy's office, when Kraus wanted you in the stockade?"

I kept my mouth shut.

"Were you listening?"

I nodded. But I couldn't seem to let it go. "If I don't do something, every dickhead on this post is going to think I'm afraid of Starker."

Ruker smirked. It wasn't a smile, but at least he smirked. "You fucking well *are* afraid of Starker."

I thought about it. Maybe the big bastard was right.

I had one last try. "I need something in return."

For the first time since I had entered the room, Ruker glanced at Garcia. "And just what the hell might that be?" Ruker asked, turning his eyes back to me.

"I need to get off this post. Forever."

For a moment Ruker did not move, and said nothing. Then he shoved his big hands into his pants pockets and jiggled his fingers, like he was playing with his balls.

"Get the hell out of this office," he growled.

And I did.

Garcia had not said a word. In fact, he had not moved.

Thirty-Seven

The Inner Compound
North Depot Activity
Romulus, New York
August 1961

There was a small buck deer hanging from the heavy wire of the middle fence and smoke was coming out of its asshole. I stared at the deer's asshole, the wisps of warm smoke curling gently upward. I could have sworn the deer was white. A ghost deer.

It wasn't just the asshole—smoke was coming from all over the deer; it seemed to flow through the hide, the hair, the entire animal seeping a gray and rancid smoke that drifted slowly out into the still air and rose softly up through the brilliance of the floodlights to be lost instantly in the hot night sky just above the lights. The smoke was lost in the blackness, but the stench of burning hair and meat hung shroud-like in the heat.

The middle fence was ten feet high, crackling with electricity, and the deer's delicate antlers were tangled just high enough up in the wire to let one of its hooves touch the ground, daintily, the deer dangling in a grotesque dancer-pose. A dancer cooking in the night.

One of its ears was missing, torn off maybe, but I couldn't see how that had happened. The one eye I could see was open and staring, wide with panic, clouded with death. There seemed to be smoke coming from the eye, but I couldn't be sure. What I was sure of—there were still huge charges of electricity coursing through the deer's body.

This was not the first time that something had died on the electric fence. I had heard stories about woodchucks, rats, birds, snakes, and other assorted life being found dead on the middle fence. And it was seldom accidental. It was called "fencing"—swinging an animal around your head and then flinging it over the inside fence, only for it to be caught on the middle fence—and fried. The army swore that would not happen, said an animal had to touch the ground while it was touching the middle fence. But I didn't believe it.

But this was a *deer*, for Christ's sake.

I did not know how long the deer had been there, but it could not have been long; no other MPs had arrived and I knew that when the deer first touched the middle fence alarms had gone off in the guard house, less than a mile away, and riot squad MPs had scrambled into pickup trucks with machine gun mounts on the back and were rolling as silently as they could toward this exact spot in the fence.

The smoke didn't seem to be lessening and the rancid odor was still drifting past my face. I leaned against the inner fence, my fingers poked through the cyclone wire, hanging, sagging there in parody of the deer.

I was safe from the electricity; only the middle fence was electrified. Beyond the middle fence was the outer fence, as far from the deer as I was. Beyond the outer fence was Upstate New York, free and clear, with nothing to worry about but the Canadian summer, warm and brilliant all the way to . . . wherever Canadian summers went.

And the Communists. Everybody worried about the Communists. The Communists were everywhere. We were told about the Red Menace every day, in no uncertain terms. President Eisenhower believed it. Maybe President Kennedy did, too.

I didn't believe it. I wanted to, but I just could not.

The three fences were of equal height and equal distance from each other, running parallel around the inner security compound of North Depot Activity. On the outside of the fences was the world and on the inside was a bunch of MPs and ordinance personnel, all of us trapped in some unholy marriage, scurrying across the tops of buried storage buildings stuffed with nuclear warheads, the MP security guards and ordinance guys like green bottle flies buzzing over the eggs of Satan, some of us caring for the eggs, some of us not. But all of us in there together.

I suddenly woke up. What the hell was I standing there, for? I hadn't reported the deer—the alarm system had taken care of that—and nothing good could happen to me if I were there when the riot squad arrived. Lt. Ringer and Sgt. Kraus would ask a lot of questions and I would end up back at the guard house, explaining why I couldn't possibly have thrown a deer, even a small one, over the inner fence.

I swept my feet around, trying to wipe out any tracks I might have left. Ringer might see all that disturbed dirt, of course, but there were at least three patrol trucks on duty that night, and there was no way he could prove I was the one who had been here, as much as he would want to, *really* want to. Probably, Ringer and Kraus wouldn't even notice, and I was sure that no one on the riot squad would point it out to them.

The patrol truck, engine idling and lights off, sat on the narrow road behind me. I leaped across a small drainage ditch and grabbed the door handle. Something across the road in the edge of the trees caught my eye. There was a slender broken tree there, the trunk snapped almost halfway up, the top of the tree hanging twisted, the uppermost branches now touching the ground. There had been a few rainstorms, but nothing heavy enough to break a tree. To hell with it, it was just a tree in the woods. I jumped into the truck and pulled away down the road and into the warm darkness of a summer night in Upstate New York. It was three o'clock in the morning and if I didn't get caught up in the investigation of the deer I would be off duty in another four hours.

It was Starker. I knew it. Starker had "fenced" the deer. But how the hell had he gotten it over the outer fence, and then hung it on the hot wire? Kraus would assume one of us had done it, but that didn't matter. Kraus was smart enough to be suspicious, but dumb enough not to figure it out. Just smart enough to know that he was stupid.

But there was another question . . . *how the hell did Starker get his hands on a deer in the first place?*

Starker.

He had done it, and I knew why. It was not about the fence. It was about the deer.

After the funeral detail, they sent Starker somewhere for "psychiatric evaluation." I wondered what there was to evaluate—the guy was *crazy*. He was gone for two weeks, and then one morning he was back. *He always came back.* How did he do that?

Me? For a brief moment I was a joke. I was the guy who, literally, had fucked a casket.

In his office, Ruker had told me something that I did not really understand, although I had pretended that I did. So I did not go after Starker when he came back. Some of the other MPs thought maybe I was chicken shit, but nobody tried to prove it.

Kraus said that Starker and I would never, ever, be picked for funeral detail again.

Big fucking deal.

They trained us not to drive a regular pattern on guard duty, so I could be anywhere in the inner compound at any time. I didn't have to be where the deer was. I drove to the far back of the compound, knowing that the riot squad had come stumbling out of the guard house and had probably arrived at the deer, hanging there, cooking slowly in the bright floodlights. They would be piling out of the trucks now, Buster Keaton-like, incredulous, watching the smoke come from the deer. They would try to hang back, knowing that Ringer would have to go to the guard house and call for authorization to have the fence turned off—and then some members of the riot squad would have to drive an MP pickup truck carefully down the lane between the fences and take down the deer with its eyes still smoking, steaming, its guts swelling, its hair stinking in the warm air.

There was nothing on the MP radio and I knew there would be radio silence until the riot squad had confirmed that it was only a deer, that there had been no actual intrusion, that the Communists had not broken in.

The riot squad. As far as anyone knew, the riot squad had never actually been to a riot.

I hid on the north side of the compound, parked, engine off, lights out, staring out through the three fences where the night pushed in against the floodlights. Beyond the lights, in the blackness, the silence of the heavy, damp summer smothered the land.

A heavy voice graveled its way out of the radio. It was Kraus. The miserable son of a bitch wanted to know where I was. I was sitting in the dark in the middle of the night in the middle of North Depot Activity.

I was nowhere.

And that's when the passenger door of the truck opened and Sabolino got in.

Thirty-Eight

The Inner Compound
North Depot Activity
Romulus, New York
August 1961

Sabolino heard Kraus on the radio.

"Tell him where you are," Sabolino said.

"Why? So the bastard can try to blame the goddamn dead deer on me?"

"You ain't nowhere near the deer. He can't prove you ever saw the deer. The deer ain't in your world."

I looked over at Sabolino, leaning back against the door of the truck. Even in the darkness I thought I could see the sneer on Sabolino's face, thought I could see the rise and fall of his thick chest in his small body. *How,* I wondered, *can a man so small seem so big?*

"If you know about the deer, Sabo, then you know more than I do. I only got there after the thing was on the fence."

"Yeah, I was there," Sabolino said softly. "Saw the whole thing."

He turned in the seat to face me.

"Starker," he said softly. "You ain't gonna believe how he did it. He went to a lot of trouble just to kill a little biddy deer."

There was something darker in Sabo's voice than I had ever heard.

"He gonna pay. He got to pay," Sabo said softly.

I waited. Sabo said nothing else.

"Well, c'mon, Sabo, how did he do it?"

Sabolino ignored the question. Instead, he reached into his pocket and pulled something out, held it out to me. "Bannerman said

I should give you this," he said, and he dropped an eight-ball into my hand.

It was not a toy, it was a real eight-ball, right off the pool table, except this one was not shiny anymore. It had marks and gouges and was discolored. It looked like an eight-ball that should have been thrown away.

Or fired out of a cannon.

Sabolino pulled the little radio out of his pocket. Shit, I thought, here we go with the bullshit preaching again. And I was right. But at least it was a different preacher. Or was it? All those idiots sounded alike to me.

Sabo held up the radio.

"You know what that reminds me of?"

Yeah, I knew.

The one thing I liked about Sabolino was that religion gave him a hard-on.

Sabolino must have told me the story a dozen times. Maybe two dozen—I lose count when I'm having fun. And I knew the story was going to come again, now.

Sabolino had once fucked a girl in church. Or maybe she fucked him. I could never figure it out from the way he told the story.

He was just a kid, going to church as he was told, sitting there in a pew in the far back, alone, as far to the left end of the row as he could get, his shoulder almost touching the wall, with no one near him for row after row of blank and empty wooden benches, the benches solid, shiny from the rubbing of thousands of soft cheeks of the women and the hard asses of the men, sinners all.

Sabolino was Catholic, but he didn't go to Catholic school. But he knew about Catholic school. He knew that any kid who went there was never supposed to think about getting laid. If he did, Sabolino knew some mysterious alarm would go off in the kid's pants and a flash of lightning would burn his dick off. Sabolino was sure of it. His brother had told him so. Sabolino was glad he didn't go to Catholic school, because he thought about getting laid all the time. When he wasn't thinking about killing somebody.

He was sitting there, bored. So he did what he always did when he was bored. He folded his jacket in his lap, stuck his hand inside his pants and, very carefully and very gently, started playing with himself. There was always something constructive you could do in church, if you just put your mind to it.

She came in and sat beside him, trapping him against the wall. He had seen her around the neighborhood and knew she was a Catholic-school girl; she had on a dark green pleated skirt and white blouse, and she was wearing a dark, flowing raincoat with a tiny, white school emblem on the left shoulder. She sat, her eyes straight ahead, clearly intent on what was happening in the front of the church. But she sat *next* to him, *against* him, her hip touching his. Why did she do that, Sabolino wondered. He would wonder about it for the rest of his life.

He turned his head slightly toward her. Her dark hair came down over her collar and he could see the shine of it in the softly colored lights that filtered down through the stained-glass windows. Her lips were full and her nose was slightly over-large and she was the most beautiful girl Sabolino had ever seen. And she was there, next to him, in a dim and nearly empty church and it was a miracle. No girls ever sat next to Sabolino if they had any other choice. Ever.

He was afraid to move his hand—he *couldn't* move it without her knowing. He was caught there, his hand under his jacket and wrapped around his erection.

For the first few minutes, she didn't move either. She kept her eyes straight ahead, her breathing calm and regular. And then he noticed—could feel it—that she breathed a little more rapidly, her chest rising and falling quickly as something in her built up tension. She edged closer to Sabolino, rubbing his leg with hers.

And then her hand was on his arm, under his coat, following his arm down to his hand and then inside his pants. Her fingers were firm but gentle. She knew exactly where she was going and what she was doing, he would tell me, his eyes glazing. She pulled his fingers away from his dick and replaced them with her own, and she squeezed until the pressure backed up through his chest and into his neck and he thought his head would explode.

She didn't really move her hand, he said. She just squeezed. But somehow she pulled his dick out through the fly and his erection was driving up against his jacket. They sat motionless, Sabolino wondering how long it would be before he came and dripped down on the dark wood of the pew. He didn't know how long he could stand it. He wondered if God could see him. He turned slightly toward her and waited for the lightning. He knew his dick was going to be burned off, but it was worth it.

And then she moved. She eased her left leg over his lap and casually slid her arm along the back of the pew, to brace herself. The back of her skirt was pulled up and as her leg slid over him he could feel her thigh, and then the softness of her cheeks. She twisted slightly and when she released the pressure on his dick he realized that he was inside her. His eyes began to glaze and he squinted them shut, trying to understand what was happening. But it was too late for that. Dimly, in the background, he could hear the priest.

He waited for the lightning.

He tried to look into her face, but she would not look at him. He started to drive his hips up into her, but her hand was still down there and she held him still, not letting him move. The muscles of her vagina clamped tight, and then released, and then did it all over again and again in wave after wave of soft-iron stroking that sent shocks to his feet, that curled his toes and sent messages to his head that curdled his mind.

Sabolino and the priest finished at the same time.

He slumped in the seat, head back, eyes closed. He felt himself slide out of her, but he didn't feel her move. And when he sat up, she was gone.

He never saw her again.

For the next year or so, every time he walked past a church he got an erection. And he would come in his pants before he got halfway around the block.

". . . never saw her again," he finished, his voice dropping.

It had to be true. Sabolino's story never varied, the detail never varied.

His erection never varied.

And it was the only story Sabolino ever told. To anybody. Ever.

"One more thing," Sabolino said, pulling is hand out of his pocket again, "just so's you don't think I can't figure things out."

He held out a short piece of pipe, not much longer than his hand, turning it slowly, the pipe dimly lit by the fence lights. There was a cap on one end, a large hole bored through the center. Some sort of lever had been welded to the cap, above the hole.

"Watch this," Sabolino said. And from somewhere inside his coat he fished out another cylinder. It looked like a goddamn brass banana but it was a large, spent shell, the end blown open from having been discharged. He pushed the shell into the opening in the pipe. It fit perfectly.

"What the hell is that, Sabo?"

"It's just a . . ." he hesitated, "a . . . model, one'a them things you make to see you got it right."

He pushed open the truck door and disappeared into the night.

Thirty-Nine

North Depot Activity
Romulus, New York
September 1961

No one ever asked me about the deer. After we got off guard duty that morning, Kraus held the platoon outside the barracks on the pavement in the bright morning sunshine. He wanted to know if anyone knew how the deer got there. Hell, I didn't know how the deer got there, but I knew who put it there. But Kraus didn't ask me that. And I wouldn't have told him if he had. Screw him.

Kraus kept up the questioning for two weeks.

Kraus dismissed the platoon and we went back to the barracks and turned our weapons into the armory, another room, like the guard mount room, built to repel the Communists. We shoved our weapons through the opening in the heavy wire mesh of the window, the armory guys checking each one as they put the guns on their racks. No one on NDA, except MPs on guard duty, was allowed to carry a weapon, to have a weapon in his possession, or to be in possession of live ammunition. The armory guys counted each round of ammunition turned in by each MP.

I wondered about the variety of the weapons. Seems as though we had a few of just about everything the army was using at the time, or didn't have any other use for: .45 caliber pistols, our standard sidearm; stubby 12-guage riot-type shotguns with thick stocks and bayonet mounts; short little .30 caliber carbines; .30 caliber M1 Garands, left over from World War II and Korea; even some .45 caliber "grease guns," short, chunky little submachine guns that had a habit of misfiring, or parts falling off in your hands. Our patrol trucks had heavy, waist-high machine gun mounts on the back, welded in the middle of the bed. The mounts were for .30 caliber machine guns. There were no .30 caliber machine guns at NDA.

To have an unauthorized weapon was a security violation. At NDA, every fucking thing could be made into a security violation, and the punishment would fit the crime. Open the wrong door— maybe a reprimand, maybe confined to the post. Have an unauthorized weapon—go to the stockade. It was Kraus's favorite game, trying to catch his own men in security violations. It was what he lived for. I only hoped it would be what he eventually died for.

And the funny thing was, we did not have a stockade at NDA. If they really wanted to lock your ass up, they had to send you to some other place.

Or maybe all of NDA was a stockade. Made sense to me.

The routine of the depot, at least what we MPs knew of it, was as dull as the guard duty. The whole idea of the depot was to remain as unobtrusive as possible, to be quiet, to have no incidents of any kind, to hide from everybody—right there in the middle of the Finger Lakes in beautiful Upstate New York.

And that was the routine of the MPs. They wanted us to stay low, stay quiet, no incidents. And that is what we tried to do, most of us, anyway. Me included.

All I wanted was to stay clear of Starker, and to keep Kraus from finding some way to put my ass in jail.

Every morning there was guard mount for the MPs and an hour or so later the civilians arrived to work, most of them driving in from Geneva, eight or nine miles away, and from other small communities. A few of the top people on the depot were civilians, but, mostly, they were just grunts like us, doing jobs that MPs or or-dinance people were not trained to do. They seemed to come and go like ghosts, driving their cars slowly along the depot's one main road, never making a wrong move, driving or walking past the guard posts, flashing their security badges, seldom looking the MPs in the eye. The depot was like a funeral; the civilians were the mourners. Once the mourners arrived at the funeral, the depot was quiet as a tomb.

As MPs, we never paid much attention to the civilians. I guess, during the time I was there, I looked at their security badges thou-sands of times as they passed in and out of the main gate and I don't remember any of them. None.

Well, except one. She worked in the badge office, right next to the guard shack at the main gate. I remember her, sure enough. I remember Jane Russell.

Forty

North Depot Activity
Romulus, New York
September 1961

Nah, her name wasn't Jane Russell. She just *looked* like Jane Russell. Her name was Antonia DiPaulo. Everybody called her Toni.

The first time I saw her I was standing guard duty with Bannerman at the main gate, right next to the badge office.

It was late summer in Upstate New York. Where once the unstoppable cold had rolled down from Canada, now the heat came in layers that collected around your boots and always, always, ended up in your crotch. And all summer long, every time I worked the main gate, I had never seen Jane Russell, even though she had been working in the badge office, right there in front of us, all the time.

The badge office. You opened the door and stepped inside. And the first thing you saw was Antonia DiPaulo. Toni.

I had never seen a woman with tits like that. Sure as hell, I had never seen them in West Virginia, not even at Myrtle Beach. Maybe those women in the whorehouse in San Franciso had bigger ones, but they sagged and flopped. I thought that Toni's tits floated in place, drifting along out in front of her like clouds rubbing together in the mists of sweat.

Bannerman and I were working the gate. It was late afternoon and I knew the civilians in the badge office were getting ready to go home. There were a few civilian cars parked in the lot out in front of the badge office, but nothing that stood out.

Until the big, black Cadillac sedan pulled in. It was not a limo, but it had to be the biggest damned car ever to roll into the parking area. The thing was long, shiny, had tinted windows and looked like something out of a bad Mafia movie. The guy driving did not get out, just sat there with the engine running, windows rolled up, and I knew he had the air conditioner going full blast. I could barely see him through the dark windows but he sat turned in his seat, as though intentionally keeping his face away from the guard shack.

Sort of pissed me off.

Standing guard duty at the main gate meant you were responsible for everything that happened there, including anything that happened in the visitors' parking area.

And, besides, I was bored.

I left Bannerman in the guard shack and walked over to the car, rapped on the window with my knuckles. The guy did not move, just kept his head turned, staring away from me.

I rapped again. Harder.

I could see his body shift, turning slightly toward me. The window came down an inch or so but, still, he never looked at me.

"Get the fuck away from my car."

It was just a flat statement, no real emotion, not even irritation, as though he were reprimanding a mildly unruly child. The guy's voice was low, gravelly, and when he spoke it was like he was just clearing his throat. He still did not look at me but I could see more of him, now. He was an older guy, his hair slicked back and shiny, his shoulders broad and heavy. He was wearing a black suit and black gloves.

Gloves? It was September, for Christ's sake.

I stepped back from the car, put my hand on the butt of my .45 and started to lift it from the holster.

"It's okay, private . . ." She was looking at my chest, trying to read my name tag.

I was looking at *her* chest.

" . . . Stone," she said finally.

She had come out of the badge office and was standing close to me, her hand out, reaching, but not touching.

I was looking at Antonia DiPaulo. I was looking at her wondrous tits. She was wearing a white blouse that looked like silk and I realized it had been carefully tailored, cut precisely to fit, and display, those amazing tits that flew out in front of her, parting the universe, announcing their power over mankind.

"I don't know your name, Miss . . . Miss . . ."

"DiPaulo," she said. At least, I think that's what she said. The vision of her tits was plugging up my hearing.

"And please forgive my driver, Carlo. He's just trying to do what he was told to do. I will see that it does not happen again."

She turned and walked quickly to the other side of the car and opened the back door. She stood for a moment, looking at me across the top of the sedan, the late afternoon light flicking tiny bursts of dark red from her black hair.

And then she got into the car and it drove away.

Her driver? A woman working out here in the middle of nowhere has a driver?

For a moment, I stood there like I was made of rock, watching the car disappear down the access road, my mind in lock-down. I did not know which was more stunning, Antonia DiPaulo's tits, or the fact that she had a driver.

I really did not pay any attention to the other cars in the lot until I heard an engine start. I glanced over toward the car as it pulled slowly from the lot and followed the big black sedan down the access road. There were two men in it. I could not see the driver, but the passenger, hunkered down in the seat trying not to be seen, was Fleet.

I turned and started slowly back toward the guard post, glancing at the badge office as I moved. Ruker and another guy were standing in a window. Ruker was staring down the access road, watching the cars drive away. The other guy was looking at me, no expression on his face. It was Garcia.

And then I realized that I still had my hand on my pistol and that the damned thing was still halfway out of its holster. Still slowly walking, still looking at Ruker and Garcia, I pushed the pistol down. Ruker was now watching me, and I thought I saw him slowly shake his huge head.

I tried to put Ruker's ugly face out of my mind.

Besides, it was turning into one of those late evenings when everything seemed right. There was little traffic through the main gate, no one gave us any shit, the badge office was closed, Ruker was gone—I never saw Garcia leave, but I never really saw Garcia do anything—and Bannerman and I were standing in the soft light and warm evening air, waiting for the dark. Actually, it was kind of nice.

And then Bannerman fucked it up.

"You know her?"

"Nope. But I damn well intend to cure that."

Bannerman walked out in front of the guard shack. He seemed to be staring down the empty access road.

"Leave it be," he said softly.

"What?"

"You remember Ruker telling you to leave Starker alone?"

"Jesus Christ, how the hell did you know that?" In July, Ruker had told me that. July! In his office, and only Ruker, Garcia and I knew that. And Bannerman?

Bannerman ignored the question. "We are supposed to be buddies, you and me. So I'm going to ask you to do something, sort of like Ruker did. And for the same reason."

He paused. I was not going to say a damn thing.

"Leave the woman alone," he said.

The shit was getting a little deep. "Look, Hank, everybody keeps telling me to leave people alone. Screw that! If I want to—"

And then we saw the headlights coming hard through the twilight. It had to be an MP vehicle.

And it had to be Kraus. And I knew the evening would go from just being fucked up to pure shit.

"We need to finish this conversation, Hank."

Bannerman did not answer.

I did not know it at the time, but Bannerman and I would only have one more conversation, and it would not be about Antonia Di-Paulo.

The little fat man parked his truck in the parking lot behind the badge office and walked to our guard shack, going directly inside, not speaking to us.

He picked up the phone. "Okay, I'm down here. Now what? . . . sir." Kraus added the "sir" almost as an afterthought. I knew he was talking to Lt. Ringer.

Kraus stood with the phone to his ear. "How do we know something's really down there? That part of the fence has lights, but it ain't got no alarm." He listened to the phone. "Shit, uh . . . sir . . . anybody could'a left that info with the company clerk. Don't really mean . . ." He stopped, listening. "Yes, sir, we will check it out. Yes, sir, according to procedure." Kraus slammed the phone down, muttering under his breath, "Fuckin' idjit."

Bannerman and I stood outside, trying to pretend Kraus was not there. A single car came to the gate, stopped, got checked, and went on down the access road.

Kraus stepped outside. "Stone, according to the lieutenant, there's some kinda security problem with the fence south of the badge office." He nodded toward the building. "I am relieving you of your duty here at this post. You will walk the fence to where it makes that turn back to the east and report back here with whatever you find. You clear on that?"

I thought about making him explain it again, just for the hell of it. I also thought about kicking him in the balls. But, what the hell, at least I got to take a walk away from the guard post. And, after all, leaving Bannerman there with Kraus was actually sort of funny.

The first hundred yards or so were easy going, a stroll through small bushes and some young trees that had been trimmed back so we could see the Communists when they attacked the post. But the vegetation got gradually thicker and I had to push my way through, scratching up my spit-shined boots and holster. (Yeah, we spit-shined our holsters.)

I had to use the flashlight that hung from my web belt. All I saw that I thought did not belong was a long, thick plank that had been thrown into the weeds near a small stand of trees. I did not see anything else nearby and I thought maybe the plank had been left there by a crew working on the fence.

And then I found the dog.

There was a thin rope around its neck and it was hanging from the barbed wire at the top of the fence. A piece of the rope hung down below the dog's head and there was a small rock tied to the end of it. The dog's belly had been slit and its guts pulled out and dropped in a loose tangle, the bottom of the tangle pushed through the chain link to form a loop. There was no way to tell whether the dog had been dead from the hanging when its belly was slit. But I knew. The dog had been alive.

It was the dog that Sabolino fed at the edge of the woods.

And I knew, I was goddamned positive, who had killed the dog.

"Didn't find anything, sergeant. Must have been some sort of prank." I didn't look at Bannerman. He knew I was lying.

"You was gone long enough," Kraus muttered. "I gotta take a piss." He turned and left, his truck lights growing smaller as he drove toward the inner compound.

We stood motionless in the circle of pale yellow light thrown by the guard post's floods.

Bannerman just waited.

"Sabo's dog," I said quietly. "The little one he feeds out there—"

"I know what dog it is," Bannerman said. "What's with the dog?"

And I told him. " . . . and there was this rock hanging from down around its neck."

Bannerman stared out into the night. "A rock?"

"Yeah, a goddamned rock . . ."

There was no movement anywhere on the post. We were as alone as two men could be, there in Northern New York State, hiding from the Communists.

"Wasn't a rock," Bannerman said.

"What? It sure as hell was a rock! I saw it, just hanging there, around that dead dog's scrawny neck!"

Bannerman looked at me. "Wasn't a rock. It was a stone."

"Stone? What the fuck's the difference . . . ?"

"Goddamn, Jesse, wake up! You don't get it! It was a Stone. With a capital 'S', for Christ's sake. A Stone. It was a message for you, Jesse."

"A message . . . ?"

"Yeah, Jesse. Your guts will be the next ones on the fence."

I guess Bannerman told Sabolino about the dog. I sure as hell didn't. I had buried the dog and told Bannerman where, but I don't think he told Sabolino about the grave.

And I told Bannerman who I thought had done it. And I think he told Sabolino.

I was very, very glad I was not there when Bannerman did that.

And I wondered what it would be like, to hang on a fence.

Forty-One

The Marvelous Bar
Geneva, New York
October 1961

We were preparing for another 24-hour shift of mind-numbing guard duty.

Our platoon was in formation, standing guard mount in the parking lot in front of the barracks building, the warm, early October sun not yet edging over the top of the building, just enough snap in the air to tell us that winter was hunched off to the north, waiting.

Kraus was reading something from a clipboard, his voice droning. I was not paying attention. I'm not sure anyone else was, either. Lt. Ringer was somewhere off to the side, waiting for Kraus to finish reading, then he and Kraus would walk down each row of men, inspecting, hoping to find some infraction.

Over Kraus's shoulder I could see the door to the barracks snap open and Sgt. Murphy stride through. He came straight to Kraus, said something to him that none of us could hear, and then left as quickly as he had arrived. I thought I saw Kraus's face turn slightly red. He was slightly pissed.

The inspection went fairly well—which always irritated Ringer and Kraus—and Kraus brought us to attention, preparing to tell us to "fall out" and send us to our assigned posts for the day.

And then Kraus said, "Stone, you will not be pulling guard duty today. Report to the badge office."

He did not look at me when he said that.

I stood in front of the counter at the badge office. I did not know why I was there and no one, not even Sgt. Heffner, the guy in charge, paid any attention to me. In fact, no one looked directly at me.

I didn't mind. From where I stood I could see Antonia DiPaulo.

She glanced casually in my direction. I could swear that there was a flash of recognition, but maybe I was wrong. Her back was to me. I could not see that magnificent chest but through her snug blouse I could see the indentations of her bra as it struggled to keep control of those tits.

I wondered how Heffner managed to get through the day in the presence of those tits. Surely, they must have occupied his every cogent moment . . .

"Stone."

Jesus H. Christ, there was only one voice like that. I wheeled around and looked at Ruker.

"With me, Private Stone." And he disappeared down a narrow hallway.

Garcia sat at a metal desk in the far corner of the small office. His handsome face was expressionless, but, even so, I thought I could sense that he was not exactly happy with my being in the room.

"I'm borrowing you, Stone. You are on temporary duty with me until you are told otherwise."

"Yes, si—" Then I decided to come right out with it. "What the hell am I supposed to call you?" I noticed the signs of a tiny grin on Garcia's face.

"You don't call me anything, private. Nothing at all. If you should ever think you have occasion to do so, my name is Ruker. You do know that, don't you?"

"Yes. I do." I decided that I would never utter Ruker's name. Just the use of his name was a bad omen.

"Sit down, and I'll tell you what your job is."

I sat.

"But before we get to that, when you leave here you will go to the armory and turn in your issued weapon. And then you will come back here and take this."

And he handed me a .45 so bright and shiny that it glistened in the lights. Fully loaded. Starker's.

I sat in the middle of the night in one of Ruker's civilian cars, wearing civilian clothes, in a civilian town, across the street from a civilian bar. This was what I had been assigned to do by Ruker—stay awake, observe, take notes, report. I was hunkered down behind the wheel of the car—turns out he had three of them—wearing a dark ball cap, my eyes just barely high enough in the window to see out. I had the windows rolled up and the doors locked, in some high-school thinking that that might protect me.

"So, if that is all I'm supposed to do, why do I need the piece?" I had asked Ruker.

"Jesus, you really are a hillbilly, aren't you," he said. It wasn't a question.

I was across the street from the Marvelous Bar on a narrow side street near downtown Geneva. Odd sort of name I thought. If you were drunk enough, all bars were marvelous.

It was a busy place. All evening and into the night guys kept going in and coming out, some of them staying an hour or so, some of staying only a few minutes. The windows in the front of the bar were painted over, black, only a couple of small neon beer signs showing to the street. You could not see who was leaving until someone stepped through the door. The door was inset and angled, opening into a small space where people could pause, check the street, check things out before they moved on. And almost every one of them did.

Always guys.

Some of them wearing army uniforms.

I guess I did not really understand what I was watching until a couple of guys walked out through the door holding hands.

A gay bar. That bastard Ruker had sent me to keep tabs on a gay bar.

What? Was he going to start busting guys because they were gay? Was that a security violation? Goddamn it, Fleet and Milken were gay, everybody knew it, and nobody gave a shit. We didn't want to fuck them; we just wanted them to stand guard duty like the rest of us. And they did.

Fleet and Milken. I was thinking about them, and thinking about Ruker, and then just thinking I should start up the ratted-out Chevy I was sitting in, drive out to NDA and just sleep in the parking lot until daylight.

And then three guys walked out of the bar, pausing in the darkness of the inset doorway. Even in the dim light, I knew it was Fleet and Milken, wearing civilian clothes. Milken checked the street, then handed something to the third guy, who handed Milken what obviously was a wad of bills.

A buy going down. Or was the third guy just paying Milken for services rendered?

I started scribbling notes in the darkness. Fleet and Milken. Fleet and Milken. The third guy put his arm around Milken and kissed him on the cheek. They stood that way for a moment, then the third guy let go of Milken and stepped out of the doorway and walked quickly down the street.

It was Kraus.

I sat stunned for a minute, watching Kraus disappear into the darkness, now and then seeing his fat shape appear in a random street light.

I started scribbling the notes that Ruker had told me to take.

Forty-Two

North Depot Activity
Romulus, New York
November 1961

Not all MPs were stupid.

Somebody figured out that Bannerman had fired the 8-ball out of the canon. I think they had been working on it since it happened, but I never really found out who put it all together.

When they brought Bannerman up before the company brass, he admitted he had done it.

They wanted to know why.

Something to do, Bannerman had said.

They busted him back to slick-sleeve. Bannerman had been a Spec. 4 for less than ninety days.

They kept him off guard duty for a long time, finding other shit details for him to work on. I hardly ever saw him.

I asked Ruker about 8-ball, if he had figured out that Bannerman did it. He said he didn't waste time on shit like that.

"So, what, you're just at NDA to chase Communists? Or how about the mafia? They always need chasing."

I thought—again—that he was going to hit me. But he just walked away.

I could not figure out what the big bastard really wanted. When I had left the Marvelous Bar and come back to the base in the middle of the night, Ruker was still in his office, a weak light shining from his window. When I passed through the gate, he was standing outside one of the metal doors of the badge office. I did not see Garcia, but I knew he was there, somewhere.

I pulled Ruker's car into the parking area behind the badge office and got out. When I opened the door, Ruker was standing there, his hand out. I shoved my notes into it. Ruker took the notes and walked away. He did not say a word.

I went back on guard duty, just as though I had never been parked across the street from the Marvelous Bar.

I left Starker's .45 in the car.

It was one of those early autumn days in Upstate New York when the cool morning light hung softly in blue skies and warm breezes drifted across trees that were showing signs of color. One of those days in Upstate New York that made you love the place—right up until the weather kicked your ass the next day, turning mean and gray, cold, relentless.

I had been thinking a lot about the Marvelous Bar. Fuck the Marvelous Bar, and all the faggots who hung out there—today, all was right with the world.

That is, until Bannerman showed up.

The car drove slowly up the access road toward the main gate, where I was on guard duty with Harvey Melton. As far as I knew, this was the only time Melt Down had ever been assigned to the main gate. Apparently, he had been warned about me, that maybe I worked for Ruker. He had not said more than a dozen words so far in the guard shift.

The car stopped about fifty yards away.

Bannerman got out.

From the instant he put both feet on the ground I knew he was fucked up. He started walking toward the gate, walking stiffly, placing one foot carefully in front of the other, arms tightly at his side. As soon as he was away from the car it turned and drove away, accelerating quickly, leaving Bannerman weaving along the blacktop.

Even from that distance, I could see that Bannerman was very, very drunk. Hank Bannerman could drink. God, yes, he could drink.

I stepped out of the guard shack and watched Bannerman come. Harvey Melton stood inside the shack with his hand on the phone. That was Bannerman out there, our Bannerman, the free spirit of the world, walking like a frozen zombie toward the guard shack. If Harvey lifted that phone, I was going to knock him on his bony ass.

But there was no way, I knew, that anything good could come from any of this.

Bannerman stopped in front of me. He was wearing a wrinkled white dress shirt that was hanging out of his pants, the sleeves pushed up to his elbows. His khaki pants drooped around his hips and the left leg was soaked from the ankle to the knee. On his right foot was a brown loafer. His left shoe was missing. His left eye was swollen shut and was rapidly turning black.

What he wasn't wearing was his security badge.

He leaned in toward me, trying to focus his eyes, his eyebrows raised, lips pressed together, fingers fumbling at his shirt pocket.

"Jesus, Hank, you look like Stan Laurel," I muttered, wondering if he were going to fall, and if he did, whether I should try to catch him.

"Laurel. Good ol' Stanley. Been a long time . . ." His voice trailed off, as though he just ran out of air.

"Hank, where's your badge?" He kept fumbling at his pocket. "Goddamnit, Hank, get your badge out and hang it on your pocket." I could not help looking around for other MPs, maybe Kraus, who liked to sneak up on guard posts.

Bannerman kept digging at his pocket. He had his whole fist in there.

"Hey, Jesse, I just remembered," he whispered, trying to stand still in the bright light of mid-morning. "I don't have a badge no more. Nope. No badge. Gave it up." He hiccupped, a deep one, from down around his navel. "Gave it up. Flushed it."

"You what!?"

"Flushed . . . it. Say, Jesse, you know that old hotel in town? Well, I had a few drinks there . . . and then I cut up that fucking badge,"—he pulled a switchblade out of his pocket and triggered it open— "and flushed it. Don't want to wear a badge anymore. I am not a badge, my good man, I am a good man. A man. Man. I'm not a fucking picture wrapped in a piece of government plastic." He tilted a little to the left and had to catch himself.

"And I didn't use any of that shit, Jesse. No, sir. I just drank. The rest of them was using that shit. And your friend was spooning it out."

I heard Melton lift the phone. I turned and looked at him. He got the message. He put the phone down, his face tight, lines around his eyes.

"What do you mean, 'my friend'? What . . ."

Bannerman cleared his throat and spat something indescribable on the ground. "Well, see, I had a little trouble with them . . . with those little pieces. Some of 'em wouldn't go down. Just kept swirling around and around in the water." He made a swirling motion with the knife. "So I put my foot in there and stomped 'em." He lifted his wet leg. "Lost my shoe in there, though. Water got stopped up and ran over and then some guys came in and started yelling at me and all I was doing was standing there with my foot in the toilet, wondering where my goddamn shoe was . . ." He stopped again, out of gas.

" 'Course, I had a knife in my hand . . . and then one of those bastards hit me, Jesse. Just hauled off and hit me." He put his hand up to the swollen eye, touching it gently.

From behind me, I heard Melton's voice drift out of the guard shack. "I'm supposed to call. It's in the regulations. And you're supposed to—"

"Melt Down, you dick-head," I snarled over my shoulder, "get your hand off that fuckin' phone!"

I turned to Bannerman. "Sir," I said in my most formal voice, "you are requesting access to this post, which is a secured area, and you have no visible security identification, you are drunk, and you are holding a weapon. All in all, you seem to be a bit . . . incapacitated." Bannerman smiled. "So, I suggest you go back down the road there"—I pointed down the access road toward the highway—"and catch a ride into town. Perhaps when your, uh, incapacitation wears off, you will be able to rectify this situation."

Bannerman could not believe his ears. "Incapa . . . rectify? Damn, Jesse, you got to quit reading books. You gettin' as bad as me. Pretty soon, Kraus won't be able to understand either of us." He had this big, stupid grin on his face.

"Nah, Jesse, my ride's already gone. I'll just go over there to the badge office and get me another little biddy piece of plastic." Bannerman was still smiling when he walked, staggering, away.

"No, Hank!" He stopped. "Give me the knife."

Bannerman looked down at his hand, surprised to see a knife dangling there. And then he dropped it.

Melton bounced out of the guard shack. "Why don't you apprehend that man? You know he's an MP, and you know he's on this post drunk, you know he doesn't have a badge, and you know—"

"Harvey!" I guess I shouted his name a little louder than I meant to. He flinched and stepped back. "Listen to me, Harvey. Listen carefully." I stepped forward and put my face to the side of his. "Fuck you," I said softly.

And I picked up the knife and stepped back into the guard shack.

Bannerman did not come out of the badge office.

I stood in the doorway of the guard shack, one eye on the badge office, the other on Harvey Melton, who still had not given up the idea of picking up the phone.

I don't know how much time went by, but it could not have been more than a few minutes. Seemed like an hour. And then I saw the MP truck coming down the main post road toward the guard shack. That could only mean one thing—Heffner, inside the badge office, had called the sergeant of the guard. Kraus.

The MP truck pulled off the road and into a parking area behind the badge office. Kraus got out and strolled slowly toward the guard shack, coming through the gate, no hurry, making it last. This would be a good day for Kraus; he would have Bannerman and me on enough security violations keep him happy for months.

The fat bastard took his time, his squat, jiggling frame seeming to roll across the blacktop. Every crease in his uniform was razor sharp, every piece of brass polished to a high sheen. A career soldier. One of those career soldiers who made a career out of hiding out, never sticking out, all the while sticking it to his men, every chance he got.

I stepped out of the guard shack.

"Private Stone, perhaps you can tell me why you sent a drunk MP into the badge office? Perhaps you can tell me why you didn't place the man under apprehension and call the sergeant of the guard?" His voice was calm. He was in no hurry. I knew he was enjoying this, a smile on his piggy little face. He would milk it for all it was worth.

"Sergeant Kraus, our security regulations require that we identify people by their badges. That man in the badge office is wearing civilian clothes and he has no badge. Therefore, I couldn't identify him, sergeant. Therefore, I don't know him."

Melton had backed all the way out the other side of the guard shack, hoping Kraus wouldn't notice him.

"Private," Kraus said in his gravelly voice, "I have been waiting for this. I have known from the time you stepped off that bus that you were a fuck-up. You got away with striking Sergeant Olsen, but this time you are going to learn a little lesson about how we operate Post No. 1, the main gate to this secured facility. Oh, and Bannerman? Hell, he's just a bonus."

"Uh, sergeant, could I speak to you privately for a moment?"

I moved a few steps toward the gate. I wanted some space between me and Melton.

Kraus moved with me. I took another step or two. He followed, but he wasn't happy.

"Where the hell are we going, soldier? The mess hall?" He took another quick step or two and came around in front of me.

"Sergeant Kraus," I said quietly, using the best college voice I had, "I am very aware of your enmity towards me—"

Kraus screwed up his face—he didn't know what 'enmity' meant.

"—and, of course, Private Bannerman. But I have a trade to offer you that might set things right again, or at least let us move past this situation."

"You ain't got nothin' to trade, and this time that fuckin' Ruker ain't around to bail your ass out."

"Perhaps not. But, even so, maybe we could go into town sometime and have a drink? Maybe go to your favorite bar? That would be the Marvelous Bar, wouldn't it? Nice place. You know, we could even invite Fleet and Milken to join us . . . make an evening of it."

I waited.

Kraus did not take his eyes from my face, his own face growing steadily redder.

We stood that way for a full minute, each waiting for the other to set something in motion.

I glanced around. No one else was near, Melton still in the guard shack looking at us through the window. I knew he could not hear us.

"Interested in a trade, Sergeant?"

His face was the color of a sunset and I could see the veins pounding in his neck.

"What do you have in mind?" Kraus asked, his voice like grit.

"Bannerman is a good soldier. A good MP. He just gets a little warped now and then. Send him—order him—back down the access road, back into town. He knows some people in there. A girl. Let him get himself straightened out. Then he can call you and report the accidental loss of his badge. It will be a pain in the ass, but you can get him a new one. Badges do get lost now and then. Can happen to anyone."

Kraus sneered. "And so the trade is . . . ?"

"Bannerman goes back into town. You get in your truck and drive away. And we're even."

Kraus was still sneering, but looking me full in the face, his sneer delivering a promise.

"We're not even, Stone. We will never be even."

Kraus turned his head toward the guard shack where he could see Melt Down watching us through the window. He raised his arm.

"Private, call inside to the badge desk and tell Sgt. Heffner to send Private Bannerman out here to report to me. Now!"

I saw Melton grab the phone. In a moment the front door of the badge office opened and Bannerman came out, still walking stiffly, bouncing slightly because of the missing shoe, still with that stupid smile on his face. He walked up and stood next to us at some drunken version of attention.

"Private," Kraus said, "you see the access road there?" Kraus looked toward the road, raising his arm and pointing. We all looked down the road, even Melt Down. "Well, I want you to go back down that road . . ."

Kraus turned back toward Bannerman. A look of utter shock was on Kraus's face, a look so strange that it took me a moment to realize what was going on.

Bannerman was looking at me, but he was pissing on the razor-sharp crease of Kraus's pants.

"Spooning it out. Your friend," he slurred, still looking at me. "You know. Tits."

I did not know it at the time, but I would never see Bannerman again.

Forty-Three

Geneva, New York
November 1961

I was never much for contemplation, for sitting on a ledge above some canyon, probing around in my mental guts for the reason behind it all—whatever it was. I just wanted to get on with it, to do what was in front of me; to take some action, even if it was wrong. I wanted my life to reflect what I had done, not what some shrink would describe as "my emotional life as related to my well-being." Fuck that. I just wanted to *do* something.

And right now I was doing exactly nothing.

I was back across the street from the Marvelous Bar, parked again in Ruker's car, wearing civilian clothes, my jacket collar turned up against the chill, trying to stay awake, a pad and pencil on the seat beside me, Starker's .45 stuck under the seat. I had read detective stories—it was too damned obvious to stash a pistol under a seat. I fished the big gun out and held it, thought about firing off a shot into the Marvelous Bar and then high-tailing it out of there. Just for the hell of it. Yeah, I thought about shit like that, all the time.

But I didn't do it. Instead, I searched around in the car for some place to stash the gun, a place I could reach fairly easily if I had to. Goddamn, I was actually thinking about using the gun.

I ended up sticking the gun up under the dash, jammed among the wires and other crap under there. It seemed to hang there well enough, and I thought I could reach it.

This time, Ruker had given me a small pair of binoculars, although I didn't know what good they would do in the middle of the night.

I knew Fleet and Milken were inside the bar. Other guys kept going in and coming out, but I didn't know any of them.

So all I could do was sit there and think; ask myself questions. Like, why did people keep telling me to stay away from things? Why did people stay away from me? I seldom saw Hays Tucker anymore, and when I did he hardly looked at me. Why did Ruker tell me to leave Starker alone? Did he want to take Starker down himself? And then there was Bannerman, telling me to leave the woman alone. The woman? Tits. Antonia. Toni.

Toni was spooning out the shit, Bannerman had said. But Bannerman had been drunk out of his mind.

I reached up to my neck and fished out the small silver chain that hung around my neck and squeezed the odd-shaped piece of turquoise that dangled from it. I had had the turquoise put on the chain back at Ord, on the one and only day they had let me off the post.

"C'mon, Wendell," I said softly, "help me out here."

It was past midnight. Way past. I was thinking about heading back to NDA when the door to the bar opened again and a bunch of guys came out and stood in a loose group on the sidewalk. They stood in the weird colored light of the small neon beer signs, talking quietly, nodding, stuffing their hands in their pockets. And then, almost as though on signal, most of them moved off down the sidewalk, still in a group. I was thankful that not one of them had looked across the street at my car.

Except the two that were left. Fleet and Milken.

They seemed to talk quietly in the alcove of the doorway, then stepped out and to the side, leaning up against the building, in plain view—even in the bad light—of anybody driving by. They seemed to get comfortable, Fleet pulling a foot up to press against the wall behind him. But the thing that bothered me—they were staring right at my car. I could hardly see their faces, could not see their eyes, but there was not a doubt that they were staring at me.

Staring at me.

I tried to stay mostly out of sight, cramming myself down into the driver's seat as much as I could. I eased Ruker's binoculars up to my eyes and peeked over the door. I was surprised to find out that I could see both their faces clearly, could see that they were smiling, could see Fleet raise his hand and wiggle his fingers in my direction.

I put the binoculars down.

I leaned forward slowly, my chest against the wheel of the car, feeling under the dash for the .45 I had stashed there. I got my fingers on the handle but the hammer must have been tangled in some wiring. I couldn't pull the damned thing loose. I leaned far to my right and pulled harder. I thought it moved—but it didn't really matter. My face and body were suddenly covered with bits of glass when the window on the passenger side exploded into the car. All of a sudden I just forgot about the gun.

I twisted hard in the seat, trying to clear my face, feeling the glass work its way down inside my shirt.

A light came on, flaring wildly into the car. I could not see who was holding it, but in the edge of the glare I could see the big pistol pointed full into my face, the grip steady, the barrel unwavering, the big hand wearing a glove. Whoever held the pistol had done this before.

And then I heard the worst sound of my life.

"He's a cop," the almost-whiny voice said.

Starker.

I heard the door unlock and then the big guy reached inside and grabbed me, pulled me out onto the sidewalk, dragged me a few feet from the car, then let go of me. I could feel the dirt and trash on the sidewalk grinding under me as I moved. I was a big guy, in good shape. Goddamn it, I had been a *cowboy*! He couldn't do this shit to me. But he did, easily.

And then he kicked me in the ribs. I pulled myself into a ball as best I could, waiting for the next kick, trying to orient myself. I would run, hell yes, I would run. But which way?

The big guy leaned over me and I finally saw his face.

Carlo. Jane Russell's driver.

He raised the pistol, not to shoot me, but to hit me. A hand appeared on his arm.

"Allow me," I heard Starker say. And Starker kicked me in the face.

Forty-Four

Geneva, New York
November 1961

Concrete is soft.

I remembered the concrete of the sidewalks and basement stairwells of San Francisco and I always thought it was hard, man-stone hard, grinding against my skin when the Indian and I tried to sleep in short patches in the doorways before someone rousted us and sent us back out into the rain.

But now it was soft. My face was pressed into it and one of my arms was folded under me and the back of my hand was pressed down into it by my own body weight. But that did not matter. The concrete was soft. I know it was. I was there.

There is a pain that journeys beyond reason.

There is a pain that drives so deep into the mind that body parts refuse to respond. Arms and legs do not work. Mouths do not open. Guts refuse to untangle.

And it was all mine. Now.

Carlo and Starker had brought that pain, Starker with rage, Carlo with expertly placed shots delivered without emotion, just another day's work.

I was pretty sure I had been beaten to within a shallow breath of my life, had pissed in my pants, my bowels loose. Beat to shit, you might say.

I must have been awake, but I could not open my eyes. There was gentle sound washing against my ears but I thought maybe it was just ringing in my head.

I was in a dream world.

I thought I was in the middle of a white room, turning slowly, seeing the dim shapes of people coming and going, people putting their hands on me, pulling, turning, dragging at my clothing, tiny points of pain darting into me when they were near. People who floated and then did not float. People of the dream world. People who came from the place Wendell Klah went to when he went away.

Nah. It was just the nurses, changing my tape and giving me shots.

I thought maybe it was raining, but I was not sure. There seemed to be a sense of water, maybe water washing against something, maybe me, but I could not open my eyes or move any part of my body. If it were raining, then I was already wet and it did not matter.

And I *was* already wet.

I wondered how long it would be, before I could move.

And then I was not awake anymore.

I was face up, my eyes closed. I kept trying to take a deep breath but my chest was too heavy for the effort. My lips were stuck together, my tongue swollen inside my mouth.

I could hear the sunlight clattering gently against the ceiling of the room. I could *hear* it. I knew it was there. It had bounced in there after hitting the water on the lake, glittering aimlessly inside the room like a sprinkling of ice crystals. I could hear it.

I opened my eyes. I could see through a window and I saw the lake and I knew I was alive.

I was not tied up. Somehow, I sensed that my arms and legs were free. I started to raise my arm and pain was suddenly let loose in my body. I lay there for a moment, my arm still hanging in the air. I was waiting for the pain to go away, but it did not. I knew it would not.

I moved the arm, kept it going through the pain until I touched my chest. I was wearing some sort of thin gown and underneath it I was wrapped in heavy bandages from my neck to below my rib cage. I kept my hand going through the pain until it touched my head. I felt my face, my fingers tracing gently across my forehead and down to my chin. But I did not really touch my face. Like my chest, my entire head was wrapped in bandages, holes left for my eyes and nose, a tiny, round hole for my mouth. And I knew terrible damage had been done to me.

I was one miserable son of a bitch.

And to make things worse, somewhere in the background, I could hear Ruker's voice.

"You got made. How the fuck could you get made? You fucked up my case, you goddamn hick."

I was in some kind of hospital. I was lying in a white hospital bed, with white hospital sheets, white paint on the walls. I must have been on an upper floor. When I managed to turn my head and look out the window, I could see the lake in the distance, the sunlight clattering off the wrinkled surface. Once, I saw a small boat far out on the water. I could barely see that there was one guy in the boat. He seemed to be fishing. I thought it was the most beautiful thing I had ever seen.

All I could do was lie there and think—not my best skill, or so it seemed—about how the hell I managed to get into this hospital bed. I had been in Ruker's car, parked across the street from the Marvelous Bar, sitting in the dark, watching the bar, just as Ruker had told me to do. Watching Fleet and Milken.

But then Fleet and Milken were watching me, hunched down in the front seat, the top of my head barely showing above the bottom of the window. They were watching me . . .

No. They were watching the car.

They knew the car.

I didn't get "made," like Ruker had said. I was already made—they were waiting for me.

A nurse was there by the bed, bending over me. She smelled like the flowers that grew in the patches of sunlight on Black Hawk ridge only better. I tried to see her face but she kept moving around, straightening the sheets, checking my bandages.

"What's the matter with me?" I muttered.

"You must have been in a fight. I think you lost."

Her voice was soft and silky. There was something familiar about it, but my mind was fuzzy and I could not get a fix on it. I would have to work on it.

"Are you in pain?"

And suddenly I realized that I *was* in pain. Odd, how the nearness of a woman can make you forget your pain.

"Yeah . . ."

"I'll fix it," she said softly, "in a minute."

She pulled down the sheet and I felt her take my hand. She opened my fingers and put something squarish and hard in my palm.

"This was left at the badge office for you."

"Badge off . . . office?" I was having trouble making the words come out and sound right. "Badge office? Toni? Is that you, Toni?"

She pulled the sheet back up over me and started to move away.

And visions from another part of my life started to flood across the front of me mind. "Badge office? Who left . . . whatever it is . . . at the badge office?" I tried to squeeze my fingers, maybe feel what it was that was in my hand. It didn't work.

"I don't know," she said. "Never saw who it was. I just thought I would bring it to you. You know—now you owe me."

I thought I could actually hear her smile.

I tried to raise my head and tilt it to look down at my hand, but the pain came again.

She moved something at the side of the bed and I realized there was an IV in my arm. She must have shoved a needle into the line. Almost instantly I could feel the pain being drawn from various parts of my body and I knew I would be asleep in a matter of seconds.

"Who was in the badge office. I need to know who was in the badge off . . . Toni?"

I fell asleep. But not before I could feel her hand wrapping around my dick.

I must have slept the rest of the night. When I opened my eyes the window was gray with light and the air in the room was still with dawn.

My arm seemed to move a little better and I dragged it slowly up to where I could see it, and reach it with my other hand. I opened my fingers.

The thing was almost the size of a tennis ball, but with flat sides, dirty, wrapped with so much rough, black electrician's tape and handled so much that it was ragged. A scrap of cloth had been glued to one side, my name written on the cloth in perfectly formed letters.

I would never get the damned thing open with my hands. I twisted slightly, trying to see the table beside my bed, the pain again shooting from places I did not know existed. There was some cutlery from the evening meal still there. I got my hand on the short, dull knife—and then noticed that my chain with the turquoise was lying there. I used the knife to hook the chain, brought it to me, and fumbled at it until I got it, once again, around my neck.

I went to work on the tape, my movements clumsy, painful, my fingers not working properly. I sawed at the tape. I fell asleep. I awoke and sawed more tape. I nodded off again. It took almost an hour to unwrap the tiny box inside. The box was stuck hopelessly to the tape and finally fell away.

The tiny doe-colored leather pouch that fell into my hand was butter-soft, the top puckered closed with a long, slender leather thong. On the side of the pouch a precise, delicate miniature cross had been beaded into the leather, the beads glowing softly even in the weak light. A cross. Never in my life had I owned anything with a cross on it.

And maybe I did not own this one.

It took a couple of tries before I could pull open the top of the pouch. Two odd-shaped, shiny pieces of turquoise fell out into my hand.

I had not cried in a long time. I cried now.

I fumbled at my neck, fumbled for the chain. I got it over my head, its attached piece of stone now lying with the other two. I ignored the pain and used both my hands to turn the tiny pieces of turquoise until they aligned.

They fit together perfectly. I had a whole stone.

Forty-Five

Hospital
Geneva, New York
November 1961

Ruker sat beside my bed, his bulk completely hiding the straight-back chair he was sitting in. If Ruker was there, I knew Garcia would be there, probably standing in a corner, but I could not move my head enough to see him.

"You look like shit," Ruker growled.

"Fuck you, *sir*." I tried to stick the 'sir' in his ear, but he didn't take the bait. I was feeling better, better enough to mess with Ruker—at my own risk. I didn't think even Ruker would hit a guy in a hospital bed.

Of course, I might have been wrong.

"You were parked across the street in the dark. What did you do to attract attention?"

"Attract!" I couldn't believe my ears. "I didn't do anything! Fleet and Milken, they knew the car. The bastards just waited, leaning against the wall, staring at the car. They *knew* what was going to happen!"

Ruker didn't say anything. He turned and looked at another part of the room, probably looking at Garcia. He turned back to me.

"We may have made a mistake," he said, his voice losing some of it gruffness. "We may have to move a little faster than we wanted to."

"Yeah. Maybe you should have moved before they beat the shit out of me." Ruker ignored me. "So," I said, "how do I explain all this to the army?"

Ruker almost smiled. But not quite. "We wrecked the car. Just drove it into a tree. The army thinks you were in it. Thinks I sent you into town and you fucked up. It wasn't a hard sell." He waited, but I said nothing. "Had it towed to the parking area behind the Badge Office so everybody could see what a fuckup you are." He paused. "There was nothing in the car. Nothing." He waited. I said nothing.

"You probably aren't going to get promoted for a while."

It was a joke. The big bastard was making a joke. I said nothing. I had not planned on ever being promoted, not for any reason. And now Ruker had made sure of it.

"Stay here. Take it easy for a while. We have some shit we have to do." *We*. He must have meant Garcia. I sure as hell was not going to do anything else for Ruker. He went on: "And then you'll come back to the base, pull some guard duty. Try to behave yourself."

"Fuck you, *sir*."

Ruker ignored the comment. "You see anybody else from NDA at the bar?"

"No."

"Kraus wasn't there?"

"No."

But not everybody from NDA had been *in* the bar. "How come you don't ask me who the fuck put the beating on me?"

Ruker looked off at Garcia again, but said nothing.

"Starker was there. He's the reason for the bandages on my face."

I waited. Ruker still said nothing. "You once told me to stay away from Starker. Starker didn't stay away from me."

The big prick still said nothing.

"He's going to kill me. You hear me, *sir?* Probably would have done it this time, 'cept there were other people around."

"So he hasn't killed you, yet?" I thought he tried to smile again. He didn't make it.

"What the fuck? NO! He hasn't killed me yet! What the hell kind of question is that?"

"Well," Ruker said, raising his big ass out of the chair, "if he kills you, let me know."

I could have sworn I heard Garcia make some sort of a grunt, maybe his attempt at a laugh, but I couldn't be sure.

Ruker shoved is hands in his pockets.

"I'm not going to wait for that. I'm going to take care of it," I said, waiting for him blow up.

His expression did not change. He slowly started for the door. I heard Garcia move and I could finally see him.

"Did you hear me? I'm not waiting!"

"Yeah, yeah, you're an impatient man. And you haven't even been killed yet."

Fuck him.

"One more thing," I grunted. "Starker didn't do this alone. I could take Starker by himself. No problem. There was another guy."

They both stopped, waiting.

"Carlo, the asshole who drives the Caddy. He was there. He pulled me out of the car. He's a pro."

Ruker and Garcia looked at each other, then slowly started out the door.

"One *more* thing," I said, enjoying it now. "My nurse here. Comes in and gives me pain medicine. She's Toni DiPaulo."

That stopped them, again.

"Yeah," I said, "Toni DiPaulo. And you sometimes park your piece-a-shit cars out behind the badge office. And I'll bet, just every now and then, you and Garcia talk in the hallway at the badge office." I hesitated, just a second or so. "Very clever of you, *sir*."

And then it hit me.

"You motherfucker! You knew she would make the car. You fucking *knew* it! I didn't get made by a couple of faggots! YOU SET ME UP!"

Ruker stepped back to the bed. "Tryin' to get 'em to make a move. And they did," he mumbled. "Might have been a mistake."

They moved toward the door, almost in step with each other.

"You gonna leave me here? With no guard on the door? What the fuck is that all about?"

They turned to face me.

"You dumb hillbilly. You aren't important, don't you understand that? If they wanted you dead, you would be dead already! Jesus Christ, I could wheel that damned bed down into town and park it in the middle of Senece Street and nobody would give a shit! Get over it—you aren't important."

He paused, thinking about something. "'Cept, of course, when you fuck up." And he laughed.

They turned back toward the door.

"Fuck you, *sir*. And while you're at it, fuck that son of a bitch who never learned to talk!" I pointed at Garcia.

And they were gone.

When Ruker and Garcia left I tried to go to sleep but my head was a cracked ball of inhuman pain and it was all I could do to keep from screaming. I had talked so much and yelled at Ruker so much that I had released pain I didn't even know was there. But it was. I had also messed up the bandages on my head and the hole where my mouth was supposed to be had slipped up over my nose. A nurse came in, pumped me full of pain killer, and changed my bandages.

The nurse was not Antonia DiPaulo. By now, I had figured out that DiPaulo was not a real nurse and I never really expected to see her again. But she had been in my room, had stuck a needle in my IV line. She could have killed me. Why didn't she? Ruker has said that if they had wanted me dead, I would already be dead.

Maybe I just wasn't worth the killing. That was a sobering thought—that I wasn't worth the killing. I would have to work on that. I was in over my head, running around in a mess that I did not understand. I did not even know who the real players were. I knew about Starker, and Kraus, and Fleet, and Milken . . . but I was sure they were just like me—flunkies.

And I knew about DiPaulo—Tits. She didn't kill me. And she had wrapped her hand around my dick.

Over the days the pain slowly went away and the nurses stopped coming so frequently. I could move all my body parts and could even—slowly and painfully—drag my ass out of bed to take a piss. I still wore the bandages but they had been changed a number of times and seemed to be lighter, thinner. On my head and face the openings were larger and I could shove real food in there.

Ruker came by only once, to tell me that Antonia DiPaulo had not come back to the badge office. He expected that she would not. He said it didn't matter. There were other things he was more interested in. He did not say what they were.

We did not mention the .45.

Forty-Six
Hospital
Geneva, New York
December 1961

There was no moon on the lake and the room was almost black. The painkiller was slowly draining from my body and I could feel all the small places where pain came from and I wondered if there would ever be another time when something in my body did not hurt. I lay there in the darkness, half asleep, thinking about the pain in my life, pain I had inflicted, pain I received from others. Physical pain was nothing much. It was all the other kinds of pain. . . .

The door to the room opened slowly and through the fog of my drowsiness I could see the white figure coming across the room. I paid no real attention—I had gotten so used to the nurses that I did even wake up when they came into the room.

But this one slipped her arm under the sheets and put her hand on my dick.

Antonia DiPaulo.

Strange and wondrous things happen when you least expect them.

I braced my elbows against the mattress and tried to sit up but she put her hand in the middle of my chest and pushed me down. Gently. She bent over me, looking at my eyes through the bandages, her raven-black hair falling down through the darkness of the room and touching me. Even in the darkness, I thought I could see tiny dots of light in her eyes.

She moved her hand across the side of my face, tracing the bandages with the tips of her fingers, letting her fingers find the opening to my mouth, gently putting her fingers in there, drawing her fingernails across my lips. I opened my mouth slightly and she felt the movement, bringing her fingers down against them a little more firmly, prying gently. I opened my mouth and she slipped her fingers in, moving them gently, touching my tongue.

Fingers, fingers. The woman was making love to me with her fingers, including the ones still wrapped around my dick.

But that was not all.

There was a tiny light on the wall at the head of my bed. She took her fingers out of my mouth, reached up, and snapped it on. The thing gave out hardly any light, but in the dense black of the room it seemed like a floodlight.

And I could see Toni's face. And I could see the Tits of Paradise, bulging beneath the prim top of her nurse's uniform.

She followed my eyes. She reached up and unbuttoned the top button of her uniform, and then another button. And another. She was not wearing a bra . . . and then those breasts, the most perfect pair I had ever seen, were loose in the world right in front of me. They stood straight out, the nipples so dark that they looked black in the weak light.

I raised my hand slowly, letting her see the hand coming to her breast. I cupped that magnificent, firm, warm tit in my hand, unable to make my fingers do anything except stay there, motionless. She waited. Still, I was frozen in place with the wonder of her. She put her hand over mine and gently moved my hand in small motions on her breast, caressing it, pressing. Loving. Absolutely . . . loving.

Inside my bandages my mouth was open and I sucked air in like I was drowning. She took my hand away from her breast, then leaned forward over me. She guided the nipple through the hole in the bandage and into my mouth.

I don't know what was going through my mind. All I could do

was suck that magnificent breast . . . and then she pressed forward, pressing her breast against my face, as though she wanted to shove more tit through the hole in the bandages. Her breast expanded from the pressure, spreading up and over my nose and I could not breathe and I absolutely, positively did not give a shit. If I suffocated, I would die knowing that sheer perfection had killed me.

And then, I remembered that *I had another hand.*

I dug my left arm out from between Toni and the bed and fumbled down her leg, finding the bottom of her skirt. I put my hand under there and stoked her leg. It was bare. I moved my hand up until I could feel the bare cheek of her ass. The *bare* cheek. Antonia DiPaulo was wearing nothing underneath the prim nurse's dress.

She had come here to fuck me.

I moved my hand down her ass and she spread her legs slightly so I could get my fingers in there and then my whole hand found a home in the warmth and wet of that fine thing that men search for their whole lives.

She got tired of the foreplay. She let go of my dick and with one quick whip of the sheets and a flip of her dress she threw her leg across my body and planted herself on me with the agility of a gymnast. I got my hand out of her crotch barely in time.

But not quite. We were not quite . . . fucking. She held herself above me, slightly touching me, me straining to rise to meet her, she not allowing it. I was in mortal dick-pain. I would gladly die from being fucked to death, bit I probably was going to die from *not* fucking.

She leaned her face into mine. "Listen carefully."

I listened. Oh, Jesus, I listened.

"What is Ruker going to do?"

And then, of course, it was clear. Antonia DiPaulo did not give a shit about me. Antonia DiPaulo was just doing her job.

I waited, feeling my dick shrink to the size of a worm.

"Fuck you," I mumbled. "Yeah, I would like to do that—fuck you. But, this time, you lose. I don't know a goddamn thing about what Ruker's up to. Never did. Never will. So whatever you're gonna do next, get it over with."

She might fuck me. She might not. Either way, I could not have cared less. I would go with it all the way, no matter what that way was.

"I guess you really are just a soldier, like Carlo. You do what you're told." She stopped. I waited. "You were not supposed to get hurt this badly. They were just supposed to pull you out of the car and rough you up a little. It was just family business."

She set me up. I already knew that, but I wasn't going to tell her.

"So, who changed the rules?" I pointed to my bandaged head.

She reached out and touched my leg, but she did not say a damned thing.

"Who changed the rules?" I asked again.

She reached across me and turned out the tiny light and the room bounded into darkness. I could hear her walking away.

I tried one more time. "Who changed the rules?"

I heard her stop. "Carlo had to stop Mr. Starker from killing you."

The door opened and closed.

I knew I had to wait until I was stronger. I wasn't strong enough to do what I wanted to do. What I thought I *had* to do.

The next morning, I held my right hand in front of my face. It trembled, but only a little.

The next day it trembled less.

It would not be long, now.

It was great to almost get laid just before killing somebody.

It was time to kill Starker.

Forty-Seven

North Depot Activity
Romulus, New York
December 1961

I knew the crazy bastard was down at the end of the long hard barracks hallway and I thought if I concentrated, really concentrated, I could hear the rasp of his stinking breath coming through his ugly rat-nose.

I had stayed in the hospital until I was strong enough that my hands trembled only a little, strong enough to handle a pistol properly, strong enough to jack the slide back without pain racking through my body.

The pistol was simple. In the middle of the first night when I got back to the base I simply went down to the parking area behind the Badge Office and untangled the pistol from beneath the dash.

It was hard, the waiting, but I didn't want anything to go wrong when I killed Starker.

There was no use looking to anybody else for help with Starker. No one would go near that crazy mutherfucker. Well, except Sabo. And Sabo was the last guy in the world I wanted to have near me at that moment.

It was up to me.

I lay on the narrow metal bunk in my cramped room in the empty third-floor barracks, my feet toward the shaft of yellow light showing where I had not completely closed the door. Washed out light from a pale moon seeped through the single window behind my head, wavering across the big nickel-shiny .45 that I held resting

265

on my crotch, the muzzle pointed down between my boots, toward the door. I could see the front sight silhouetted against the shaft of light. I gripped the pistol with both hands, like King Kong must have gripped his dick, and I waited. When it was time to fire, I hoped I would not blow my own goddamn foot off.

Starker was out there. I knew he was. I had made sure that Kraus had told him I was here, back from the hospital, in the room, waiting. I could feel him, smell him, could sense the warped craziness that seemed to flow out of every pore of his body. But mostly out of his eyes. And sooner or later he would walk past the doorway. I knew he would glance inside. I would not have to do a thing to make him do that. After all, that was why he was here. He would look inside, that mean smirk on his rat-face, and he would see the pistol pointed at him. Just before I pulled the trigger.

I wondered, if you were looking down the barrel of a pistol when the trigger was pulled, could you see the bullet coming? Jesus Christ, I hoped so. I wanted Starker to see the bullet coming.

Now that I had made the decision, really made it, no going back, it all seemed so clear and simple. He would be dead, and I would be free, at least in my own mind.

For a brief moment, one of those moments that actually is a thought, a question, an idea that lurks in the back of your mind, waiting—one of those moments that you refuse to recognize, one of those made itself known:

How did I sink to this, to be lying in wait, to actually want to kill a man?

Fuck it. Now was not the time to answer that question.

There were only three things that could happen here. One: I could shoot Starker, and the other MPs would storm the third floor and either take me or shoot me. Either way, they probably would beat the shit out of me. It would not take them long; hell, this *was* an MP barracks. And who the hell cared? I still was not fully recovered from the other beating. Two: I could shoot Starker and maybe make it out of the building before they caught me—but they would catch me within minutes and then they would take me or shoot me. And beat the shit out of me. Three: I could shoot Starker and make it completely off the base, maybe sneak through the gate, maybe climb the fence, maybe . . . Hell, I had not thought that far ahead.

I really did not give a damn!

No matter what, Starker would be dead. And that was all that mattered.

There was a fourth thing, of course. Ruker could find me and get me out of this shit. Make me disappear. He needed me, I thought. He *owed* me, goddamnit! But I had not seen Ruker since his last visit to the hospital. It was as though the huge son of a bitch had simply faded into the cold mists that hung over everything, here, in the dead of winter.

Ruker had told me to leave Starker alone, that he had other things to do and Starker was just a distraction. Fuck Ruker. It was too late for me to leave Starker alone. His time had come.

Ruker. On the other hand, maybe it would be better if the MPs just went ahead and killed me.

I considered it self-defense. For almost my whole time in the army I had known that Starker was going to kill somebody, probably me. It was just a matter of time. When I thought about Starker, really thought about him; when I thought about what he had done and how he had done it, slowly building to larger and larger invasions of my life; when I saw the thin, flat light behind his beady little eyes. . . . I knew that Starker had been put on this earth to kill me.

And the goddamn army was helping him do it.

One of us had to die. Probably both of us. I no longer cared.

I had walked away from a lot of shit since I had been in the army. But I would not walk away from *this* thing. Not if I killed Starker right here in the goddamn MP barracks.

I wanted to use the .45. I *had* to use the .45. It was just the right thing to do, to use *his own pistol*, the pistol that Starker had used to fuck up my mind and my life, that he had used to tie us together. I wanted to gut-shoot him. I wanted the joy of it, wanted to know the huge .45 slug had entered his belly, wanted to *see* it, wanted to know the giant bullet was expanding, tearing guts to shreds, blowing out the back of him, leaving a hole large enough to stuff my fist in.

But I would not go down easily after I shot him. I would not just sit here and wait for the MPs. I would actually try to get away, thinking maybe the other MPs would be so glad to be rid of Starker that they might actually give me a head start. So I would shoot the son of a bitch, then I would just stuff the .45 inside the back of my pants, slip out past the gate guards and be gone. If I got past the guards, I might have a few hours head start before anybody in the army knew I was off the post. I knew I would have to keep running, that I would have to find a place, maybe a lot of places, where they might not think to look.

Bullshit. When I pulled the trigger on a .45 inside a building made of cement block, glass and metal it would sound like setting off a grenade in a tunnel. The other MPs would be on my ass instantly, like flies on a dead hog.

There was a round in the chamber and the pistol's safety was already off, but the hammer was down. When Starker glanced inside my room I knew he would be holding the bayonet. Then he would see the big .45 pointed at his belly and I would see the expression on his narrow, rat face when he realized the old cliché had caught up with him—he had brought a knife to a gun fight. He would know the pistol was loaded, would have no doubt that I was going to kill him. I wanted him to hear me haul back the hammer, those tiny clicks that sound like nothing else on the planet. I wanted to scare the shit out of him, if that were possible, just before I killed him. I wanted the son of a bitch to stand there with shit in his pants, knowing he was going to die.

I wanted him to see the bullet coming.

I wanted him to eat the fucking bayonet.

There was only a single, small light that burned in the hallway during the night. I waited for the shadow Starker would make as he passed that light. I waited for him to glance inside the room, waited to see that smirk. I gripped the pistol and waited for Starker's face to appear.

The noise was a light tinkling sound, a tiny, metallic, almost musical note that floated down the hallway.

Starker, flicking the tip of the bayonet against the stone-hard wall of the hallway.

Starker, putting me on notice, announcing that he was coming to split me like a butchered hog.

Starker, telling me he, too, did not give a shit. And never had.

The metallic noise again, closer now.

I wondered if he knew I had the gun.

Of course. Of course he knew about the gun. Why else was he making the noise? The bastard had no intention of poking his head inside my room.

I hauled the hammer back and slid carefully off the bunk and turned onto my stomach in the middle of the room, never taking the pistol off the doorway. I had been out of the hospital less than a week and the hard floor brought into clear focus the beating I had taken, my pains reawakening in all the vital parts of my body.

I belly-crawled to the door, grunting slightly. I didn't know how far away Starker was and I wanted to be able to get my right arm through the door, get off a couple of quick rounds. It was time for Starker to die. I didn't give a shit who heard the shots.

I gathered my feet under me, took a deep breath and dived head-first out into the hallway, sliding across the slick, shiny tile, trying to turn as I slid, both arms out in front of me, trying to bring the .45 to bear on some spot just in front of me.

But Starker was back at the far end of the hallway, his arm in full motion toward me, throwing the bayonet.

I triggered off two quick rounds, the flat thunder of the shots trapped inside the hard surfaces of the hallway, a noise like two freight trains coming together in the universe. Twice. Pounding inside my head.

I heard the bayonet clang off the floor in front of me and then it bounced out of my vision. I didn't know if he had any other weapons but it did not matter anymore, maybe had never mattered. We were in it, now.

And in the middle of all that, Starker disappeared.

I jumped up and charged down the hallway, fired twice more, quickly, not really aiming, just trying to get bullets flying.

I didn't see where the bullets went, but it didn't matter. Starker was gone.

I ran down the hallway, charged down the flights of stairs, and hit the heavy entry door at full speed.

I had to finish this.

I had waited, like the Indian said. Now the Earth was turned in a direction that only I could see.

When I killed Starker, the MPs would not have much trouble following me. I was leaving a trail of blood.

Forty-Eight

North Depot Activity
Romulus, New York
December, 1961

I left a blood trail along the hallway, down the stairs and out through the heavy entry door. But that was okay—I wanted the trail of blood to lead straight to Starker.

I heard the explosion before I got to the entry door. It shook the big door, shook the building, shook me. It was an explosion out of a war movie with the sound turned up to 'pain.' A sound I had never heard before. It was worse than the practice grenades, worse than a .50 cal. machine gun being fired single-shot, and it had happened just outside the door of the barracks.

I lowered my shoulder and crashed through the door, the shiny .45 stuck out in front of me, holding it in my right hand. For some reason, my left arm didn't seem to be working the way I wanted it to, but this was not the time to try to figure that out.

The tilted world was black with night and cold as only NDA could be cold in early winter. There was only the pale yellow light from the stairwell behind me spilling out through the panes of reinforced glass in the door, making weak blotches in the emptiness.

There were pieces of Starker in all the blotches of light.

Sabolino sat on his ass in the center of it all, some sort of tube in his hand, a pipe, the size of a baseball bat. There was smoke drifting out of one end of the pipe and Sabolino kept looking from the smoke to his left hand, holding it up in front of his face, looking quizzically at the blood sliding down his wrist, making a black, wet patch on the sleeve of his fatigue blouse.

A body lay in the edge of the light. I could see the arms and legs and maybe something that looked like a rib. The head was untouched, an expression of utter disbelief on Starker's face. Starker's chest was shredded, large parts of it gone, steam drifting up from the gaping hole and disappearing into the frigid night air. I could not see the parade ground but I knew there were pieces of Starker's chest everywhere. It was almost as if I could smell the pieces. But it wasn't pieces of Starker I smelled. It was gun smoke.

A canon. Sabo had made a canon. And from the looks of what was left of Starker, it was one helluva canon.

The heavy door swung shut behind me and I stepped to the side and stood just at the edge of the light, the shiny .45 at my side now, dangling from my hand.

Sabolino held up his bleeding hand, staring at it in the weak light, fascinated. Two of his fingers were missing. "Didn't git the trigger part right."

"Jesus, Sabo . . ."

"He made a cater . . . a caterpuller," Sabolino mumbled. I could see his breath when he talked. "It was a deer, Jesse, just a little biddy white deer. Just like the little biddy dog."

I looked at what was left of Starker. Caterpuller? What the hell was he talking about at a time like this?

"Was going to shoot him in his car. Was on the way to do that, shoot through the whole fuckin' car. Kill him in the night, just like he killed the dog. But then he come runnin' out the door. Seemed like a good time to get it over with."

From somewhere out in the darkness I could hear men yelling, the yells punctuated by the sounds of boots pounding across the parade ground.

Sabolino heard the boots coming, closer now. He grunted, pulled his hand tighter against his chest.

"You dumb fuckin' hillbilly," Sabolino rasped, the pain seeping through his words. "Don't you know when it's time to run? Don't you know what kinda shit is gonna come down here?"

Starker was dead. And in the middle all the shit that had happened here, was still happening, all I could think of, all I could feel, was a soft rolling cloud that came in through the night and covered me. Relief. I was free.

"Look at me, asshole!" Sabolino gritted the words through clenched teeth.

"You fuckin' run, hillbilly! How many times I got to tell you? You standin' there with a piece, rounds fired from it. You think they gonna care which one of us killed that asshole?"

I knew where to run, and so I ran.

For a few steps. I turned back toward Sabolino, in time to see him pull his arm into his chest, his head dropping forward.

"I won't forget this, Sabo," I said quietly.

"You fuckin' will," he grunted softly.

I ran again.

I remembered the plank. I knew exactly where it was. I found it easily, even in the dark. It was long and thick and I wondered where it had come from. And then I wondered at the rootlessness of my mind, that I could wonder things like that at a time when my ass was hanging in the wind like some tattered flag from a lost battle.

I jammed the .45 into my pocket.

The plank was unbelievably heavy and when I tried to pick it up pain danced through my left arm from my elbow to my hand. I dropped the damned plank. I did not want to take the time to really look at the arm, but I had to know what was going on. The nearest security light on the fence was enough for me to see that my left sleeve was soaked in blood, and that the blood was now soaking the entire left side of my fatigues. I found a slit in the sleeve. I had a knife in my pocket—I always had a knife in my pocket—and I cut the sleeve off just below the shoulder. Starker's bayonet had gone through the sleeve and driven deeply into the fleshly part of my lower arm. Blood was still flowing from the wound.

I cut a strip off the bottom of my fatigue blouse and wrapped it around my bleeding arm, then cut another strip to tie it in place. I pulled the wrappings tight. I needed to stop the bleeding.

Jesus, how much time had I spent, messing around with a stab wound? I stood still, trying to control my breathing, listening. I heard nothing. Not a sound.

I grabbed the plank again, heaved it up, letting its weight carry it forward, and I managed to get it leaning against the fence. It didn't seem to be leaning straight, but I really didn't care.

It was time to go.

Starker was dead. The Mexican was gone. The Indian was gone. Yvonne was gone, left behind far and away in another world. If there were something, anything, left of my life, I had fucked it up, whatever it was. It wasn't anybody else's fault. It wasn't Starker's fault. Whatever I was, was the result of the decisions I had made.

So I decided it was time to go.

I backed away from the end of the plank, took a deep breath, and charged at the heavy wood like an ox charging the end of a diving board. When I hit the middle of the board it sprung slightly and I vaulted up, enough to get my chest on the other side of the barbed wire. I flailed my legs and gripped the wire, struggling against my own heavy body, struggling to keep all the flailing from ripping off my shirt-bandage. And then I was over the fence, with countless rips in my hide from the barbed wire.

And, officially, AWOL.

I flopped around on the ground, disoriented, finally getting my feet under me. I grabbed for the pistol in my pocket. I didn't know if I could actually shoot another MP—other than Starker—but at least I could pretend.

The .45 was gone.

The trees were spindly and thick, standing tangled and twisted. I knew they were second growth, maybe third, cut and then left to re-grow in a dense, living barrier to anyone trying to run into, or out of, the area around NDA. And the undergrowth was even thicker, a green, spiny wall that only Sabolino's dog could penetrate. But I had to get to the two-lane blacktop off to the west. Then maybe across the road and on down to Seneca Lake, maybe steal a boat, just stay in the dark along the shore, maybe make it all the way to Watkins Glen. The stumblebum MPs would never think to look for me in a boat in the middle of the night.

Yes, they would. I was a stumblebum MP and that is one of the first places I would look.

Yeah, I had to do all that, in the winter, wearing only my fatigues, which were pretty much ripped to shreds.

I would never get through the bush. No matter what I did, I would make too much noise.

I eased off to the north and found the access road, then ran down the edge of it, trying to keep my boots from making flopping sounds. If a vehicle came by—probably an MP truck—I would slip into the woods and lie low until it was safe.

But no vehicles came. Now and then I would stop and listen, trying to hear anything coming from back at NDA. I heard nothing. No yelling, no sirens . . . nothing.

I slowed to a walk. If they weren't chasing, I was not going to run. But I had to keep moving to keep warm.

I don't know how long it took me to get to the highway. It could have been ten minutes. It could have been an hour. I was breathing deeply, trying to control my heart beat, my mind still darkened with the death of Starker and the sight of Sabolino sitting in the light, his mangled hand in front of him.

But he had set me free. Everything I loved, or hated, was gone. All I had to do was get the hell away from NDA, find myself a weapon, get a coat, steal something that would move, and I was gone for good.

Gone where? Where was there a place for me? And how would I get there, even if I knew where "there" was? I fingered the small leather pouch that hung around my neck, the pouch with my turquoise, and two other pieces in it. *Two other* pieces. I had tried not to think about how those pieces got there, in the pouch, the pouch now taped to my bandages. In the entire world, only one of two men could have put it there.

The pouch with a cross on it.

Whatever it meant, I might never figure it out.

So there I was, running again. I was good at running away, I just wasn't too good at getting anywhere.

I saw the highway a few yards ahead. I stopped and listened for traffic, but there was none. Holy shit! Maybe I would make it, after all.

There was no reason to hide. No one was chasing me; there was no traffic. I stepped out of the weeds and put a foot on the pavement. A step. My first step on a real road that led to . . . somewhere.

Anywhere.

I stepped firmly out on the road and took a deep breath.

Sabolino had set me free.

And that's when the car's lights came on, pointed exactly at me. It was parked across the road, probably had been there, waiting, all the time I was coming through the woods . . . knew exactly where I would be coming out. There was a figure standing motionless to my left, just inside the light. The figure was not hard to identify. It was that silent asshole, Garcia, and he was holding a big, shiny .45, pointed directly at me.

Forty-Nine

Lakeside
Romulus, New York
December 1961

We did not go back to the base. Whatever was going to happen from now on, Ruker said, was going to happen out of the reach of Kraus and the rest of them.

They had put me in the car and we were driving slowly down a narrow road that seemed to slope away in front of us. Ruker drove. I was in the back. Garcia sat in the passenger seat, turned slightly toward me, the .45 somewhere down out of sight. It was Starker's gun. Garcia had been on his way to the barracks to pull my ass out of there—they knew I was going to shoot Starker—and had seen the whole thing, had seen Sabolino waiting, had seen Starker burst through the door, had seen Sabolino fire his cannon. Had seen all the rest of it. Followed me to the fence, watched me go over. Had picked up the gun.

Ruker said they let me go over the fence so the army would officially declare me AWOL. He would straighten it all out later, he said, as long as I did what I was told.

The road ended in a small parking area, a cabin off to one side of it. It was one of those cabins that people in town built to use on weekends, come out to their 'lake place', fish, drink, fuck around. Literally. The cabin was only a few yards from Seneca Lake. There was a dying moon but it gave enough light to glitter from the water and give the place a postcard type of character, the perfect little hideaway for a loving couple.

Loving couple my ass—the cabin belonged to Ruker.

Inside, the place had all the charm of a barracks room. It was basically one room, a military cot up against the far wall, a tiny sink and an even smaller stove. I did not see a refrigerator. A round table sat in the middle of the room. We sat at the table and Ruker went into a closet and brought out three bottles of beer. I was surprised to feel how cold the beer was. I thought maybe there was a refrigerator in the closet, and then I realized that I could see my breath—it was nearly freezing in the cabin.

"I told you to leave him alone." Ruker's voice sounded caged in the small room, like a man speaking into a barrel. Garcia, as usual, did not say a word.

"You know what the son of a bitch did to me. How the hell could you expect me to leave him alone? Sooner or later, he was going to kill me. Damned near did it at the Marvelous Bar."

Ruker glanced at Garcia, one of those glances that people make when they are deciding something.

"Okay, hillbilly, maybe you're right. Maybe Starker was building up to something." He paused, glancing at Garcia again. "He tried to hang a neighbor kid. Got a belt around his neck. Got the belt over the top of a door before his old man came in and stopped it."

"WHAT!?" I could not believe what I was hearing. "And they let the bastard get into the army?"

"It don't matter anymore," Ruker said. "It's over, so here it is— we knew Sabolino was building the cannon, we just didn't know what he was going to do with it. Didn't think he would kill Starker over a goddamn dog and a deer."

"A deer? The deer on the electric fence? Starker killed the deer?"

"Hit it with his patrol truck. Probably didn't mean to. So many deer inside the inner compound that the MPs have to try to herd them out of there, now and then. Broke the deer's leg. Bastard was crazy, but smart. He made a catapult. Bent over a small tree and flung the goddamn deer over the fence. Probably didn't plan for it to hang up on the hot fence, but it did. Deer was probably still alive. Guess Sabolino took some serious exception to the whole thing. Anyway, Sabolino saved your ass.

"Saved my ass? He saved me from killing Starker. As far as I can tell, my *ass* is still pretty far from being saved."

"Sabolino will never see a free day for the rest of his life. He saved you from that."

"Get fucking real. They won't put Sabo away forever for killing a fucking psycho drug dealer like Starker."

"No," Ruker said, letting out a deep breath, "they will put him away forever for killing the son of a general in the United States Army."

They left me in the cabin for three days. There was nothing to do but wait for whatever Ruker had in mind, so I spent the days looking out the window at the cold water of the lake, a frigid breeze blowing down from the north, the buzz of an electric always in the background. Ruker had a collection of military manuals in a wooden crate. I dug out the ones on survival and tried to figure out how to stay alive in the desert. I had never been in the desert and, according to the manual, it was nearly impossible to make it out of there alive. I read it anyway. Twice.

Ruker brought me some canned food. He left it on the tiny front porch and drove away. If I had not heard his car, I never would have looked outside and found the food. Bastard.

And then I discovered there was nothing in the cabin that I could use to open the cans. But I had my knife. I cut open the cans and then used the knife to dig out the beans, or whatever was in the can. I did not pay that much attention.

There was a tiny bathroom, but now and then I would go outside and piss off the porch. It gave me some sort of satisfaction.

Ruker would not tell me what happened at NDA. I didn't know what happened to Sabolino. I didn't know if they raided the Marvelous Bar, or whatever other places the no-necks in Geneva were using to buy and sell drugs.

I didn't know what happened to Antonia DiPaulo.

So I read about digging a survival ditch in the desert so I could stay out of the sun. And other stuff. And I waited.

It got colder.

When Ruker and Garcia finally did come back to get me, they had all the stuff from the locker in my barracks room. I did not have much in the way of civilian clothes, but they had brought it all.

Before Ruker said anything, he went to the wall over the bunk and pulled a couple of planks loose, reached in and took out a black briefcase. It was hard, looked like some sort of plastic. He handed the case to Garcia.

"I want you to do one more thing for me," Ruker said, "and then we're even."

That really pissed me off. "*Even*? I take a beating for you that damned-near killed me, and we're *even*?"

"Listen, boy," Ruker growled, "there's a mountain of shit coming down over there on NDA, and all I have to do is tell 'em where you are. I don't give a fuck about a beating. I want the slimy fucks who've been selling H to the troops. You can be a part of making that case, or you can kiss my ass and walk out of here. Your choice."

He waited. He knew damn well I had no choice. All I had was Ruker. If I didn't do what he wanted, I was screwed.

"How do you fix it? I mean, I'm AWOL. How do you fix that?"

Ruker glanced at Garcia. "It's already fixed. I told the CO that I had you on temporary duty, working a big case. Told him you would be back when it was over. He didn't really give a fuck. He's a bird colonel—all he's worried about is a general named Starker who is on his way to North Depot Activity. Why the fuck do you think I wanted you to leave Starker alone? I didn't want all this shit coming down in the middle of my investigation."

His investigation. That's all the bastard cared about.

A long time ago—at least it seemed like a long time ago—I told Ruker that I wanted off NDA, forever. This was the time to press the issue.

"I'm not coming back. Ever."

"Yeah, I know." His voice was lower than I had ever heard it.

I went over to the window and stood looking at the lake.

"So, what do you want me to do?" I mumbled over my shoulder.

Fifty

Inner City
Oakland, California
January 1962

It was that time of day when the light died willingly behind cracked buildings and trash-strewn vacant lots, as though it could not wait to cover the city with darkness to keep decent people from seeing what crawled there. The sun slid down behind the highest buildings, leaving a thick, tired heat that boiled through the streets and seeped into the gaps of the boarded-up windows that stared vacantly into a neighborhood where no sane person ever walked alone.

Ruker and I sat quietly in the car. It was January, but sweat ran down our faces and soaked our shirts. Ruker said the sweat was from tension. I said my sweat was from being trapped in a car with him. He did not laugh.

We moved only when we had to, staring vacantly at the abandoned cars and dented garbage cans that lined the sidewalk. The cans seemed to be a permanent part of the street, overflowing with trash so old that it had become solid, petrified, and I knew the cans had not been emptied, or moved, in weeks. Months.

We were parked between two cars that had their windows smashed, one of them with all the wheels gone. Once, about an hour ago, Ruker got out of our car and pretended to be looking at something on the back of the car in front of us. Actually, he was pissing on the car. When he got back in his seat he said, "I should'a taken a shit. They'd never notice it, this part of town."

But they would notice us. We were wearing civilian clothes, but no one would ever take us for civilians.

This was what I owed Ruker. One last stakeout. Only this time Ruker was here with me. If the shit came down, like at the Marvelous Bar, Ruker would be in it, too. That made me smile. And I knew what I was: I was just fill-in, muscle, meat, another pair of hands, somebody to keep Ruker company. I was there because Ruker had spirited me away from NDA. Now I was officially attached to him, and Garcia. That was okay with me. At least I wasn't in the stockade, Ruker had seen to that. I guess I owed him. But, all in all, before this was over, I would think maybe the stockade was not such a bad deal.

I had to take a leak. Even though lights flickered dimly in the near-dark and I knew I would not be noticed, I was determined not to take a leak in the street. I was, I told myself, more civilized than Ruker. Even if I was, according to him, a fucking hillbilly.

Ruker sat silently beside me. I had learned that he could sit, or stand, not moving, for a longer time than anyone I had ever known. Sitting there in the dark and the silence, I thought about all the things I did not know about Ruker. I didn't know what his rank was, or even if he was in the same army as I was. I had never seen him salute anyone, refer to anyone as "sir," or take his hat off when he entered a building. At NDA he came and went whenever he wanted, never reported to anyone. I had learned that he usually carried a briefcase that he never seemed to open—the black briefcase he had taken out of the wall at the cabin. The briefcase was with us now, behind Ruker's seat. All I knew was, Ruker was supposed to be an investigator and that no one gave him shit, not the officers, not the enlisted men, not the civilians.

And he could do things like have other MPs assigned to him. Me.

We were watching the bar across the narrow street, one of those pathetic saloons that seemed to be painted into the landscape by a set designer for a low-budget horror movie. The door of the bar was set back from the sidewalk and there was black grillwork on the windows. A single, flickering neon beer sign glowed dimly, almost unreadable through the smoky smudge that covered the glass. I wondered why anyone would ever go in there.

This was the third day of the stakeout and I was bored to a level of actual pain. But Ruker didn't seem to be affected by anything. With his heavy shoulders and thick arms, his massive hands resting on the steering wheel, he looked like an overgrown child driving a toy car. And for three days I had not seen him smile. In fact, I'm not sure I had *ever* seen Ruker smile.

Before this was over, I would see him smile. Once.

Fleet and Milken were gone. Ruker had personally taken them to another post—he never said where—but not before Ruker had pulled every tiny bit of information from their bodies. I saw them just before they left with Ruker. Fleet and Milken had never been that tough to start with, and when I saw them they looked like their skins had deflated and were hanging, sagging, on their bones, dark circles making targets under their watery eyes. As I watched the dark green army sedan pull away from the main gate I knew I would never see Fleet and Milken again

Ruker had not had time to pull anything out of Starker. Sabolino had seen to that. There was not enough left of Starker to hold anything.

And some of those bits of information pulled out of Fleet and Milken somehow connected the no-necks in Geneva to . . . well, to someone who was supposed to show up in that grimy bar across the street. At least that's what Ruker said.

And so we were in Oakland, at this bar, waiting for some cheap-ass snitch to slide inside and tell Ruker's real partner, Garcia, where the pipeline started, and where it ended.

Hell, I knew were it ended—it ended, at least part of it, in Geneva. It ended at NDA. And then I realized that NDA was not really big enough to make it all worthwhile. There must be other military bases involved. Was that why Ruker was here? Jesus Christ, was that why *I* was here?

Inside the bar, Garcia was sitting at a filthy table, trying to drink enough to be a customer, and not drink enough to be drunk. Garcia and Ruker had been partners for a long time—I did not know how long. Every time I had seen Garcia he had been in a perfectly tailored uniform. Except, now, he wasn't. For this stakeout, Garcia had gone to a Salvation Army store and bought some crappy clothes to wear so he wouldn't stand out. He looked like shit.

Not stand out? Bullshit, I thought. We didn't live here, didn't live in this neighborhood. The only way we would not stand out was if we were dead, our bodies piled in the street.

The snitch was supposed to meet Garcia in the bar. We parked our car across the street four hours ago and just sat there, waiting, smelling the stink of the street and waiting for the lights to go on behind the blinds that were drawn down over every window we could see.

For the last hour we had seen no one on the street so we stayed where we were. I was edgy, but Ruker wasn't. That was fine with me. I had learned that I didn't like being around Ruker when he was edgy.

And then we heard the rumbling.

The noise started in the far distance, a growl that grew in your stomach before you actually heard it, slowly and steadily edging up until you could feel it in the metal of the car. The sound climbed to your spine and crumbled into your brain and you knew that whatever was causing it was not going to be good.

"Bikes," Ruker said, trying to squeeze his bulk farther down into the seat.

I slid down, tucking my knees under the dash.

There were six of them. They rolled slowly up the street toward us and then turned in toward the bar, wheeling out again, finally backing the bikes into the curb. They killed the growling engines. The riders swung off the bikes and strutted around the machines. Three of the bikes were shiny, glistening even in the pale light, mirrors twinkling, chrome burnished. But the other three bikes were different. They had pieces of leather, feathers, chains, beads, hanks of rope, studded belts and other crap of unknown use or origin tied, bolted and strapped to every square inch of surface. They looked like garbage magnets. They looked like shit.

"Rat bikes," Ruker muttered. "I didn't know this was a rat bar. What the fuck."

I had never seen a rat bike. I didn't know what they were, or what Ruker meant. In fact, I seldom knew what Ruker meant.

The bikers were mostly big guys, fat, greasy hair hanging down to their shoulders, wearing heavy boots and studded leather vests with no shirts. Only one guy wore a helmet, a World War II German type with a spike sticking out of the top.

The bikers strutted into the bar.

Ruker was suddenly tense, nervous, balled up like a pending explosion. I knew he wanted to go into the bar. But he didn't.

The bikers came out of the bar in a bunch, jostling each other, joking, laughing. They seemed high. They ambled to their bikes, fired them up, rode away.

"How long were they in the bar?" Ruker wanted to know, his heavy voice sounding like it was from some inarticulate throat.

"Seven minutes."

"Seven minutes is not long enough to be in a bar because it's a bar," Ruker growled.

Before I realized it, Ruker was out of the car and halfway across the street, his heavy legs and huge feet pounding the rutted pavement. I jumped out of the car and ran after him. Ruker pushed through the door of the bar. I knew he would not charge into the middle of the room—he would immediately slide to the left, just inside the door, quickly sizing up what, if anything, was going on. I went through the door and moved a step to the right.

The bar was as dim as a crypt. A haze of smoke hung from the ceiling and the smell of stale beer, stale bodies and piss seemed to ooze out of the woodwork. There was no one at the tables or on the stools. The bartender was behind the bar, smoking a cigarette and leaning on a broom. The three of us stood absolutely still. And then I saw Garcia on the floor. Garcia was face-down. He looked loose, broken, his arms and legs splayed out at odd angles, some sort of white powder scattered all over his body.

The hospital was one of those that sat on the edge of hell and, nightly, scooped up broken humans.

Garcia was on the third floor. He was in a coma and the doctors didn't know if he would ever come out of it. The bones around both eyes were scattered fragments, ribs cracked, spleen ruptured, one lung collapsed, an arm broken. Somewhere inside Garcia a bleeder was oozing into his guts and the doctors didn't know where it was.

The white powder that had been sprinkled on Garcia was talcum, the stuff you buy for babies.

I thought Ruker would stay at the hospital and wait for the end, but he didn't. He looked at Garcia, talked with the doctors, paced the hallways and, once, punched his huge fist into a tilted serving cart, scattering dishes crusted with day-old food. He went to a pay phone and talked for a long time. And then he left before I knew it. He didn't wait for me and I had to run to catch him in the parking lot.

We stopped the car at a grassy park and we slept in the car. We ate greasy sandwiches and drank weak coffee and slept in the car some more. And then it was almost night again.

We sat quietly in the same car in the same place across the street from the bar, the car now beginning to stink from the sweat of our bodies and from the hate that bled out of our eyes. The street was the same, except for a trashed-out deuce-and-a-half that I noticed about half a block away. The huge, blocky truck had one fender missing, its windshield cracked, its paint faded, and I dismissed it as another piece of shit that belonged in this neighborhood.

Last night when the ambulance left with Garcia there were wraith-like people in windows and doorways, watching. I could see their eyes and sometimes their faces but I knew they were not smiling. They saw us get into this car, parked in this same spot, and follow the ambulance. And there we were again, obvious and exposed. Ruker didn't seem to care. For twenty-four hours he had not spoken to me, or to anyone, and I knew enough not to ask questions.

So I was surprised when he spoke.

"We're going inside. Follow my lead and don't get in the way. If there comes a time when you don't want any part of this, just walk away."

I followed him into the bar.

Two guys sat on stools, talking with the bartender. The rest of the place was empty.

The bartender was surprised to see us. He started toward the other end of the bar.

"No," is all Ruker said. The bartender stopped.

The two guys got up and started around us toward the door. Ruker held out his arm, like he was directing traffic.

"Take your beer and go to the back. Stay there and keep your mouths shut." Ruker's gravelly voice was so low I could hardly hear what he said. He walked slowly down the bar toward the bartender.

"Make the call," Ruker said, nodding toward the phone at the end of the bar.

"What call? I don't make calls for . . ."

He never got to finish. Ruker grabbed a barstool and whipped it into the bottles behind the bar. Shards of glass and sprays of cheap whiskey flashed toward the bartender. The guy flung his arms up to shield his face and didn't see Ruker come across the bar. Ruker was on him like a giant on a gnome, picked him up and threw him toward the phone. The bartender slammed into the wood and sank to the floor, bleeding from a hundred cuts. Ruker dragged him up, grabbed the phone, and smashed it into the guy's face.

"I told you, make the call," Ruker said quietly.

Ruker was still inside the bar.

I was back across the street in the car, where Ruker told me to be. Cover the street side, he said. I took out my .45 and jacked a round in the chamber.

Yeah, *the* .45, Starker's .45 that Garcia had given me back at the cabin. It was fully loaded and I had extra magazines in my pockets.

I didn't put the gun back in my shoulder holster. I snapped on the safety. I sat holding the shiny gun in my lap.

I didn't have long to wait. I heard the rumbling again.

The same bikes. The same riders.

When the bikers shut off their machines and swung down, Ruker was standing in the doorway of the bar. And suddenly there were two things that I knew—that Ruker might be the angriest man who ever lived, and that we were no longer investigators on official duty. We were straight out of the history books. We were vigilantes.

There were six of them, and two of us. I didn't want to go across the street. I argued with myself: this was Ruker's fight; Garcia was Ruker's partner; Ruker was not thinking clearly, or not thinking at all. Why should I pay the price for that? I was more civilized than Ruker. Why should I go over there to be beaten so badly that not even my dental records would identify me?

And then I realized I was halfway across the street. At some point, I had jammed the .45 back into its holster, and I had a military baton stuck down inside the back of my pants.

The first biker, the guy with the spiked helmet, rushed the door and I saw Ruker's right hand shoot out at his neck. Ruker grabbed the man and spun him, slamming him against the doorway, fingers digging into the guy's throat. The biker was sagging, knees bending, the air, and the fight, gone from him. The other bikers seemed stunned.

I saw a flicker of motion to my right and suddenly there were two guys standing on the sidewalk, not bikers, guys who wore loose black pants, black t-shirts, boots, their hair cut so short they were almost bald. They moved at the same time, using their feet, and two bikers were on the pavement. It happened so fast I didn't know what those guys did, or how they did it. The bikers just went to the ground and stayed there, each of them clutching body parts and screaming.

The other bikers were moving, one toward Ruker, the others toward the two guys in black. Ruker had been holding his man with one hand. Now, he dropped him, unconscious, to the ground and moved out of the doorway, shooting a straight right at the face of the man in front of him. The guy threw up his arms to block the shot and didn't see Ruker's right leg coming up at the same time. The leg, as big as a tree trunk, thudded up between the guy's legs and he doubled over instantly, puking on the sidewalk. Ruker kicked him in the ribs and the puke shot all the way to the front of the building.

One of other bikers reached the guys with the black pants. He never got to raise his arms. One of those guys whipped out a short piece of heavy cable and, spinning, slashed it across the biker's face. Blood splattered all the way to where I was standing—immobilized in the street, not believing what I was seeing.

The last biker broke away and ran for it, toward me. I dragged out the baton and whipped it across his face. I felt it sink into his skull and he screamed, grabbed his nose and rolled off to the right. I caught him, whipped him with the baton again and again, his ribs, the sides of his knees, his collarbone. When he went down, his feet flew up, and I whipped the baton through one of his ankles, hearing the bone shatter.

One by one, Ruker dragged the jangling, bleeding bikers onto the sidewalk, two of them still unconscious. The guys in the black pants did nothing, just stood there, expressionless, as though viewing a boring movie.

The bikers all carried heavy wallets hooked by shiny chains to their belts. Ruker ripped the wallets off their pants and tore out the insides. He found driver's licenses and collected them all, looking at each in turn. He turned to me.

"Four licenses have the same address," he rumbled. "That'll be the clubhouse."

Ruker kept the licenses, but kicked the wallets down a sewer at the curb.

The first biker groaned and sat up, his spiked helmet pulled back on his head. Ruker carefully, almost gently, unbuckled the helmet and lifted it from the guy's head, put his fist inside and drove the spike down into the biker's thigh. The guy screamed and went limp. He was unconscious before he slumped sideways and hit the sidewalk. He didn't move and I thought he was dead.

The two guys in black checked the street, the front of the bar and a couple of the abandoned cars. They seemed to find nothing that concerned them. They did not speak to Ruker, or to me. In fact, they did not speak at all. They turned and walked away and I thought we were rid of them.

I was wrong.

They climbed into the junked-out dual-wheeled truck and started it up. I could tell from the sound that the engine of the truck was not junk. The truck pulled away from the curb and eased toward us. The driver took the truck easily over the row of bikes, the huge wheels crushing frames, tanks, and spokes like an angry child might crush cheap toys. The truck rolled over the last bike, stopped, and then backed over them. And then again. And then the truck was gone.

Ruker disappeared inside the bar. In less than a minute he was back, dragging the bartender. The guy's face was still bleeding. Behind him, inside the bar, he had turned the lights up and started music playing on the filthy jukebox. He left the door open.

He handcuffed the bartender to the heavy grating that covered the windows.

"If any of their friends show up, you'll be the first thing they see. They're going to wonder why you're standing up, when everybody else is on the ground. In the meantime, this place is open for business to any neighborhood patrons who might want to drop by."

The bartender started to cry.

We climbed back into our car and pulled slowly away. As we left, I turned in my seat and watched as two winos materialized out of the darkness, edged around the bartender, and wandered in through the door of the bar. A few people had opened their bolted doors and were peering into the night. In the distance I thought I could hear sirens but I was not sure.

It was a neighborhood that I wouldn't be caught dead in. But it occurred to me that I might be.

Ruker looked across the near-dark street at the piece-of-shit house, a two-story frame that leaned slightly toward the sidewalk. One of the front windows was broken. A flight of mismatched steps led up to a front porch that was held together with nailed-on two-by-fours. Rusted pieces of what appeared to be engines and other motorcycle parts were piled against the cracked railings. Inside, a naked light bulb shined dimly in a narrow hallway. Four bikes—two of them showroom-shiny and two rat bikes—were parked on the bare earth below the porch.

The lots on either side of the house were vacant, weeds growing knee high, piles of old tires and random pieces of metal sticking up like insane tombstones.

Ruker took out a tiny flashlight and looked at the drivers licenses clutched in his huge hand. He looked at a few of the nearby houses, most of them dark, their doors probably bolted against the other evil and moving things of the neighborhood.

"That has to be the place. Even without a street number, you can't miss a fucking shit hole like that."

He pulled out his .45, pressed the slide slightly to the rear, making sure there was a round in the chamber, clicked on the safety and stuffed the gun back into the holster on his belt. He looked at me.

"You don't have to be any part of this. If I step in shit in there, I'll tell 'em I sent you back to the hospital, check on Garcia. That is, if I'm in any condition to tell anybody anything."

I looked at Ruker and said nothing. Darkness ticked heavily against the windshield. And then I knew that I *was* in this, that I was *already* in this, that I was in it back at the bar when I first got out of the car with a gun and the baton and that no matter what happened I would *never* be able to separate myself from what happened here. This was a time, and a place, and a weight that would be in front of me, on me, forever. I knew what was going on inside Ruker, because it was going on inside me.

This was judgment day, and I was one of the judges.

I was tensioned, a spring bent to the breaking point.

I was calm.

I dragged out my .45 to jack a round into the chamber, only to remember there was one already in there. I checked the safety and jammed the gun back under my arm.

We took our batons and climbed quietly out of the car.

There was no one on the street. I felt eyes on me, but, then, I always felt eyes on me when I was with Ruker.

We crossed the street and stood in front of the house.

I could hear Ruker breathing.

"Want 'em all?"

"Yeah," Ruker growled, "I want 'em all."

"Then I'll take the back."

"Two minutes," Ruker said.

I checked my watch and then eased away and slid along the side of the house and around the back porch, feeling weeds grab at my pants and stumbling now and then over metal junk. The back door was closed. I slipped up a short flight of creaking steps to the porch and tried to see through a back window, but there was something covering it on the inside.

I looked at my watch. Fifteen seconds to go.

The first thing I heard was a crashing sound and I knew Ruker was through the front door. There were a couple of screams, some cursing, one curse cut off in mid-curse, as though the man's throat had closed. None of the screaming and cursing was Ruker's. He was working silently.

So far, no gunshots.

I moved back toward the railing and tried to relax, tried to be ready.

The back door exploded.

A huge man thundered through and I knew instantly that if I gave him a half-second to act that he could take me. I dived to the side, whipped the baton across his shins as I went down. I lost the baton. I heard him scream. He pitched forward and slammed face-first into the porch, bouncing forward and down the steps and before he could get up I was on him, wrapping up one of his arms and twisting and I felt the arm come loose from its socket. He screamed again and I drove the heel of my hand into his nose, feeling the bones flatten. He twisted hard toward me and swung his good arm at my head. I caught his forearm on the side of my head and the hit rolled me over backward. As I was rolling I was dragging out the .45 and trying to swing it toward him. His face was directly in front of me and the swing of the .45 caught him on the ear. He went down and went quiet, his head back and at an odd angle. I ripped the .45 across his throat, hearing something tear in there.

I didn't want to just hit him with the .45, I wanted to blow a hole in his stinking biker heart. I pointed the gun at his chest and I thought about it. But I did not fire.

I left him on the ground, charged up the steps and blew through the back door, the .45 in front of me.

Ruker was standing in the middle of the room. Two bikers were crawling down the narrow hallway toward the front of the house and Ruker was watching them go. Almost casually, we followed behind them. My eyes flicked from door to door, the .45 on the door as my eyes get there. But there was nothing.

Just inside the front door, Ruker reached down and grabbed an unconscious biker by his leather vest. The two crawling bikers were on the front porch, trying to get to their bikes. Ruker kicked them down the steps. We followed, Ruker dragging the last biker down the steps.

The bikers never got to the bikes. Ruker saw to that. He grabbed one and jerked him up into a sitting position, leaning close into his face.

"You tell your 'brothers' I'm dissolving the chapter." He shook the biker. "You understand?" He shook the biker again. The biker said nothing. Ruker slapped him so hard snot and blood flew from his nose. "You understand?" The biker nodded his head, Yes.

Ruker brought his fist down hard on the bridge of the guy's nose, and I knew the guy would never breathe properly again.

Ruker looked at me. "Where's your guy?"

"Out back, maybe strangling."

"I'm going to light it up."

"I'll do the bikes."

Ruker disappeared inside the house.

I found a long, heavy piece of scrap metal with a pointed end.

I kicked the bikes over and drove the point through the tanks, gas dribbling out onto the bare ground.

Ruker came out on the porch. Behind him, a light began to flicker in the hallway.

I had matches in my hand. Ruker took them and, almost casually, dropped a lighted match on the gasoline-soaked earth. The flames that shot up were so heavy that the bikes disappeared inside them.

We climbed into the car and Ruker started the engine.

"You clear?" he asked.

Something jumped in my mind. "Wait a minute."

I rolled out of the car, scrambled around the flames that were eating the bikes, along the side of the house to the back. I pulled the .45 and stepped around the corner. The biker was where I left him. I could not tell if he were breathing, and I did not check. I eased up on the porch. Inside, I could see light flickering and hear popping sounds. I scouted the porch and found nothing. I jumped down to the ground, took out a small flashlight and did a quick search. I found the baton in some weeds.

As I ran back around the house toward the car, there was a small explosion and a window blew out behind me. And then I was in the car. Ruker drove slowly back to the hospital. There was plenty of time.

And I realized that he was smiling.

Two days later, Garcia died.

Fifty-One

Cottage, Seneca Lake
January 1962

After that, Ruker never mentioned Garcia.

I never mentioned the biker at the back of the house, never mentioned that I did not know if he was breathing.

Technically, I never went back to North Depot Activity.

I went back to Ruker's plain little cottage by Seneca Lake. Ruker did not want me to be found, so I stayed there, eating out of cans and reading Ruker's military manuals. Now and then he would bring me a newspaper or a paperback that someone had left in the badge office.

For once, Ruker talked, keeping me up to date on what was going on.

He covered our trail, saying that we pulled out of the surveillance before the fight at the bar. He said Garcia was working alone. There was no way to connect us to the fire at the biker pad. But Ruker said two bikers died there. I tried to get Ruker to find out which two bikers died—whether one was in the backyard. But he did not seem interested. When the fire department arrived, he said, they just scooped up the bodies and got them out of there. They knew one guy had been in the backyard, but did not know if he was one of the dead ones.

I was still officially "attached" to Ruker on temporary duty, and I began to wonder how long "temporary" would last.

The army brought in some other guys, slick guys, guys who also never smiled and never shook hands and wore custom-made suits.

The slick guys kept hanging around, and there were days when I did not see Ruker at all. But Ruker said not to worry, the slick guys didn't give a shit about me. It was Ruker they were interested in.

I never found out who the other two guys were, the guys in the truck at the bar, the guys in the black clothes, the guys whose feet moved too fast for me to keep up with. I asked Ruker, but he did not answer.

Somewhere in there Christmas had come and gone. I did not even notice. But I wondered about Antonia DiPaulo, and whether Christmas meant anything to her, wondered if she bought Christmas gifts with the family drug money. I actually thought about going into Geneva and trying to find her. But then I came to my senses.

I dozed on the cot, the electric heater still buzzing and barely keeping up with the cold that flowed off the lake and into every crevice known to mankind.

I heard the car and I waited for Ruker. He filled the door when he came in and I realized again how big he was. He lowered himself into one of the two straight-back chairs.

"You got any personal effects here?"

"A few odds and ends," I said.

"Put 'em in this bag." He held out a burlap bag.

A burlap bag?

"How about in the barracks? You got any personal stuff there?"

"No. Not that I know of. You and Garcia cleaned it out before we went west. Never kept any personal stuff in there, anyway."

Ruker was looking out the window at the lake. "We crossed the line out there," he muttered. "No, I crossed the line. You were there for the ride." I didn't say anything. I knew damned well we had crossed the line so far we could not see it behind us. "The army is changing," he said. "I'm not sure I can change with it."

"So what do we do now?"

Ruker turned toward me. "You've been transferred. You are now a grunt in the CID. You belong to me. It's supposed to be temporary, but I'll get it fixed permanently."

CID? Criminal Investigation Division? What the hell did I know about being in the CID?

"Yeah, I know," he said, "you don't know shit. But you'll learn. You'd better learn, or you will not live to finish your hitch."

And then I realized—he *had* fixed it. I was leaving NDA. Forever. "Where the hell am I going?"

He stood up. "Look, Stone, you have to get away, far away. You have to go somewhere out of their line of sight. You understand? So I'm leaving. And you're leaving."

"What the hell does 'leaving' mean? Where am I going?"

"You won't know until you get there. And, Stone, you will be taking one of my cars. For a while, I don't want you on any airplanes." He pulled a thick envelope from inside his suit coat and handed it to me. "Everything you need to know is in here."

I was driving. I was not sure what that meant. I was not sure I wanted to know.

"General Starker. What happened with him?" I had forgotten to ask. It seemed like Starker was gone from my life and my mind.

"Nothing. At least not yet. Came on base, picked up the psycho's remains, left. His little experiment to use the army to 'fix' his psycho son didn't work out too well. But it wouldn't surprise me if he didn't start storming around Washington trying to get everyone at NDA thrown in the stockade. And I ain't going to be here when that happens."

"Did he know I was going to kill his son?"

Ruker turned away and said nothing.

"When am I leaving?"

"Now."

And he handed me the black briefcase.

Two days later, just before nightfall, on a narrow two-lane black-top that crossed a high ridge in the Appalachians, I pulled off at a wide spot in a turn, killed the engine and got out, looking at the mists beginning to form in the hundreds of valleys I could see stacking away in the distance. I took out the briefcase, laid it on the hood of the car and opened it. Inside, the case was lined with something like black velvet, and nestled into the bottom was a .45 caliber sub-machine, a "grease gun." Fitted into the lid of the case were six magazines, long black sticks of terror, each holding thirty rounds of ammo.

I took out the gun. I had fired grease guns before, but this one seemed different. It was polished, almost shiny, as though it had been worked on. Worked on? What the hell would that mean to a grease gun? I raised the bolt cover, stuck my finger into the hole and pulled the bolt back. The gun worked smoothly, no slop in anything that moved. I jammed one of the magazines up into it, pulled out the wire stock and clamped it against me, pointed the thing out over the ridges and leaned on the trigger. I ran off all thirty rounds. The noise was a string of connected explosions that pounded through the mountains over the scream that I realized was mine. When the gun stopped firing, I was still screaming.

Thirty rounds in memory of Ruker. And Garcia.

Not nearly enough.

I cradled the empty gun in my arms, pressing it against my chest, a tiny curl of smoke drifting out of the muzzle. There was something unfulfilling about firing the gun, about the noise, the bullets whipping into the Appalachian ridges. And I realized that I had wanted someone in front of the gun. I had wanted it to be real.

I was not more civilized than Ruker.

I was not more civilized than anyone.

I put the gun away and got back in the car. I had hundreds of miles to go before I crossed the border.

Fifty-Two

On The Beach
Honduras, near the Nicaragua Border
March 1964

It was the best café I had ever been in. I wanted to stay there, to live there, to drop out of the minds and sights of any who were in search of me, who knew that I was alive.

Heavy wooden tables and benches nestled into the sand floor. The wood had been scrubbed so many times with sea water that the surfaces were velvet to the touch. The roof was made of banana leaves and palm fronds, stitched together with some sort of tiny vines that twisted and bound like miniature snakes. The roof was held aloft by heavy timbers of wood so hard that there were no nails driven into it. There were no walls. The café was open to the air, to the beach, and the sea. The counter was bamboo, and meant only to keep customers out of the kitchen. There were no stools at the counter. The kitchen was an area directly behind the counter where a length-wise half of a 55-gallon barrel rested atop a stack of concrete blocks. Lying across the top of the barrel were pieces of heavy metal grill that looked as though they might once have been the shelves of refrigerators. At the other end of the counter was the café's cooler, a heavy wooden box lined with thick pieces of foam that had been picked up along the beach. The box was half filled with ice left over from the fish truck that left the village before dawn each day. As the ice melted, it simply ran out of the box and down into the sand. There was no electricity in the café. There was no gas, not even propane. When night fell, the only light was from the glow of two kerosene lamps attached to the center pole that supported the roof. The lamps did little to hold back the night. In this café, at night, you ate mostly by touch.

I sat at a small corner table near the front—the side nearest the ocean. I was less than twenty yards from the water. There were only three other customers, all men, all sitting at separate tables off to my right.

It was the best café I had ever been in. Except for one thing. One of the other men was Ruker. I had not seen him come it.

The sun drifted slowly into the ocean and the shadows of the jungle behind me darkened, the darkness spilling onto the beach and into the café. I could not see any of the men clearly. Even so, I could recognize Ruker's giant form, a figure out of nightmares that I didn't even have. I sat turned slightly so that he was in my field of vision.

I dug my rubber sandals into the cool sand, sipped a beer from the cooler, watched the small waves, and waited on my food. The menu was simple, never varied, everything cooked on the barrel-grill: fish—whatever had been caught that day—rice, flat bread, coffee and beer. The cook was also the waiter, and also the owner, and when he brought my food he brought a small pottery bowl filled with something that can only be described as liquid fire, the hottest salsa I had ever tasted in a public place. He smiled when he put it on the table. He knew the salsa would demand that I have another beer.

I had been coming here every day for almost two months. It had become a habit, and I knew I was not supposed to develop such public habits. But the café was, after all, the best café I had ever been in, and that had to count for something. I had begun to feel less tense, less hunted, less the hunter. I had begun to fantasize about living there, sleeping under a *palapa*, wearing nothing more than I had on now—sandals, shorts, large floppy shirt—fishing for my food. Coming here was a habit. It was a habit I would risk.

Less hunted. And now Ruker was here.

The cook brought my second beer, and I paid him, and I knew he would simply go home, leaving everything as it was until he came back tomorrow. If he decided to come back tomorrow.

I sipped my beer, listening to the soft sounds of night at the edge of the jungle, hearing the overlay of light surf. Two of the other men were gone. There was only me and the one other guy—Ruker. I kept him in my peripheral vision. He did not seem to be eating and there was no beer bottle on his table. He sat and stared at the ocean, now a black, moving sheet beyond the beach.

I tipped the bottle up and emptied it and realized that Ruker was moving toward me. I had not seen him get up from his seat. He was in no hurry, walking casually, but there was no doubt that he was coming to me. He was still Ruker, large, bear-like. I could see the size of his hands even in the kerosene light.

I tried to stay relaxed, turning slightly away from him and reaching up and under my shirt, my fingers wrapping around the grip of the shiny .45 that hung under my arm. I slipped the pistol out of the holster, moved it down to the bottom of my shirt, eased off the safety and transferred the gun to my left hand, away from Ruker, who was still ambling toward my table. I turned slightly toward him, my left hand pointing the gun at him under the table. I put my finger on the trigger.

He stood at my table, looking down at me.

He seemed thinner, now, but not really smaller; his bulk blocked out the light from the lanterns. He wore old army fatigues that looked thin and well used.

He sat down at my table, turning slightly so that I could see his face in the gold light of the lanterns. The lines in his face were deeper, the crooked nose somehow more crooked, bent more to his left, as though it was over there by accident and he never really cared to put it back.

He leaned forward slightly, put his elbows on the table and folded his big hands. I could see his gnarled knuckles and the scar tissue that ran down from them.

It was a full minute before he spoke. "You don't need the piece," he said, his voice a rumble in the night. "Besides, you should trade that thing off for something that doesn't shine. Anyway . . . you don't need the piece."

"I'll decide that."

"What are we, enemies now?"

"I don't know. I know what I'm doing here. You sent me here. A long time ago. What are you doing here? Are we doing the same thing?"

He turned his head slightly and stared off toward the ocean. I thought he had lost some of his intensity, some of the hard covering that had been part of him.

"Looks like we've both graduated to other things . . . chasing different kinds of bad guys, now," he says, still looking at the water.

"Depends on your definition of 'bad guy,' I guess."

"You're not as careful as you used to be. Pretty obvious of you, eating here every night."

"Maybe I don't give a shit anymore." I waited for him to say something, but he did not. "Maybe there comes a time when just staying alive . . ." I didn't finish.

Ruker turned his face back toward me.

"The two dead ones . . . you ever get that figured out?"

For a moment I did not know what he was talking about. And then I did.

"I got their names, but not their locations. I don't know if one of them was in the backyard."

"Did it matter then? Does it matter now?" He was not being sarcastic. He really wanted to know.

I thought about it.

"It mattered for a while. But not now," I mumbled, angry that he has made me think about it. "Nothing much matters now."

We sat silently. And then he looked back at the empty counter.

"You think there's a beer back there?"

I nodded.

He got up slowly, as though his legs were tired of moving his big body. He shuffled across the sand floor to the cooler. All the time, I kept the gun on him.

He brought back two bottles and put one down in front of me, unopened. He put the cap of his beer bottle against the table and pushed. The cap flipped off. He drank long and slowly.

He looked at me.

"It takes two hands to open a beer bottle," he said.

I did not answer, and did not touch the bottle.

He reached across, took the bottle and opened it, putting it back in front of me.

"So, it has come to this?" he asked.

"I don't know. You didn't find me here by accident. You've been tracking me. What do you want?"

He drank again, long, slow swallows.

"Maybe nothing," he said. "Maybe nothing."

He pushed back from the table and stood, sensing that the muzzle of my gun was still following him under the table.

"You once thought you were a civilized man," he said softly. "You read Whitehead. Whitehead said that civilization was a very fine veneer—the more you rub it, the thinner it gets." He looked away down the beach. "Who you been rubbing up against, partner?"

"I don't remember that you read much."

"I don't. Never read the man. Whitehead. You told me what he wrote, about the veneer."

He picked up the beer bottle and walked out from under the café roof and stood at the edge of the light from the lanterns. He turned slowly back toward me.

"You still have the briefcase," he said, a small note of lightness in his voice.

My left foot automatically nudged the case sitting on the sand under the table.

"Yeah. Same case. Same contents."

He stood quietly for a moment, then raised the beer bottle and held it there, above him.

I didn't want to, but my arm and hand seemed to move without my will. I took the beer bottle in front of me and held it up.

"Garcia," he said.

"Garcia," I said.

He drained the bottle, turned, and threw the empty out into the ocean.

"You're not clear. I tried to fix it. Too many people involved. Some army, some not. Your enlistment is up, but maybe someone'll be looking for you for a long time. You can probably stay here," he said, "but I'm not sure I would." I could read nothing in his voice.

He shuffled away down the beach, his huge body growing smaller as he moved away, until his size seemed almost normal. And then the night took him in.

So that's why he was tracking me, to tell me that he couldn't fix it. I think I had known that all along.

I waited three days, just to make sure, but he never came back.

I wandered through the tiny village, always alert for any figure that stood a head taller than most, wider than most, but I never saw him.

And then I realized that whatever debt I owed to Ruker I had already paid. In fact, there was not a single thing that I owed to anyone. I had paid it all.

I looked at the café, standing dark now, standing abandoned. I loved it. But I knew it would not even be there in another year. Maybe sooner.

I spent one more evening at the café, drinking beer, watching the ocean. But things had changed. Somehow, I was no longer free there. Ruker had seen to that.

I could stay there, but I knew I would not.

By the end of the next day, I was gone from that place.

And there was only one other place I had to go.

Just to make sure.

Fifty-Three

Crum, West Virginia
August 1964

I had to go back. As I said, just to make sure.

I came to the town in the middle of a dog-days night when the darkness has a thickness to it that you can actually feel. Even so, I knew that place.

I had come across the border like some returning tourist, feigning a hangover, several days of beard muddling my face, shirt hanging out of my pants, carrying everything I owned in an ancient rucksack with a one broken strap that I had slung around my shoulder. I carried the briefcase.

No one gave a shit.

I hitched up the Mississippi and then the Ohio River to Huntington and caught a ride with a guy driving a new Chevy who said he was going to Williamson. I had money, a bunch of money, and could have bought a bus ticket—hell, I could have bought the guy's Chevy—but I had missed the only bus of the day and I did not want to wait another night, or spend another day hanging around Huntington. And I didn't want to spend my money.

But that was not the real reason I was hitch-hiking. I had hitched out of Crum all those years ago. Something told me that was the way I was supposed to go back.

Before it even got dark the son of a bitch driving the Chevy stopped at a beer garden in Wayne and we sat in the stinking place drinking cheap beer until the guy was shit-faced and I was totally pissed off. I was tempted to drop his ass in the gravel parking area and take his car. But I did not want any trouble with the law, local or otherwise. Ruker had made that very clear. And I did not want to piss off Ruker. Even now. Even not knowing where he was, or if he were alive. Keep your head down, he had said. Keep your head so far fucking down you can't see daylight.

And that's the way I felt about Crum: I could not see daylight from there.

When we finally got back into the car I realized the guy could barely keep it on the narrow road. I thought about getting out and trying for another ride, but it was already full dark and I knew there would be little chance of anybody stopping for me this far south in Wayne County. I tried to get him to pull over and let me drive but he was one of those happy drunks who thinks that nothing is wrong with the world and it was useless trying to convince him otherwise.

The Chevy staggered along a pitted road beside a creek and finally began to struggle up Bull Mountain and I knew I had a decision to make. There was little chance that the guy would be able to keep the car on the road going *down* Bull Mountain and I had not survived Starker, Ruker, the bikers and the army just to die with some drunk on an unknown road just outside of Crum, West Virginia.

By God, I was not going to die in Crum.

So, at the top of the mountain, I told him I was going to puke all over the front seat of his new Chevy.

He couldn't get the car stopped fast enough.

I pushed the door open, grabbed my old rucksack and the briefcase and got out into the darkness. I knew the bastard would not want me back in the car, not if he thought puke would be dripping down the front of my shirt. As soon as I got out the car rolled away down the mountain and I watched it until the tail lights disappeared. I hope the idiot made it to Williamson.

I stood in the darkness and let the realization set in, that Crum was just down the mountain and a little off to the south.

I walked down the road off Bull Mountain, a road I had walked down before. There was heat and stillness in the night and I began to sweat, feeling that heaviness in my chest that I get when I'm walking into something I fear. But I had decided to do this, and I was going to do it. I had to find out.

Somewhere through the darkness I heard a train, the rhythmic sound of wheels on tracks clicking up through the night and before I realized it I was walking in time with the clicking, rushing downhill, the sound of the train roaring against my face, heading as fast as I could go into a time and place that squeezed so tightly that I thought I could not raise my arms.

I stopped, dead still, in the middle of the road.

The train was long gone. The roaring was in my head.

And so was the music.

The music that played inside my head when I was where I should not be, when deep shit was near at hand, some sort of sound track not of my making, music that I could not identify, that I did not understand, music that would follow me at times like these for the rest of my life. It was not as though I marched to a different drummer. Hell, *there was no drummer*, different or otherwise. There was only the music.

It with me then, there, in the silence of the long-gone train.

It is with me now.

The path to the old house ran away from the road and up the hill. I stepped onto it, my feet seeming to know exactly where to go. The stone school building was behind me, across the road and the tracks, but I did not try to see it. There would be time enough for that. I climbed the path, one slow step at a time.

By the time I reached the house there was small light in the sky behind the ridge behind me. I stepped softly onto the sagging planks of the porch and carefully put down the rucksack, not wanting to awaken anyone in the house. I carried the briefcase. There had once been a rocking chair on the porch but it was not there; there were no chairs of any kind on the porch. I leaned against the porch railing and looked down into the valley and across to the school. Light was just coming to its face and the face had not changed.

The school.

I had completed the circle, gone from here, gone to there, looking all the time, never finding. I was back in the county where I was born, in the tiny town where I was sent to go to school. And back to the school, itself.

I watched the light crawl across the roofline and grow stronger on the stone face of the school. The light did not sparkle on the windows, only passed through and was sucked into the darkness of the classrooms and hallways, never making its way out again.

It was late August. School would open soon, but not yet. There would be no one at the school today.

I eased off the porch and around the side of the house, seeing the small barn out to my left, a piece of its tin roof missing. That did not seem right. This was my aunt and uncle's hour, Mattie and Oscar, the people who had sheltered me when I was here, going to school in Crum. I knew Oscar would not leave the roof open like that.

Between me and the barn there was a wellbox, some planking nailed across its top, the small beam and pulley lying on the ground beside the box. I did not see a bucket.

I knew there was a small shed tacked on to the back of the house. I turned the corner. The door of the shed sagged open, hanging from the upper hinge. I did not have to look inside. There would be nothing in there.

I looked anyway.

There was nothing in the shed, not a piece of old broken furniture, not a scrap of cloth, a piece of paper. Nothing. For long minutes I stood with my hand on the edge of the door looking inside the small room, at the one window at the far end, at how the ceiling sloped down from the house, at the hole in the wall of the house where the back of the wood burning stove once showed through, the only source of heat for the shed.

My mind searched my body. I felt nothing.

I let go of the door and stepped backward, idly wondering how long the door would hang from that single hinge. It was a door hanging open, and out of some old habit I pulled it slowly closed, trance-like.

The hole in the wall of the house where the back of the wood-burning stove once showed through. . . .

The stove was gone.

The realization brought me out of my trance. I went around the house to the side door and turned the knob. The door opened easily and I stepped into the kitchen. The kitchen, and the house, were empty.

The highway through Crum seemed more narrow, the railroad track closer to the pavement. That's the way it is, I thought, places always seem bigger in our memory. Even Crum.

I kept walking, toward the memories of Yvonne.

The house was still there, but even without climbing the hill up to it I knew no one was living there. From the pitted highway I could see the sagging railing where Yvonne and I had leaned onto each other, pressing, the sweat of our bodies forming a bond that I still felt.

I could taste her. She was in the heavy air. She left her scent on the very wood of the old place, the way she moved, the way her skin shone on crisp winter mornings.

But this was not a crisp winter morning, the air now so thick I could hardly breathe.

Directly across the brittle pavement, nestled into the side of the hill, was a tiny garage, its sides being bowed inward from the hard press of the hill. Its roof caved in. The heavy wooden door still guarded the tiny space and even from where I stood I could see that a heavy, rusted lock still dangled from the hasp.

A door and lock guarding only my memory.

Yvonne had driven her brother's car out of that garage, and then tried to run me down as I stood stupidly in the gravel by the pavement.

When I had crossed the border back into the United States, I had called information in Myrtle Beach.

There was no Yvonne Staley listed.

I did not climb the hill to the house.

There is only so much pain a man can stand.

I sat on my ass in the deep shadow of the front porch, leaning back against the wall of Mattie and Oscar's house. I sat stone-still, watching the tiny valley along the Tug River come alive with light. I was high enough on the hill to see people, but not close enough for people to see me. But there were no people to see. I scanned the highway and the dirt lane just beyond that separated the railroad track from a ragged field in front of the school, a football field. But there was no one.

I heard the thick whining of a diesel engine and I watched as a bus rolled slowly into sight, coming from the direction of Huntington. It pulled off the road and stopped in front of a tiny general store that sat beside a railroad crossing down and off to my right, far enough away that the bus seemed toy-like, far too small to make the noise it was making. The general store was closed. I could not see the door of the bus. When it pulled way, a woman and a young boy stood in the gravel and the rapidly rising heat, the boy holding the woman's hand. They stood quietly, not talking to each other, the woman looking around as though searching for something.

And then the woman looked directly up the hill at me.

I knew she could not really see me, me humped up in the shadow at the back of the porch, but her eyes were fastened on the house, her face and body still, as though waiting for something to happen, something to move, something to appear.

I did not move.

The woman seemed to tire of looking, her shoulders slumping slightly. She looked down at the boy, maybe saying something. And then she pointed up the hill at me.

No, not at me. At the house.

The boy looked briefly, then turned his face toward the school.

For a moment, for just a fraction of a moment, I wondered what it would be like, to be here, in a house—a home—and watch my woman and my boy get off the bus, maybe after a shopping trip to Huntington, see them look up at me, here on the porch.

The woman dropped her head and seemed to take a deep breath. And then they walked slowly away along the railroad track, the woman still holding the boy's hand. I could not see where they went.

The image was gone from my mind. And I thought I was losing my mind.

And they were the only people I saw all morning.

Crum, West Virginia.

I had to go back, just to make sure, but I did not know how to make sure. I did not know what to do.

And then I realized that I did not have to do anything. It was there in front of me. It was there inside me. It would always be so.

I looked down the hill at the old school, and the row of houses that started off to my left, along the dirt lane and just beyond a small cemetery that seemed abandoned, tree branches hanging heavily over the leaning gravestones. I felt the tightness start in my chest and for some reason my breath came a little more sharply. I sat forward and gripped the porch railing, pulling myself up into a crouch.

Ready to run.

But not yet.

I had some food in the rucksack and I hid out in the hollow old house, listening for echoes, then walked slowly out behind the old barn, planks beginning to slough from its sides, and climbed the hill. When I got into the trees along the upper ridge I turned and looked back, but the low hardwoods and tangled undergrowth held everything from sight. It was just as well.

I thought it was Monday morning, but I wasn't sure. It didn't matter.

I thought about going down the hill and walking along the railroad tracks, maybe seeing someone I knew, had known. I ran names through my mind, times, places, things I had done. None of it clicked into place; none of it mattered.

I had come back. And I had made sure.

This was not my home.

I pulled myself up by the railing and took one last look at the sagging door that I had left open. The room inside was no longer inviting. I picked up the rucksack and the black briefcase.

I walked back around the house and stood again in front of the door to the shed. The first time I had stood there, I was twelve years old.

I would never stand there again.

I fingered the tiny leather pouch hanging around my neck.

With the stones inside.

With the cross so finely beaded.

The cross.

La cruz.

I knew the Mexican was alive.

Maybe the Indian, too.

I had a plan.

I did not go down the hill and walk along the railroad track; I went down the hill and stood by the side of the road away from the river. Cars on that side of the road would be going toward Huntington. Should be easy to catch a ride, if there were any cars. I had not seen one since I had come out on the porch of the old house. I could wait.

A car came into view. I put out my thumb, but the driver did not stop.

I heard another car, but it was going the other way, toward Williamson. It was not a car, it was a truck, and I heard it grinding down from the bottom of Bull Mountain long before I could see it.

There really was no decision to make; one direction was as good as another. I walked across the road and waited. There was more than one way to get to where I was going.

Epilogue

Two days after Jesse Stone left Crum, the woman and boy from the bus walked into Crum School. The woman registered the boy, her son, in the second grade. His name was Jesse Stone Staley. There is no record of how long they stayed in Crum.

About the Author

Lee Maynard, also the author of *Crum* and *Screaming with the Cannibals*, was born and raised in the small towns and hollows of Wayne County, West Virginia, where his relatives have dwelt for over two hundred years. His work has appeared in *Columbia Review of Literature, Appalachian Heritage, Kestrel, Reader's Digest, The Saturday Review, Rider Magazine, Washington Post, Country America, The Christian Science Monitor,* and many other publications. Specializing in the novel, Maynard has taught at many national and regional workshops, including the Appalachian Writers Workshop, SouthWest Writers Workshop, and West Virginia Writers' Conference. He has served as Writing Master at Allegheny Echoes.

An avid outdoorsman and conservationist, Maynard is a mountaineer, sea kayaker, skier, and former professional river runner. Currently, he serves as President and CEO of The Storehouse, an independently funded, nonprofit food pantry in Albuquerque, New Mexico. He received the 2008 Turquoise Chalice Award to honor his dedication to this organization.